SUICIDE CLUB

RACHEL HENG

LARGE
PRINT

First published in Great Britain 2018
by
Sceptre
an imprint of Hodder & Stoughton

First Isis Edition
published 2020
by arrangement with
Hodder & Stoughton
An Hachette UK Company

The extract from "Kindness" quoted p.vii first appeared, in a
different form, in *Words Under Words: Selected Poems* and is
reproduced here with the permission of Naomi Shihab Nye

A catalogue record for this book is available
from the British Library.

ISBN 978–1–78541–874–7

Published by
Ulverscroft Limited
Anstey, Leicestershire

Set by Words & Graphics Ltd.
Anstey, Leicestershire
Printed and bound in Great Britain by
T. J. International Ltd., Padstow, Cornwall

This book is printed on acid-free paper

SUICIDE CLUB

n a near-future New York, medical technology has
rogressed far enough that immortality is now
ithin reach. Lea Kirino is a "lifer", which means
at a roll of the genetic dice has given her the
otential to live forever — if she does everything
ght. But Lea's perfect life is turned upside down
hen she spots her estranged father on a crowded
dewalk. His return marks the beginning of her
ownfall as she is drawn into his mysterious world
f the Suicide Club, a network of powerful
dividuals and rebels who reject society's pursuit
f immortality, and instead choose to live — and die
- on their own terms. In this future world, death is
ot only taboo, it's also highly illegal; and soon Lea
ust choose between her estranged father and her
—— ance to live forever.

Ple
shc

w\

R
Te
s

ι

SPECIAL MESSAGE TO READERS

For my father, Geoffrey Heng (1957–2017)

Before you know what kindness really is
you must lose things,
feel the future dissolve in a moment
like salt in a weakened broth.
What you held in your hand,
what you counted and carefully saved,
all this must go so you know
how desolate the landscape can be
between the regions of kindness.

Kindness, *Naomi Shihab Nye*

Prelude

The man stood in a windowless room. He wore a tuxedo, black as coal, cut sharply against the cliffs of his shoulders. The room was empty, except for the glass bottle and box of matches at his feet.

Some watching the video that night would have closed it at this point, taking it for advertising or spam. But others watched on, intrigued by the formality of his dress or the hard glint in his eyes. Those who kept watching would have heard him state his name and age. They would have heard him explain the reasons for what he was about to do, how long and hard he'd deliberated before coming to this decision. Why he did not want to live another two hundred years. They heard him say that his family had no part in this, and that he had chosen to dress up for the occasion.

Once the man finished speaking, he picked up the bottle from the floor, tipping its contents down his throat. His Adam's apple bobbed under the fleshy creases of his neck as he drank. When he finished, he gave his invisible audience a long, silent look.

"They leave us no choice," he said at last. "DiamondSkin^{TM}, ToughMusc^{TM}. Replacements. Think how much easier it was when you could just take a kitchen knife to your wrists and watch the life pour out of your veins."

More observant viewers would have seen that a trail of clear fluid was now trickling down the side of his mouth as he spoke.

"Something has to change. In being robbed of our deaths, we are robbed of our lives."

He struck a match. The flame shivered under the cool, fluorescent lights.

"They leave us no choice."

When he touched the tip of the match to his outstretched tongue, the flame seemed to pause for a moment, as if wondering where to go. But then he breathed in and the flame grew and grew, filling the alcohol-soaked cavity of his mouth, darting down his throat and up his nasal passages. The man spoke no more.

CHAPTER
ONE

The cake was a huge, tiered thing, painted with butter-cream and decked with tiny red flowers, floating on a glass pedestal in the middle of the crowded room.

No one talked about it, or even looked at it. But every now and then, someone would linger a little too long by the drinks table, pretending to assess the various bubbly greens on offer, while peeking at the cake out of the corner of their eye.

Todd stood dutifully by Lea's side, a slender flute of pale cordial in hand.

"Lovely party," he said, nodding as if someone had asked him a question. He beckoned at her with his glass. "Great drinks. I'm really enjoying the Spirulina Spritz."

Lea smiled absently. Her eyes flitted over the crowd, taking in the navy dresses and delicate silver jewellery, the tasteful suits in varying shades of grey. The flowers on the cake stood out like pinpricks of blood in an otherwise bloodless room. Even the bronzed faces, framed by shiny locks, so well hydrated and evenly boned, seemed grey to her.

But it was a success, by all accounts. The party was a success.

She wouldn't forget to smile. Healthy mind, healthy body.

"There they are! My favourite couple."

"Natalie," Todd brightened, tilting his head in welcome.

Natalie delivered her air kisses with the forbearance of a celebrity deigning to have their picture taken. First to Todd, then to Lea, careful not to actually touch their cheeks.

"You look — wow — so great," Todd said, still nodding. Lea suppressed the urge to grab his head and hold it still.

She did look great though. Her sheath dress shimmered in the candlelight, shadowy indigo. It looked as if Natalie had been poured, a creamy liquid, into the sleek dark length of it.

Lea flashed a smile, mentally cataloguing her own appearance. She measured her straight black hair against Natalie's glossy brown curls (Natalie's was more luscious, more full of life), the burnt umber of her skin against Natalie's pale, freckled visage (prone to UV damage and melanoma, so here Lea had a clear advantage). Natalie's face was angular and long, which together with her large front teeth, gave her an equine aspect. Lea, on the other hand, had never lost her baby fat and her cheeks remained full and plump, lacking in angles altogether. It was something which had bothered her as a girl but that she prized today. As with most lifers around the same age, their bodies were as similar as their faces were different, nearly identical in stature and muscular tone.

4

"Please," Natalie said. "Don't patronise me. Can you see these lines?" She pointed to one smooth, rouged cheek. "I know you can, so there's no need to be polite. I've had the worst week, just the worst, must have taken at least three months off my number. But I don't want to talk about it."

She pressed her lips together. It was evident that she did, in fact, very much want to talk about it, but no one said anything.

"Lea!" she said suddenly. "Tell me all about you! You are naughty, always keeping things to yourself." Natalie glanced coyly at Todd.

"Trust me, I'd love to have some secrets. But with friends like you . . ."

They burst out laughing. Todd laughed too, right on cue. Their laughter was rich and cascading, a golden ribbon unfurling through the party, making people turn to look, people who were until then perfectly secure of their position in life but at that moment felt something was missing.

More friends arrived to join the group, and the flirtatious barbs continued. Lea was up for a big promotion, which she made sure to slip in casually while complaining about how much more work she was getting. She felt the information sink in and waited for the reaction it would generate. Sure enough, Jasmine jumped in with a cautionary tale about how promotions tended to turn co-workers against you; after all, that was what happened to her when she was the first lifer at her firm to get to director level before she hit a hundred.

The conversation fizzled, and they cast their gazes about, looking for a new topic. Some pulled out their tablets.

"So," Natalie said, lowering her voice conspiratorially. "Have you seen it?" She tossed her hair, the lush ringlets giving off the faint scent of coconut. Her neck was firm and smooth. Like the flank of a racehorse, Lea thought.

"Seen what?"

Natalie rolled her eyes, pushed her shoulders back. Her left shoulder, Lea noticed with satisfaction, was slightly lower than the right. Lea drew herself up to her full height as well, glad that her sleeveless silk top showed off the definition of her upper arms, the symmetry of her clavicle.

"The video, of course," Natalie said.

No one looked up from their tabs, but Lea felt the air freeze. She saw the man's eyes, hard and shiny, pupils perfectly opaque, like a fish. His mouth, filling up with heat and fire, melting into brown and black and red, flesh vanishing into smoke and flame.

"Oh God," a tall man with poreless mahogany skin said. He sipped on his vitamin spritz and shuddered. "Can we not talk about that again, Natalie?"

Natalie's new fiancé, Lea remembered. She looked at him closely, taking in his height, posture, muscle tone. She noted the dark intelligent eyes, long lashes, elegant, broad forehead.

"What? We know everyone's thinking about it," Natalie said.

"Unfortunate, unfortunate, very unfortunate. How could we not?" Todd bowed his head.

"Exactly!" Natalie crowed.

"They're sick," someone else chimed in.

"Disgusting."

"Antisanct."

"Imagine children watching that."

"Imagine *us* watching that. Who knows how many months you lose watching that kind of thing?"

"Right! Just think about what it does to cortisol levels."

"Pure spectacle, that's what it is."

"And to do it like that. I feel nauseous just thinking about it."

Suddenly Lea could smell it — the acrid burn of flesh, the eye-watering sting of smoke. The man's eyes filled with a hard, unfamiliar conviction, a deep sadness. Something inside her lurched. Revulsion, she told herself. Shock.

"Are you okay, Lea?" Todd said. "You look a little pale."

Everyone was looking at her now.

"Oh yes, Lea," Natalie said, eyes wide with concern. "Now that Todd's mentioned it. How are your Vitamin D levels, darling? I can recommend a clinic, you know, if yours aren't quite up to the mark."

"Perfect, actually." Lea smiled, ignoring the barely veiled insult. "And no, thank you. I would never leave my Tender. Jessie and I go way back — she was assigned to our family when my mother made senior VP."

"Of course," Natalie said. She pressed her lips together and turned back to the others.

It won't kill you to be nice. At least try.

I am, Lea thought. I am trying. Irritation flared in her belly. She saw her mother's face, the thin sorrowful lines emanating from the corners of her eyes. Then she heard her voice in her head again: *Wrinkles are caused by the loss of elasticity in the skin, a consequence of wear and tear that can be delayed, but not eliminated, by Repairants*^{TM}.

Ever practical, her mother. Even after she'd been dead for decades. Her spine had remained upright till the very end, her downy hair as black as it had always been, kept neatly cropped close to her skull by monthly visits to the salon. Her skin retained its elasticity far better than some of her lighter peers, who had withered decades earlier. Her muscles stayed firm, her feet smooth and well-groomed, her mauve lips full. Such were the benefits of being the CEO of Talent Global and having access to Tier 4 benefits.

Uju had lived to a hundred and forty-two — forty-two years older than Lea was now. It had been a good outcome for someone of her generation, someone who had been in her sixties when the Second Wave began. For Lea, however, a hundred and forty-two would be failure. Three hundred was now the number to beat.

Don't waste it. I gave you everything. Everything your brother couldn't have. Her mother's voice was quiet now, but Lea heard in it the ache that always made her snap to attention, that threatened to open up the wound that the decades, so many of them, could not heal.

She looked around the room at the sleek, glossy haircuts, the smooth foreheads and ramrod spines. The beautiful, wealthy, life-loving people conversing in low voices, politely laughing and clinking glasses from time to time. She took in the premium vitamin spritzes, the crystal flutes, the high ceilings and expansive view of the city down below. The space she had rented for the party was usually reserved for corporate functions, but select employees at the HealthFin trust fund she worked for were able to book it for special occasions.

No, she hadn't wasted anything, Lea thought. Her mother would surely have been proud.

"Happy birthday to you, happy birthday to you, happy birthday dear Lea!"

The room burst into thunderous applause. Cameras flashed. Lea smiled the way Uju had told her to eighty-eight years ago: *Your eyes, make sure to use your eyes, or it looks like you don't mean it.*

She picked up the knife and sliced into the bottom layer of the cake. The styrofoam gave a high squeal when the plastic blade went through it, but even as she winced inwardly, Lea never let the smile leave her face.

CHAPTER
TWO

The sidewalk was a slipstream of browns and greys. The jacket-clad men and women all walked in the same way — elbows pinned to their sides, heads down, gaze directed at the heels of the commuter in front of them.

Lea didn't know what it was that made her look up. Perhaps it was something in the air, the smell of summer giving way to fall, that first nip of coolness brushing her cheeks. Perhaps it was the delicate ankles of the woman in front of her, clothed in dark mesh. Or the leftover buzz from her birthday party the night before, a desire to take in the expanse of the street, the eggshell blue of the morning sky.

When she saw him the air went out of her lungs. He was crossing the road some way ahead of her. He moved slowly, unaware of the disruption he was causing to the flow of commuters around him. Lea could see the looks of annoyance on their faces as people were forced to veer off their usual unthinking paths. The impatient clicks of tongues and issuance of sighs filled her head. He, however, did not seem to notice, and only kept walking at the same ponderous pace, one heavy footstep after another.

This old, oblivious man couldn't be her father. Yet she couldn't tear her eyes from him. She saw how his once-black hair had faded to grey; how thinly it sat against his scalp, the unkempt edges of it curling at his lined neck. She scrutinised the curve of his jaw that used to hold more flesh than it did now. She watched as he brought his chin to his chest and his hand to his nose, pinching its base as if preparing to go underwater. The gesture was unmistakeable.

Lea felt a violent jerk in her chest. A pressure on her diaphragm, a tightness in the throat. Eighty-eight years since the day he'd disappeared without saying goodbye, and there he was again. On the other side of the road, as if he'd never been gone at all.

Let him go. Uju's voice to twelve-year-old Lea. *We have to let him go. It's better this way, after what he's done. He doesn't belong in your life.*

The crowd was bearing the man further and further away, despite his slow pace. Now he was on the other side of the street, disappearing down the sidewalk. Soon he would be out of sight.

Her mother had been right then and she was almost certainly right now, especially now. Everything Lea had worked so hard for, decade after decade, was about to pay off. She'd done it with her mother's support and discipline, yes, but she'd also done it in spite of her father, everything that he'd done and was.

Lea bit down hard on the inside of her cheek, sucking the soft flesh between her teeth. She started elbowing her way through the crowd.

"Watch out!" A stray shoulder rammed into her chest.

He was getting further away. Only his lack of speed allowed her to keep her eyes on him; he was like a pebble in a stream, forming ripples in the crowd that surrounded him. Now all she could see was the top of his grey head, bobbing amid the swirling human currents.

The traffic crossing was too far away. Lea craned her neck as she continued pushing her way through the crowd, but he was turning the corner on the other side of the street, and would soon be out of sight altogether. She made a sharp right.

Sorry. Excuse me. Sorry, sorry. Pardon me. Sorry.

She found herself at the edge of the sidewalk. Vehicles sped past, their tinted windows hiding those powerful enough to use car pools at peak hour. On the other side of the road, her father was about to turn the corner, about to disappear again. For the second time in eighty-eight years, she was going to lose him.

A gap opened in the flow of traffic. Lea stepped out into the road.

She woke up with the familiar cold of tiny electrodes attached to her bare skin.

"Lea Kirino, one hundred years old."

The voice came from a woman in Tenders' maroons, standing next to the bed. She was reading from a tablet. When she lifted her eyes from the screen, Lea saw that they were the dark, damp colour of moss.

"Happy belated birthday. Could you tell me what happened?" the Tender said.

"I was walking to work. I was late —" Lea stopped. Work. The Musk presentation. She stiffened and tried to sit up, but her head felt thick, her brain swollen. "What time is it?"

The Tender placed a hand on Lea's shoulder. Her touch was gentle, but surprisingly heavy. Lea sank her head back into the pillow.

"What happened?" the Tender asked again. "Why did you step out onto the road like that?"

Her father's face in the crowd. The sagging cheeks, the thin neck. Lea thought of the white envelopes that were slipped under her door every few months, the statutory declarations she had to make stating that she did not know where he was. They were still looking for him, decades later. What was he doing in the city?

"I was late for work," Lea said again, her thoughts whirling. "I was trying to take a short cut. The cars — they didn't stop."

The Tender was looking at her with eyebrows drawn together, two deep lines between them. Lea wanted to tell her not to frown, to remind her of the importance of a neutral expression in preserving skin elasticity. But she could tell from the Tender's skin that she was well hydrated and pH balanced.

"How bad was it? Will I need to have anything replaced?" Lea recoiled. She had managed thus far to keep all of her limbs organic, no mean feat for someone who had just reached a hundred. It was only when the

13

Tender failed to reply that Lea noticed the white stripes across her maroon sleeves.

"Which division is this?" she asked.

The Tender tapped a silent note into her tablet. Its red recording light blinked.

"Late for work, you said."

"Yes. Why does that matter?" But Lea's heart was sinking even as she asked the question. *Directive 109A: Reckless pedestrian conduct in undesignated zones.*

"Look, I know it was an undesignated zone," Lea said. "But you'll see, just look it up, my record is spotless. It was one tiny mistake, surely this doesn't matter?"

The Tender was listening carefully now, head tilted to one side. "Where did you say you were crossing again?" Her cool gaze didn't budge.

"Somewhere along Broadway. The intersection with 32nd Street. Maybe 34th."

The Tender's fingernails clicked neatly against the polished glass of her tablet.

"And where do you work?"

"Borough One West. Why does that matter? You haven't answered me — how bad was it? Am I okay?" Lea spread her hands out underneath the sheets, feeling the webs of skin between her fingers stretch. She wriggled her toes and bent her knees. Around her, the electrode wires rustled like a bed of grass. Her body felt normal, as far as she could tell. But she'd heard that these days, replacements felt normal too.

Posters lined the wall, comforting and familiar in their thin metal frames. A fat-encrusted artery stretched out like a sock ("Meat kills"); a raw, torn joint ("Switch to low impact today"); the ubiquitous glowing red eyeball ("Fruit — #1 cause of diabetes blindness"). Recessed ceiling lights cast a warm but insistent glow, leaving no corner of the room unlit. Lea recognised the album streaming from invisible speakers as *Sea and Mandolin*, dubbed one of the most calming tracks of the decade. Nevertheless she felt her cortisol levels ticking up. What was this Tender doing? Certainly not her job. Lea looked around the room for a feedback box, but except for the bed, the room contained no furniture or equipment.

"Borough One West," the Tender repeated. "Why would you try to cross where you did, then?"

"What?" Lea said. Because I saw him, she thought. Because I couldn't lose him again. But she couldn't say that.

"Where you crossed. That would have taken you further east."

"This is ridiculous. I have to get to work." Lea sat up.

The Tender eyed her, but didn't say anything. After a few seconds, she tapped another note into her tab. It silently spat out a single sheet of paper.

"Your treatment plan," she said. "You sustained no injuries, only minor bruises from when you fainted. Shock. The car barely grazed you, its sensors were perfectly operational."

The paper was wafer thin between Lea's fingers and so translucent that it looked like it would dissolve when touched. A deep red cursive rolled across the page,

15

curling elegantly around words like "occipital curvature index" and "ventromedial prefrontal cortex".

"You'll need to attend some follow-up sessions."

Lea read the sheet again, her eyes darting unevenly across the page, but she couldn't make any sense of it. It was like no treatment plan she had ever seen before. The weekly sessions were at a different clinic than usual; no supplements were prescribed. No rehabilitative exercises.

"What is this?" Lea asked, looking up from the sheet of paper.

But the Tender was already gone.

Lea turned the page, dread collecting in the pit of her stomach. She was under Observation. But that made no sense; people like her didn't get placed on the Observation List. That was for other people — no one she knew, of course — but people she imagined were serially divorced, unemployable, or cognitively impaired. The non-life-loving, the antisanct. Lea was a good lifer. She worked in Healthfin. She was as life-loving as it got, surely the Ministry knew that?

Then it clicked: they thought she'd stepped in front of the car on purpose.

Lea let out a snort of indignation. She shook her head as she began plucking the electrodes off her body. The white circles offered little resistance, lifting off her dark smooth skin with a satisfying sluice. She placed them in a neat pile on the bed, wires aligned so that their little adhesive heads bunched together like a bouquet of white wilted roses.

16

Her clothes lay folded next to the bed. As Lea slipped on her underwear, she caught sight of her reflection in the opaque polish of the smooth walls. Instinctively, she stood up straighter, drew her abdomen in and clenched her glutes. She was the picture of a model lifer. Under Observation — she would clear that up soon enough.

Lungs expanding with the tilt of her spine, her breathing was back to normal now. She would speak to Jessie. Maintenance was scheduled for Saturday, so a special appointment wouldn't even be necessary. She could tell her everything then. Jessie would inform them that the whole thing was a big mistake, elaborate on Lea's exemplary medical and motivational history. They would remove her at once from the Observation List. Perhaps she would demand a formal letter of apology.

Lea's office was in a tall glass building in the middle of Borough One. Eighty floors of floating desks and people, and Long Term Capital Partners at the very top. There was something about this great cathedral of empty space carved out from the choked, tumbling streets outside, and stepping into the building's vast lobby always sent a small tremor up Lea's spine. Looking up, there were the soles of polished shoes, cushioned desk feet, the glazed bases of ornamental plant pots. Something naked and alive about it all, all those objects and people suspended so naturally above her, their undersides exposed and vulnerable. Often she came to work early just to linger in the lobby, but today there was no time.

Lea listened to Jiang's frantic voicemails as the elevator swept her up. On one side, people and screens and cubicles whipped by, melting into a smudge. On the other, the city soared, a forest of metal and glass reaching up to the heavens.

As the ground dropped away from Lea's feet, she thought of the way the Tender had looked at her this morning. There was something about her shifting eyes, her pale monoethnic face, that left Lea with an unsettled feeling. Even the motion of the elevator, normally so pleasurable, did not dispel this sense of unease in Lea.

When she got to her office, Jiang was already there. From the violent knitting of his forehead, Lea could tell that it was worse than she had thought. Jiang was usually very careful about his skin.

"I am so, so sorry," she said before he could say anything. "You'll have the presentation on your desk in an hour, I promise. It's practically finished. I just need to update the hourly figures." She wouldn't tell him about the accident, it might have an impact on her promotion this year. No, better to keep it vague.

Jiang was still frowning. He was not one to get angry — none of them were. They knew how bad anger was for oxidative degeneration. She wondered if she should suggest some breathing exercises.

He was pointing at something outside her office. "What are they doing here?"

Everything looked normal: well-dressed colleagues watching terminals as green numbers ticked by, sitting in QuietCoves with their eyes shut, constructively dissenting in glass-doored meeting rooms. An air of efficiency suffused the bright, sunlit space.

"Who?" Lea asked.

And then she saw them. Two men in suits, one fair and lanky, hair slicked so far back it dipped into the back of his shirt, the other, dark-skinned, square-nosed and well-built. Their suits were charcoal grey — tasteful, Lea observed, but not in the expensive fabrics her clients wore. Both clasped tablets in their right hands like bibles. They were looking straight at Lea.

"They've been here all morning asking questions, with some kind of permit from the Ministry? It's a sub-division I've never even heard of. The clients don't like it. Strangers are bad enough, but if they knew they were Ministry — well, then."

What were they doing here, and how could they have got here so quickly? She'd only just come from the clinic.

"So? Did you do something? You know, you're under oath to the company. Is it . . ." he lowered his voice ". . . extensions fraud? Because if it's anything like that, I know a guy. Not from personal experience, of course. But you know how it is, I keep a wide network."

"No!" Lea said. "Of course it's not fraud. It's — I had a kind of accident this morning."

"Accident? Did you get anything replaced?"

Something in Jiang's voice made Lea turn. An edge to it, a frisson. Was it excitement? But his expression

19

had not changed from the serious mask, tempered now with some concern.

"No! I'm perfectly fine, just look at me. This is completely ridiculous," she said. A polite yet firm smile on her face, the kind she gave clients who simply did not meet their lifespan-net-worth-index criteria, she strode out of the office and onto the main floor.

"Good morning, gentlemen. Can I help you with anything?" Lea said.

The one with the slicked-back hair and bad posture opened his mouth as if to speak, only to be interrupted by a cough from his colleague. He closed his mouth.

"You would have received a treatment plan," the interrupter said. Dewy and poreless, his skin had the unreal sheen of someone with abundant access to antioxidant treatments. He had to be high up in the Ministry.

Lea couldn't take her eyes off his skin. It was literally giving off a glow. Its unblemished expanse was like varnished walnut and it tugged at something inside of her, made her want to bring her palm against it, leave a smarting mark.

"What are you doing here?"

The two looked at each other. They were getting more attention now — polite colleagues, pretending to be absorbed in trading and leveraging, were in fact far too quiet to be doing any actual work.

"My name is AJ," the one with the perfect skin said. "And this is my colleague, GK."

GK, busy tapping notes into his tablet, glanced up.

"We are here to observe," AJ went on. GK was slouched over his tablet again. Lea resisted the urge to correct his posture — clearly he had to be further down in the Ministry, with a spine like that.

"This is a place of business. Do you know who our clients are? You can't be here."

At this, the two men simultaneously pulled out slips of paper, crossed with the same red cursive on the plan she'd received this morning. These were smaller, just large enough for the three words: Right to Observe. A gold stamp, the shape of a heart, right in the middle. Papers, like Jiang had said.

"What sub-division are you with?" Lea asked. "I'll have to provide feedback."

AJ blinked. She had his attention now. But then he smiled, flashing small, square teeth. "What about?" he asked.

"Trespassing," Lea started, but then remembered the papers. "Deliberate inducement of cortisol generation," she continued. They could lose their jobs for that.

Her colleagues were openly gathered around now. At the edges of her vision, Lea saw Jiang, tapping shoulders and cupping elbows, trying to disperse the onlookers.

GK was typing faster. Between sentences he would glance up at Lea, first one way, then the other, like an artist trying to capture her likeness.

"And if you don't leave immediately, we'll have to call security," Lea went on.

Now GK smiled too, looking up from his tablet, lips stretching thinly across his flat, pale face. "We're in touch with security. You shouldn't worry about that." He pulled out a small square of orange plastic, curved at the corners, identical to the pass Lea had attached to her keys. "We've been given full access."

Lea breathed down a rising panic. "Fine. Do what you like."

She turned and walked back to her office. Jiang followed her, closing the glass door behind them.

"They can't stay here. It's throwing the clients off." Jiang gestured at the waiting area, where a handful of clients were filling in forms and reading their latest reports. Several had brightly patterned silk scarves wrapped around the bottom halves of their faces. A couple were even wearing sunglasses. They were far too discreet to stare directly, but Lea could feel their eyes on her.

"I can't do anything about it. You heard them. I'm under Observation."

She scratched at a hangnail under her desk, the old guilty satisfaction a sudden relief. Blood swelled from the wound for a split second, before clotting in a smooth patch that would heal in moments.

"Oh," Jiang's voice changed, buckling ever so slightly, as if under an invisible weight. "Observation. I see, well. I see. I didn't hear that."

His gaze slipped from her face, travelled the length of her office before coming to rest on a spot in the middle of the far wall. He clasped his hands together, then unclasped them, then clasped them again.

He glanced out again at where AJ and GK were standing. AJ was talking to the receptionist, hands in his pockets, leaning against the desk in an unnaturally casual stance. A peel of low laughter trickled out of the receptionist's throat. She leaned forward conspiratorially, red lips barely moving. Tap, tap, tap, went GK's fingers.

"Jiang," Lea said. "You don't actually think —"

"No, no, of course not." He flashed his pink palms at her. "But — still."

"Still what?"

"Just, you can never be too careful, you know. As employers, we only want what's best for you. Healthy mind, healthy body. Maybe," he said, examining the back of his left hand as if he had never quite noticed it before, "maybe you're working too hard."

"What?" Lea's voice rose.

"We can get Natalie to back you up on the Musk account. Always good to have two heads working on a deal as big as this."

The thought of Natalie's smug, all-natural face made Lea say in a louder voice than she'd intended: "No way. I brought the Musks in. You're not handing them over to anyone else."

Sunlight streamed in from all directions. Jiang's face was like a moon, round and pitted with visible pores, several of which were dark and enlarged. Despite the icy air-conditioning, a fine film of perspiration coated his forehead.

"They'll be gone by next week, I promise," Lea said, controlling her tone. "I have a maintenance appointment on Saturday. They'll sort the whole thing out. It's just a misunderstanding."

"Okay," he finally said. "But you promise you'll let me know if — if anything comes up. Anything too cortisol-generating or rest-detrimental."

When Jiang had gone, Lea leaned back in her ergonomic chair. Except for the alarm that regulated her sitting time, the screens on her desk were completely dark. The timer meted out a fixed number of seconds before an automated voice would remind her to complete her Hourly Stretches. The numbers vanished noiselessly, green resolving into black again and again. The longer Lea stared at them, the less sense they made. Glancing over the tops of the screens, she saw GK and AJ, now pacing the perimeter of the waiting area.

It occurred to her that she could make it all go away. She could tell them who she had seen, why she'd stepped out onto the road so urgently. She could tell them she didn't want to let him get away, not again. And it would be true, in part.

But then what? What if they found him? It may have been eighty-eight years, but the Ministry had a long, unforgiving memory.

CHAPTER
THREE

Anja drew the woollen shawl across her thin shoulders tightly, sinking her chin to breathe in the fading scent of her mother. French lavender and the sea, all mixed up in one sharp whiff.

Time was measured in the beating of her mother's mechanical heart. Thud, thud, thud. Space, in the number of steps taken to cross the room to retrieve the dried meals that arrived at regular intervals.

Her mother's heart, rupture-proof, was now visible through a transparent film that had once been her skin, wrapped around a cage of bones. Anja could predict with split-second accuracy the rising and falling of each atrium, each ventricle. Each beat was exactly the same as the last. She watched it fill and squeeze, valves open and close, the ink-coloured SmartBlood™ flowing thick and steady.

Thud, thud, thud. Like the footsteps of someone pacing back and forth along the corridor of a big, empty house. The heart would be the last thing to fail. It had the longest working life and had been the newest, most cutting-edge technology. The skin had been the first. Anja had watched as it mottled and shrank away from the bones, great stains of tea brown spreading.

DiamondSkin^{TM}, they called it, self-repairing and extra tough. To a point, until her mother reached the end of her predicted enhanced lifespan, and the clinic doors of spotless glass slammed shut forever. So Anja waited, alone with her in this dark room that smelled of stale water, with nowhere to go.

When her mother first took to bed it was not so bad, because at least they could still talk. Back then, she could pretend things were normal even as her mother's muscles atrophied under the embroidered quilt and her lungs slowly collapsed into themselves. They passed their time in idle conversation, talking about anything and everything — music, Sweden, Anja's father.

Sometimes Anja would play the violin for her, the strings pressing cold and cruel into her stiff fingers. She was out of practice and it showed badly, but her mother no longer pointed out her mistakes. She didn't seem to hear the flat notes or stray beats, only smiled quietly, eyes on the ceiling, hands clasped on her hollow stomach.

Anja longed for harsh words, for her mother to point out where she was going wrong and to call her lazy, complacent. To suck the air in through her teeth sharply and stamp her feet, to rap Anja hard on her knuckles like she used to. So Anja started playing badly on purpose, notes slipping and sliding, rhythm askew, watching in quiet desperation for the slightest twitch of displeasure on her mother's face. But it never came. All that remained was that blankness. Anja packed her violin away in its dark velvet case, the shiny metal clasps making gunshot clicks as they snapped shut.

When Anja was a girl, a proper girl with ropey limbs and scattered acne, her mother used to take her swimming in the Baltic Sea. They would rise at dawn when the clouds were still asleep and the air was damp with fog. Wrapped in thick bathrobes, they'd cycle the shrub-lined path in the dim light, anticipating each bump and turn before it came. The cloistered morning seemed to go on forever, as if in a dream. But then suddenly, just as their sandalled feet started to go numb in the wind, the path would open up and there it would be: lapping, metallic, the open sea. They stripped quickly. Leaving their bathrobes in a pile, tripping lightly over rough sand and spiky little plants until they reached the edge of the surf. It was better to do it quickly, so they always plunged straight in, pushing through the suffocating chill that pressed from all sides until the sandy bottom dropped away and there was nothing left to do but swim. Her mother's limbs shone like ivory in the pink morning light, fearlessly sluicing through cold. They did this every morning of her life but then they came to New York, and there was nowhere to swim.

The day her mother said her last words, they had been talking about their beach. How the sand would rub their feet raw, the steely water blending into the sky. How every single time the sharp cold, more heat than cold, never failed to take their bodies by surprise.

27

Her mother wondering if their neighbour, Mr Andersson, was still watering their plants as he had promised, waiting for the day when they would return to their little white house by the sea. Anja reminding her that Mr Andersson was long gone, fifty years ago at least, before they even introduced life extension in Sweden. They had embraced it by now, of course, but were still a long way behind America.

It was in the middle of this reminiscing that her mother's voice box quit, the muscles clenching around shapeless sounds until they gave up forever. At first, Anja kept talking, filling in with what she imagined her mother would say. It helped that her mother's eyes were still alert, still met her own with a burning life. But eventually they dimmed. Then her skin started to fade, losing its colour and opacity. It grew harder and harder to keep up the one-sided conversation.

Now Anja sat silently in the hard wooden chair next to her mother's bed, listening to the pumping of her mechanical heart.

She told herself that her mother was long gone, her spirit extinguished like a flame in an airless room. She told herself that her mother was no longer there, that the body which remained was an imposter, a shell. A prison.

But sometimes she saw her mother's transluscent eyelids twitch, and she wondered. And always, always there was the relentless thud, thud, thud of the alien heart, a sound that haunted Anja in her sleep, in her dreams. As hard as she tried, she couldn't shake the idea that her mother was still in there. Trapped in the dark, unable to speak or see.

How long had it been now? She couldn't tell. The days smeared into one another.

Before they turned milky and white, her mother's eyes had been the colour of the sea. A clear, cold grey, the colour of ice on a freshly frozen lake. When Anja looked in the mirror now, all she could see was her mother's eyes staring back at her. Her mother's eyes, her mother's sharp nose, her mother's pale, salmon mouth.

Just to see, what's the harm? That was what her mother had said when they first arrived in New York and walked past the clinic. So they got tested. It turned out they both had good genes, excellent genes, so good that they were eligible for all kinds of subsidised treatments. They laughed it off. That was not what they were here for, no, they were here for the music. Her mother to sing, Anja to play the violin.

But the thought of living forever was a slow-burning disease she'd caught from the moment they took those tests. Her mother started living like the Americans, no longer eating meat or even fish, her hefty bulk dwindling into an efficient, gym-honed leanness. She stopped running because of what it did to her knees. Eventually she sang less and less, because they'd told her about her heart, how it was the weakest link in an otherwise immaculate genetic make-up. There was also all that excess cortisol production involved in being a musician. Occupational hazard, as they called it.

Her mother became obsessed with enhancements, and then repairs. First it was the skin, regrafted every fifteen months, then the blood, souped up with microscopic smart particles, nanobots that cleansed and repaired and regenerated. The day they replaced her heart with a high-powered synthetic pump, Anja practised the violin till her fingers turned purple and raw. At the clinic she searched her mother's face for clues as to where this would end.

Now she knew, of course. This was how. The two of them in this empty, damp room with nothing but a few instruments to their name. The treatments were only subsidised up to a point, growing more and more expensive as her mother reached the end of her predicted lifespan, until they had nothing left. All there was left to do now was wait.

Her tablet began to ring, but Anja ignored it, instead standing up and walking over to the window. She placed her hands on the smooth painted wood and pushed up. At first it wouldn't budge, so she pushed again, this time harder, and the shawl around her neck fell to the floor. The window's dusty seams creaked as it opened.

The smell of the city was crisp and sour. It hit her nose like saltwater, making her eyes well up. The streets outside were empty and most windows were dark. How many others were there, dying and unable to die? At least her mother had her.

The shrill cry of the tab bled out onto the empty streets.

Anja stepped back from the window, slipping a hand into her pocket. Her fingers closed around a card she had been carrying with her for a long time now, ever since her mother had taken to bed. With her thumb she traced the curves of embossed numbers that she knew by heart now, a phone number printed under two words in bold, red type: Suicide Club.

CHAPTER
FOUR

It was always a matter of focus, as most things were. So Lea focused, pushing every stray thought out of her mind, forcing herself to relax and breathe. She focused on the sinuous curve of Todd's shoulders dipping and rising, blurring and sharpening with the movement of his head. She focused on the damp heat of his hard flank pressing against her calves. His cheeks, crumbed with stubble, on her inner thighs. Her fingers, which had been resting gently on Todd's head, gripped a handful of hair. He sped up, but Lea closed her thighs and sat up.

"What?" he said, pink lips glistening in a blade of light.

Lea slid off the bed.

She checked the living room first. Everything was as it should be. Throw pillows neatly arranged on the mid-century couch, cashmere throw draped over its grey herringbone upholstery. White storage units lined the wall, flushed orange in the morning light. Paper lanterns scattered through the room pulsed a soft pale pink, a hue meant to energise and uplift. The spotless linen curtains hung still, the furniture mute in its coordinated palette of neutral shades. The marble floor was cold beneath her feet.

Lea walked through the entire apartment twice, checking the kitchen, bathroom, guest room.

When she returned to bed, Todd shot her a look.

"I thought I heard something," she said.

Todd propped himself up onto his elbows, worry creasing his brow. "You have to stop. All this paranoia — it's not good for you."

"You don't get it. Do you realise they were there? In my office? Asking questions, talking to the receptionist. And —" she stopped.

I saw him. My father. But the words stuck in her throat. Todd knew about her family, of course he did, but to him it was nothing more than backstory, a tragic chapter of Lea's life that was long past. As far as he was concerned, it was a thing that she had overcome.

Todd's warm toes found her tailbone. Then his fingers, kneading upwards, digging into the hard muscle that knotted her spine. When he reached her neck, Todd wrapped his fingers around the bare, smooth length of it, thumbs working diligently. She stiffened.

"What?" Todd said.

She prised his fingers from her neck, leaning forward out of his reach.

"What else can I do? How can I convince them?"

"Like I said, you don't have to convince them," Todd said. "This whole thing is crazy, Lea; they'll realise sooner or later they've made a mistake. The Ministry will sort it out. There's no point getting worked up, losing days over this."

Lea stood up from the bed and turned towards the mirrored wardrobe. Even naked, she could still pass for no older than fifty. This wasn't unique to her, of course, most lifers close to a hundred were indistinguishable from those in their first half-century. But it was how you looked as you approached your second century that really counted. Still, examining her straight spine, the well-calibrated gap between the tops of her thighs and the subtle hollows of her hips, it was hard to believe that she, of all people, was under Observation.

"Worrying about it is only going to make it worse," Todd went on. "Healthy mind, healthy body. Can't you just ignore them?"

"We lost the Musk account because of them. That could set me back by years," Lea said.

"You haven't lost it," Todd said. "They said it was on hold. Why assume the worst? Maybe if you just —"

"Just what?"

Todd looked away. He smoothed out a crease in the sheets.

She knelt down next to him, running her palms over his thighs. Under the soft surface, freckled with blond hairs like the surface of an alien planet, was a hard solidity that always fascinated her. One day, that would be all that was left, she thought, suddenly sad. SmartBlood^{TM}, DiamondSkin^{TM} and ToughMusc^{TM}, living on into eternity. She pushed away the thought of her father's face, dark with pigmentation and ridged with creases.

Todd placed his hands over hers. "I know it's going to work out. You're the best, most dedicated lifer I know, that's all I'm saying."

"But what if it doesn't? What if —"

"I'll go to the Ministry myself and tell them. I'll tell them about how you were the first lifer to give up running, even before the high impact advisory came out. I'll tell them about the way you split your Nutripaks into half-hourly portions to ensure optimal nutrient release through the day. I'll tell them about the two hours you spend meditating each night, the daily morning stretches you've never missed a single time, the —"

"Okay, okay, I get it," Lea said.

She smiled, but her insides still felt tight. The look on his face now was the thing about Todd. Why, maybe, they had now been engaged close to eight years and still hadn't set a date for the wedding. Todd, with his impeccable genes and trusting goodness, his firm belief that the Ministry was fair and reasonable. Todd, with his HealthFin family, his trust fund that meant he was able to pass his days indulging in languid self-maintenance. Todd, who had never known a sub-100 in his life, who existed solely on the plane of the genetically blessed.

But wasn't that why she was with him? Didn't she wear Todd like a band-aid, armour against her muddled past? Wasn't he her crowning glory, the last puzzle piece of the life she wanted, the life that Uju would have wanted for her? Their offspring would almost certainly be lifers, and for all they knew, could even be the first to break the threshold. Immortals. They'd have as good a chance as any, with Todd and Lea's genes.

Lea stood up abruptly. "Come with me," she said.

She took him by the hand, leading him to the smallest room in her apartment. It had originally been conceived of as a walk-in wardrobe. Now it was full, ceiling to floor, with paintings. The tall mirror that spanned the length of one wall was smudged with streaks and spots of colour.

Todd never came in here alone. He was always sweetly respectful of what he considered her odd, private hobby. Now he stared at the canvases with polite puzzlement, brow furrowed like he was trying to solve a maths problem.

"What do you think?" She spun him around to face the large easel which stood splayed in the middle of the room. "It's the city," she said, pointing to the grid, the skyscrapers, the ombre sky.

"I see," Todd said, nodding slowly. Lea could see that he didn't. Still, she picked up the canvas and held it out to him.

"Here. I want you to have it."

"I can't take this," Todd said. But when Lea didn't move, he took the painting from her gently, taking care not to touch the glistening surface. "It's beautiful," he said with a certain resolve. "Thank you."

Lea kissed him the way she always did, lips parted as if to sip from a straw, tongue coyly poised on the edge of her teeth. Hands stroking his sinewy, strong neck, reminding herself that this was it, this was success. Healthy mind, healthy body.

They did it on the floor, cold marble pressing against her thighs, surrounded by canvases and the chemical smell of liquid colour. Outside, the sky was thick with clouds.

CHAPTER
FIVE

Everyone was born with a number. They ran the tests immediately after birth. A simple swab of a wailing throat, parents waiting, hands clasped nervously, for the moment that would define the rest of their child's life. Sometimes the results came out as a mother held the baby in her arms for the first time, staring into its liquid, barely human eyes.

That was how it had been with Lea, so the story went. She had heard it countless times — how her mother had asked them to repeat themselves, and then, on hearing the same thing, insisted they repeat the test. The brusque way in which they stated that they did not make mistakes, the doctor so offended that his black moustache wouldn't stop twitching. How she still couldn't bring herself to believe it, but found herself crying anyway, tears dripping down her chin to fall onto little baby Lea's perfect, round cheeks, how she had parted her tiny pink lips and tasted salt for the first time.

It had been different with Samuel, of course. Forty years before Lea was born. Then her mother had remained expressionless, taking the news as though she'd expected it.

First there was Samuel, and then there was Lea. Uju and Kaito gave them what they thought were good American names, names that signified a new beginning for their family.

The doctors gave it a million to one chance, what had happened. It was extremely unusual. Siblings' numbers were usually within a hundred years of each other; each extra ten years of divergence were a slap in the face of probability. For one to be a lifer, and the other not — that was practically unthinkable.

Sometimes Lea wondered if a gene pool were finite and could only be split so many ways between siblings. If she had stolen something from him. But she never let herself wonder for too long.

"Good morning, Lea!" the receptionist trilled as the clinic's doors slid shut behind her. "I'll let Jessie know you're here. Won't be a moment."

Other customers, mainly women in pencil skirts tapping away at their tabs, sat in the glossy reception area. Some held glasses of khaki-coloured liquid, freshly cold-pressed at the clinic's veggie bar. Its solid pine counters, white Zen paintings, and paper lanterns all designed to soothe.

Lea ordered a ginger tea from thc attractive barista at the counter. She watched the outline of a vein in his forearm as he sliced a stalk of fresh ginger into wafer-thin strips. Perhaps he was in training to be a surgeon. He couldn't be a day over fifty and was probably finishing up his third decade in med school. These days, she'd heard, every clinic job was hotly contested by students eager to get any experience they could, even if it meant blending smoothies and scrubbing latrines.

Samuel had wanted to be a paediatrician, she remembered suddenly. He had always been good with children. He'd practised on her. She thought of him now, long-limbed and knobbly at the joints, hair brushing the floor and glasses sliding past his forehead, teaching her to do a headstand against the kitchen island. Lea laughing and kicking up before her mother could stop her.

He'd never stood a chance, of course. Non-lifers didn't have the lifespan to complete the four decades of medical training required to qualify as even the most basic of doctors.

"Lea."

At the sound of Jessie's voice, Lea's insides warmed. Jessie had that effect on people, most Tenders who worked maintenance did. The texture of her voice was golden and syrupy. Jessie was family. She'd looked after Samuel before Lea, as well as her mother, when she was still alive. And her father, before he'd disappeared.

They entered the treatment room, a space so clean and uncluttered that it felt much larger than it really was. All the equipment — regulators, sensors, scales — were neatly tucked away behind white panels, all except for the cocoon, which sat silently in a corner. Lining the far wall was a vertical garden, row upon row of shiny porcelain pots, mostly succulents, prickly turgid limbs jostling for space.

"Oh Jessie," Lea said. "You're going to be so shocked at my stats. I've probably lost a whole month just from yesterday alone."

Jessie's hands squeaked into cream rubber gloves, milky against her skin.

"Well, let's see what the damage is, shall we?" Jessie drew one finger across a screen. The cocoon in the corner of the room softly whirred to life. It emitted a pale green light, and then was silent.

Lea removed her clothes quickly, folding them neatly on Jessie's desk. Her skin prickled with cold.

"Oof." Jessie's gloved fingers met with the dark purple shape on Lea's hip. "Land yoga?"

For a moment Lea was struck with the odd thought that they could have been sisters, her and Jessie, comparing bodies in their bedroom. She wondered what that must have been like, having a sister. How different it would have been to having a brother.

There he was again, Samuel. Sitting in the corner of the room. He had his nose in a worn book, something to do with string theory or ornithology, his two favourite topics. He chewed on his forefinger as he read, nose scrunched up. Lea stared at him, wishing he would look up at her. But he never did.

You've always had his nose, her mother said. It was the only time she'd allowed Lea to indulge in what she would otherwise consider to be unproductive wallowing. Uju had always made exceptions for Samuel.

The cocoon was ready. It slid open noiselessly, revealing the narrow bed within.

Lea took Jessie's outstretched hand and stepped in. Bare skin against the rough, sanitised sheet, she exhaled one long, audible breath. The sides of the cocoon were

41

transparent, allowing her to see outside, but it was little comfort. Her heart rattled in her chest.

Jessie touched the screen again, sending the sound of a calm ocean streaming into the small space. Then, the smell of salt, fresh and bracing. Lea closed her eyes.

The lid slid over her body, a click telling her that the air lock was sealed. The sides turned opaque, plunging her into an inky darkness. She spread her fingers against the rough fabric of the mattress, then closed them, then spread them again, reassuring herself that she was still there. She squeezed her eyes shut.

She saw Samuel again, the day the coughing wouldn't stop, the day he stared at his hand for a long time after bringing it away from his mouth. Lea making herself as small as she could in the corner of the living room as her parents rushed to Samuel's side. Thinking about it now, it must have been strange, Samuel crinkle-eyed and loose around the middle, the hair on his head sparser, greyer than that of their seventy-six-year-old father.

A low vibration filled the cocoon. Lea knew the drill: the gas, the green light, then vibration again. She breathed slowly, mindfully, dragging the air against the walls of her windpipe. It would be over soon.

The second vibration came. And then, without warning, her father's face. Not the man she had seen on the street, but her father as he used to be. His skin firm with life, his eyes dark and shining pinpricks, the same shape and colour as hers.

Her father, grabbing Samuel's wrist so roughly that she saw her brother wince behind the corrective lenses.

Her father, staring shock-still into Samuel's palm, as if reading some terrible future in their lines. She found out later it wasn't the lines he was looking at, of course. It had been blood, thick and frothy, mixed with phlegm.

But it wasn't the blood that she remembered most clearly. Or what came later, the coughing fits, the cancer, the hospitals, the funeral. She had always known that Samuel would die. What she remembered was the look on her father's face that first day, the day the coughing wouldn't stop. The way his face had twisted as he stared into Samuel's hand, his mouth becoming a thin line. His eyes were blank and intractable pools, suddenly cold and foreign to her. The terrible, sad look on his face was what she remembered.

When the cocoon's lid finally opened, Lea's eyes were still squeezed shut.

"All done," Jessie sang. "Hey, you okay?"

She took three deep breaths, counting as she filled her lungs.

"Lea?"

Lea opened her eyes and sat up. Her skin prickled at the sudden chill.

"Fine," she said. "I —" Lea stopped. How could she even begin to tell Jessie? "I just never get used to those things."

As Lea dressed, Jessie turned to the three large screens that loomed over her workstation. Lines began to arch gracefully across each of them, propping up bars, connecting circles and triangles. The shapes formed familiar constellations, but they meant nothing to Lea. Only Tenders could read them.

Jessie glanced over at one screen, then the next, then the first again. Lea stared into her face, trying to decode her features instead, but Jessie's expression remained unchanged. A tiny smattering of dark freckles across her nose was the only mark on her bronze skin.

"Nothing to worry about," she said, finally. "Whatever that little shock was yesterday, it barely moved your stats. A couple of extra cleanses, some months of intensive meditation and you'll make it up in no time."

But when the numbers started to appear, filling the screen with their pert green angles, Jessie paused. "What happened yesterday?" she asked.

When Lea told her, she kept her tone light-hearted. Made it sound like a big joke: the two guys in their shiny suits, the Tender who clearly needed a refresher course in Creating A Soothing Environment (which Jessie was a master at, Lea threw in), the incomprehensible "treatment plan". She didn't mention why she stepped out onto the road.

"You'll speak to them today then?" Lea said when she finished.

Jessie turned away from the screens, retrieving a small watering can from under her desk. She said nothing until she finished watering the plants. Eventually, most were covered in fat jewels of water, and she turned back to Lea. The watering can, Lea noticed, was the exact shade of maroon as the robes Jessie wore.

"Lea," Jessie said gently. "This is Maintenance. Monitoring — they're completely separate from us. A totally different division."

"What are you saying?"

"It's not that I don't want to help," Jessie said, without meeting Lea's eyes. Under the warmth of her voice was a hard spine of professionalism, something that Lea had always known was there but never given much thought to until now.

"Oh." Lea stared at her hands in her lap. "Well, then. Should we carry on? I have — I'm meeting someone in ten minutes," she lied.

"Of course." Jessie turned back to her screens and started typing, the even clicks of the keyboard like the pattering of rain. For the rest of the session, she didn't say a thing about the bruise on Lea's hip or the Observers. It was as if Lea hadn't said anything at all.

A series of scrapings, joint manipulations and spinal fluid adjustments later, and they were done. The delivery tube next to her desk pinged, spitting out a small glass vial. Jessie pulled out a syringe tipped with a fine needle and with one smooth motion, extracted the fluid inside the vial. Lea offered her forearm automatically.

"I'm giving you some extra Repairants^{TM}. The usual antioxidants, plus a little boost to help you get over the extra stress. Oh, and good job on the Swimlates," Jessie said. "Great for your tendons."

The needle prick was nothing more than a tickle, followed by the familiar chemical rush of well-being. As she straightened her spine, Lea felt every little bone, every minor tendon, click and stretch into place. She felt the fine capillaries branching beneath her skin, laden with ripe haemoglobin and newly added Repairants^{TM}. Her skin tingled and she seemed to feel the tiny cracks and fissures in its surface close, the dead dry cells slough off, snake-like. Her muscles were limber, supple springs coiled tight with strength. The heightened awareness of her invigorated body was blissful but also agitating, and Lea stood up from her chair abruptly.

"I'll see you out," Jessie said.

They walked in silence down the short hallway towards the lobby. Lea could feel Jessie's discomfort hovering between them, but she did nothing to assuage it. It was Jessie's own fault, she thought, for not even trying to help. It was impossible that she couldn't do anything. She was a Tender.

The clinic's peach walls were lined with a series of portraits, dramatically lit photos of men and women in lab coats, labelled with titles and dates in handsome serif type. Lea recited the familiar names — *Pillai, Blackwell, Chan, Krusov, Moll* — staring into their blown-up, high-definition eyes that watched over the ebb and flow of clients. She wondered what the pioneers of the First Wave would think if they could see New York today, post — Second Wave, on the cusp of the Third. *The first Immortals already lived among them.* The phrase, so often recited that it had become a meaningless mantra, struck her all of a sudden. She thought of Samuel.

She stopped and turned to Jessie, grabbing her arm.

"You could look into it, couldn't you, Jessie? You could do it for me?" Lea said. She hated the pleading note in her voice. "The Third Wave. I've heard rumours it's happening sooner than expected. I can't have this on my record. Not now, not after how hard I've worked."

Jessie looked about the lobby, her gaze skittering away from Lea's. As she blinked, her long eyelashes cast a cobweb of shadows across her cheek.

"I'll see you next week," she said brightly, prising Lea's fingers from her arm.

"I will, yes, but couldn't you just —" Lea stopped. Jessie was no longer listening. Her eyes were fixed on some commotion behind Lea, the voice of the receptionist rising over a low, insistent baritone.

Lea turned. The scene in front of her didn't register immediately. It was, at first glance, exactly as she had left it when she'd gone into Jessie's office for her appointment. The Zen paintings, the paper lanterns, the barista manning the juice counter. It had filled up while she was gone, every plush sofa occupied by other customers. But unlike before, none of them were looking at their tabs or their phones or the glossy magazines whose open pages flopped lifelessly in their laps.

Instead, they were looking at the man standing in the middle of the room. The clinic lights did him no favours, making his scalp under the sparse grey hair appear shinier than it was, casting shadows under his eyes and mouth, revealing the excess folds of skin in his neck.

"Our waiting area is members only, sir. I really must ask you to wait outside," the receptionist was saying, her voice getting higher and higher.

"All I'm asking is whether she's registered here." His voice a rich, calming sound, commanding and strong, at odds with the decrepitude of his face.

"We don't reveal confidential client information to strangers, as I have already said," the receptionist went on. The distress in her voice was palpable. Likely a medical student herself, it was clear that she was unused to anyone other than the clinic's polished clientele.

"And as I've already said, I'm not a stranger," the man said.

"Sir." Jessie stepped forward.

Lea's father turned, and their eyes met for the first time in eighty-eight years.

Jessie was by his side now, her hand cupping his elbow. "You'll have to leave now, sir," she said. She nodded at the barista, who joined her in a flash, taking Lea's father by the other elbow. He twisted out of their grasp, pulling his arms away from them. He made as if to take a step towards Lea, but the barista grabbed him again, this time in a firm lock around his chest. He stumbled and gave a yelp.

"Hey!" Lea said sharply, stepping forward. "Stop that."

The barista looked up in surprise. "But he's a sub-100, ma'am."

"He is not a sub-100," Lea answered, walking up to them.

48

"What are you talking about, Lea?" Jessie asked curiously. Her father shrugged off the barista's grip, pulling his worn blazer straight on his shoulders. The familiar movement made Lea's chest tighten.

"It was you he was asking about," the receptionist said. Now that she was back behind the front desk and absolved of responsibility, she seemed eager to get back into the fray. The other clients looked on as well, hungry for a story.

"You know him? Who are you?" Jessie asked, turning towards the man, squinting at his face. Something flickered across her eyes. She stared at him as if he was a ghost. And wasn't he, after all?

CHAPTER
SIX

Before her father could respond, Lea grabbed his elbow and dragged him towards the exit.

"I'll see you next week, Jessie," she called brightly as the doors slid shut behind them.

For once she was thankful for the Saturday morning traffic. The flow of people swallowed them up quickly, and the clinic soon disappeared out of view. The weekend brunch crowd were out in full force, sipping flavoured protein mixes and sucking in oxygen shots as if their lives depended on it.

Lea picked the most crowded bar they could find, a few blocks down from the clinic, squeezing in next to a trio of househusbands with wailing babies. The plummeting birth rates meant you rarely saw children any more, so every passer-by stopped by the prams, cooing and tickling cheeks, making the babies cry even louder while their fathers looked on indulgently.

The dim lights in the bar hid the worst of his face, though they were sitting so close that she could still make out the clusters of milia under his blurry eyes.

"My little Lea, all grown up," Kaito said. He took a sip of the pale green cucumber slush in the tall glass in front of him and made a face. "Oh, that's terrible. How can anyone be expected to drink this?" He beckoned to a waiter. "Hi. Excuse me. Can I get a vanilla milkshake, please?"

"A what?"

"An artery-clogging, LDL-rich, triglyceride-packed concoction of sugary, artificially flavoured vanilla ice cream and whole milk," Kaito went on.

"He's joking," Lea interrupted. "*Such* a joker." She laughed loudly, waved the waiter along.

"It might be a good idea to try not to draw attention to yourself," she whispered.

Kaito sighed. He looked down at his smoothie, stirring the green slush. The spoon clinked against glass, filling the air that hung between them.

"You sound just like your mother," he said, looking up from his unappealing drink. His eyes were hooded stars in his face, as bright and mischievous as they'd always been. The curve of his mouth still sardonic, still gently mocking. "Just like your mother."

And there it was again, her mother's disapproving voice. *He could be recognised. You could be seen with him. Directive 28B: Aiding and abetting an antisanct.*

"Anyway. It's been almost ninety years. I doubt they even remember who I am."

Lea shook her head. She knew this wasn't true, but all she said was: "You're back."

Her father stopped stirring. "How are you?" he asked. The smile was gone now. It was a serious question.

"I'm —" the word caught in her throat, a tickle, a blockage, but she forced it out with a cough. "I'm fine," she said. Her voice was measured and calm, no different from when she was giving a presentation at work, talking through compound growth rates and kidney forward curves. But a pressure was building behind Lea's eyes, spreading to the upper reaches of her nose, the back of her throat. It took her a few seconds to recognise the feeling.

Lea hadn't cried in decades, and she wasn't about to start now. She looked away from her father, staring instead at the street outside, where the thick flow of human traffic carried on reassuringly. People talking and pushing and walking, all with the same smooth faces, the same upright gaits. A patchwork of browns and greys and blacks. It seemed everyone was wearing the same fall coat. Suddenly, she longed for summer, the only time of year when the streets erupted in colour and sweat.

"I was worried sick. When you dashed out like that across the road. At first, of course, I didn't realise it was you. What were the odds? But when I saw you — even with all the people crowding around, I knew. I'd recognise my Lea anywhere."

The lump in her throat grew. Like I recognised you, she thought.

His eyes traced some invisible pattern in her face, one feature to another. "I'm not used to you being an adult." Her father grinned, revealing teeth that were faintly yellow, their edges jagged and ground down. She hadn't seen teeth like that in decades. Was this how everyone's teeth used to look? "Little Lea. Somehow I expected you to still be that little girl with the big, round eyes. Always quiet, always watching. Planning for world domination. Terrifying all the other children at school."

Her chest squeezed. The tears receded. The face of a boy, pale and afraid, flashed before her eyes. Classmates quiet and crying. A fluffy rabbit, soft, white as a cloud.

"That was a long time ago," she said abruptly. "I barely remember any of it."

Kaito leaned back in his chair. He tilted his head to the side and seemed to be sizing her up. It was a look she couldn't read. "I'm sure. Eighty-eight years. Almost a century ago," he said.

She was afraid he would say more, but he stopped, looking back down at his drink.

"Aren't you — are they still looking for you?" Lea said in a low voice. She was grateful for the roar of conversation, the shouted orders and the incessant grinding buzz of the industrial juicers.

"It's good to see you," her father said, ignoring her question. "I mean, I wish it could have been under better circumstances. Without you running into rush-hour traffic in the middle of Broadway and all. But still, so good to see you. I can see you're doing well. Really well."

"I am," Lea said. For a moment she allowed herself to believe that she was seeing her father after a long trip away. That he had gone somewhere for work, for a few weeks, for a month. That they had a close, lifelong relationship, full of daily phone calls, shared Nutripak meals, long walks in the park. "I'm up for a promotion at work," she said, even though he didn't even know what she did, didn't know anything about the past eighty-eight years of her life.

Kaito grinned. "Of course you are. Bet no one else stands a chance. Bet you're *walloping* them all."

Lea blinked. Did he think this was funny, just one big joke?

"Why are you here?" Her voice was stronger now, and she no longer felt like she was about to cry or shout.

She saw the movement of the streets reflected in the bright pinpricks of his eyes and it struck her, forcefully, that her father was in there. In this shrunken body, this shell of his former self, it was still him. The same man who'd brought her a plastic dinosaur toy every time he went away on a business trip, the same man who'd carried Samuel thirty blocks to the hospital when the ambulance was stalled in traffic. The same man who'd cried when her brother closed his eyes for the last time. The first man Lea had ever seen cry.

Finally he spoke.

"I'm getting old, Lea." He smiled another ironic smile.

It hit her then that he was only a decade younger than her mother. Which made him a hundred and seventy, an impressive age for someone of his generation. They'd always known, of course, that he would outlive Uju. His number had always been higher than hers; an ancestral advantage he'd brought with him from the small mountain town in Central Honshu, Japan, to America, all those years ago.

"And, well, I've missed you," he said.

Her insides squeezed. I've missed you too, she thought. But what now? What did he think they could be now? There was no family left. Their family had fallen apart a long time ago. She had a different life now, a different purpose.

"I — I need to go," Lea said. Under the counter, Lea scraped one thumbnail across ragged cuticles, drawing blood faster than the skin could grow back.

Kaito sighed, and she saw it move through him, rising up from his chest, rippling through his face. In the lines that radiated out from the edges of his eyes and circled his mouth, Lea saw every expression he had ever made. It occurred to her that almost all those smiles and frowns and sighs had taken place outside the boundaries of her life, in some other realm to which he had banished himself voluntarily. The thought made it easier for her to give him the impersonal nod that she gave him now.

The bill arrived and Lea pulled out her wallet. Her father didn't try to pay, only watched as she handed the waiter a card. When the waiter was gone, Lea busied herself with her coat and purse.

"Look," her father said in a low voice. "I thought of calling you many times, of sending you a message, paying you a visit. Believe me, I wanted to. But it would have only made things worse. I knew Uju had done a great job of dealing with — everything. You were happy, healthy. HealthFin job. Todd. You had, *have*, a great life. And I get it, I really do. What else were you supposed to do? Sit around and pine after your deadbeat, antisanct, absent dad?"

Lea slipped off the bar stool. "I need to go," she muttered again.

"Especially after what happened at school, you know —" He stopped, running his hands over his cheeks.

Lea became aware of the unnaturally bright voices of the group next to them, the sideways glances between what seemed like choreographed laughter.

"I really, really have to go. Goodbye, Dad," she said.

But something inside her cracked when she said the word Dad, and she saw from the way he blinked that he had felt it too.

"Wait." He pulled a pen out from the inside of his blazer and scribbled something down onto a damp napkin. When he was done, he thrust it at her. "Just in case you want to — I don't know, talk. Or something." He leaned towards her and slipped the napkin into her purse.

She didn't look back as she manoeuvred her way through the crowd. It was only after she stepped out of the juice bar and was standing on the sidewalk, that she allowed herself to look. Her father had made no move to leave. He sat with his head bowed, staring at the half-drunk smoothie clasped between his hands.

The young men next to him were handing around one of the babies, whose balled fleshy fists flailed about as it was passed. The adults' faces were lit up with joy, all their attention focused laser-like on the child, their eyes and hands attentive to its every twitch. The baby began to cry, noiselessly, behind the glass window. Its face was a purple knot of flesh, glistening and ugly with need.

CHAPTER
SEVEN

When her father disappeared eighty-eight years ago, he had been a large man. Nothing like the gangly, shrunken shape he was now — back then, he'd been broad-shouldered and barrel-chested, his arms hefty lamp-posts, his legs solid trunks. Lea remembered hanging onto his neck as a child; the entire length of her arms encircling the width of it and her hands just meeting on the other side. She'd been small, of course, much smaller, when he'd left. Twelve years old, yet she remembered those months as if they'd happened yesterday.

Lea remembered Kaito as a large man, but the pictures of him at thirty, forty, fifty even, showed him to be as svelte and toned as any top-decile lifer today. In one picture he was suave in tennis whites, his long black hair pulled back from his face by a pink terrycloth headband, racket head balanced on the cracked red clay. In others he stood with Uju next to a waterfall in Peru, both carrying backpacks taller than themselves, wearing embarrassing sunhats and grinning widely. In Lea's favourite picture, her father was on a sailboat, his tanned face silhouetted against the brilliant blue sky. He leaned against the boat's prow, a tiny baby cradled in his arms. Samuel.

She wished she'd known him, this man who played recreational sports, who wore crisp workout clothes in pastel colours, whose arm was slung over his wife's shoulder with such easy affection. She could not detect the vein of cynicism that she had always associated with him. The man in the pictures was as straightforwardly life-loving as he was physically fit.

Everything started going wrong after the Second Wave. So went the family folklore, passed down to Lea by Uju. They'd had the lifespan tests and predictive treatments for decades, even when Samuel was born, but this was something different. The Second Wave, it was dubbed, when a whole raft of new Medtech measures were approved for mass distribution: first-generation SmartBlood^{TM}, an early prototype of what would later become DiamondSkin^{TM}, the first truly functional replacements. And with the new technologies, a whole host of new directives, aimed at keeping the Ministry's biggest investments — lifers — safe and healthy. The Second Wave. There would be Immortals by the Third.

"Maybe your children," Uju used to say to Lea, the excitement in her voice sheathed in a note of envy. "Maybe even you."

"Sounds terrible," Kaito would reply, shaking his head. "Who wants to live forever? Especially now they want us to give up steak."

It was some time after the Second Wave began that Kaito's middle began to swell, his wrists and ankles thickening with rolls of flesh, as if in direct opposition to the new monthly maintenance requirement and the nutritional scales that were appearing in grocery stores. He would go out of his way to seek out the burger joints and fried chicken diners that were slowly closing down, one after another. He stopped playing tennis, and their yearly hiking trips became a thing of the past.

Uju, newly promoted and reaping the benefits of being a senior official in a Ministry-affiliated organisation, was put onto Talent Global's company-wide maintenance plan for executives. And as she grew leaner, stronger, taller, Kaito became the opposite. His middle softened, his jowls grew prosperous. He bought new shirts to fit his new body, threw himself into his pharmaceutical sales job, taking on brutal cross-country trips that involved multiple stops and red-eyes, weeks away from the family.

This was the Kaito that Lea remembered. She'd never met the vital man in the pictures, the man who could have been featured in the Forty Minutes A Day campaign. The father she had known as a child made rude jokes, got into fights with Uju about Nutripak meals, clamoured for burgers and steaks; trad food, as it was now called.

Kaito had always been what her mother would call difficult, but before Samuel died, it had never caused any real problems between them. Lea remembered the way her mother would playfully smack his hand away from the fried chicken he brought home, the way he'd laugh and pull her down onto the couch, pretend to force-feed her chunks of crispy batter. She remembered following her mother to her office on Bring Your Daughter to Work Day, remembered the excited, gleeful questions from Uju's colleagues about Kaito. *And what's he up to now? And then he said what? Oh, he didn't!* She remembered being proud when they exclaimed she looked just like him. She told them more stories about her unusual, independent, rebellious father. Though she'd never admit it, Uju too was proud.

As Lea grew up, she remembered it used to be different. And she remembered when it all changed.

The summer after Samuel died, Uju had the windows in their three-bedroom apartment sealed shut, citing Directive 7077A: The High-Rise Protection Act. They lived on a low floor of an old building in Borough Five, so, technically, they weren't required to seal their windows. Not yet, at least, not until twenty years later, when Directive 7077C would be drafted to include apartments located on second to fifth floors. Still, Uju wanted to be proactive. *Anticipating developments in the pipeline* was how she put it, as if their family was a newly formed corporation responding to impending regulatory change, rather than the broken, grieving remains of what had once been a unit of four.

Time was unbalanced that summer. One moment it was a slipstream, a whirling eddy of tears and tantrums, the next it was perfectly still, a crystalline gel in which the three remaining family members were suspended. While heatwaves festered in the streets outside, their apartment stayed cold and stale, deliberately chilled, as if preserving something that would soon be gone. There would come a time when Samuel's ghost did not lurk near every set table and every empty armchair. Now was not that time. Now they sealed themselves in, protected from the heat that rose from the sidewalks and hovered, trapped, between buildings.

The air-conditioning was ostensibly what set it off. It was Saturday, Lea remembered, and she and Kaito had been home all day. Uju was at the office again, for the third weekend in a row. Lea sat cross-legged on the floor, maths homework spread out over the coffee table. She wasn't making much progress, in part because she'd missed two months of school to be at the hospital with Samuel, in part because of Kaito's fidgeting. He lay sprawled on the three-seater couch behind her, his bulk spreading over the patterned upholstery. He held a book suspended over his face, but Lea was all too aware that he hadn't turned a page in over an hour. Instead, he sighed and shifted, scratched his head loudly, crossed and uncrossed his legs.

"Can you hear it?" he asked, all of a sudden. "You can hear it, right?"

"What?" Lea answered in an irritable tone. *I can hear you*, she said to herself.

"That buzzing. It's deafening."

Lea cocked her head, and then shook it.

"I don't hear anything," she said.

"How can you not hear it?" Kaito hauled himself upright, sending a cascade of cushions over the couch edge, huffing as he sat up.

Even his breathing was loud, Lea found herself thinking uncharitably.

"I'm trying to work, Dad," she said, as kindly as she could.

"But you can't work with that noise, of course, yes, understandably. Don't worry, we'll figure out what it is." He stood up and walked over to the window.

Lea turned back to her homework. *The derivative of x^2 is 2x. The derivative of x is 1.*

Kaito clapped his hands loudly. "The airconditioning. Of course." He was staring at the vents above the window, arms akimbo.

"I really don't hear anything," Lea muttered.

"Come here, Lea. You'll hear it from here."

Lea lowered the screen of her laptop. "I'm busy, Dad, I really have to finish this."

A strange look flashed across Kaito's face. It was a look that Lea had seen more than once in recent months, a tightening of the jaw, a hardening of the eyes. She didn't like it. It made her feel empty, unsettled, alone. *Derivative: the slope of a curve, the rate of change.*

So she shut her laptop and walked over to where Kaito was standing. She craned her neck, looking up at the innocuous grey grate in the ceiling, tried her best to see what Kaito was seeing, to hear what he was hearing. She cocked her head, strained her ears, but still she heard nothing more. All she heard was the muffled noise of cars passing outside, the rise and fall of Kaito's breathing, the faint footsteps of their upstairs neighbour.

But when she turned to Kaito, he looked so eager, so expectant, that she found herself nodding her head.

"Yes," she said. "It's the air-conditioning."

"I told you!" he burst out triumphantly. "Now, pass me a chair. I'm going to turn it off."

"What?" she said. "You can't turn it off. It's so hot outside."

But Kaito was already dragging a dining chair over to the window, reaching up to the air-conditioning unit.

"They make it so hard," he muttered. "Can't even turn something off when you want to any more. Clima-smart. Intelligent cooling. State of the art. State of the art, my ass." He ran his hands around the grey metal grate, searching for the manual override button.

"Hah!" he said at last, flicking a switch that Lea couldn't see. Sure enough, the air-conditioning slowed to a stop. The air in the apartment stood still.

"We'll die of heat in here," Lea exclaimed.

"Don't be silly. We're not dying of anything," Kaito said.

He paused. The strange expression returned. He climbed down from the chair slowly. She watched as he carefully placed the chair back in its corner, his movements slow and deliberate, his face distant and empty.

Lea sighed and sat back down at the coffee table, opening her laptop once again.

With the sun blazing through the windows, it only took ten minutes before a thin film of sweat began forming on her forehead. Her armpits were hot and damp, the backs of her knees slick, the sleeves of her light cotton blouse stuck to her arms. Kaito had returned to his position on the couch, engrossed in his book once again. He had stopped fidgeting and didn't seem to notice the heat. Lea didn't say anything, only stretched her legs out under the coffee table to prevent her calves from touching her thighs, forced herself to ignore the suffocating heat. But when she heard the key in the door, her heart sank. Uju. Lea looked around the apartment in a panic, wondering foolishly if she could turn the air-conditioning back on in time.

"Hello," Uju called as the door swung open, her voice clipped and bright, full of the outside world, full of the things at work that kept her so busy, so apart from unnamed absence in their home.

"Oh my God," she gasped as she entered the apartment. "Did the air-conditioning break? Have you called someone? Why haven't they fixed it yet? Kaito, what are you doing? I'll phone the building manager right now."

"Hey," Kaito said from the couch. "Oh. Yes, I guess we could call someone. It was making this awful noise, a loud buzzing noise. It was driving me batshit crazy."

"Weird. And then it stopped working, just like that?"

Lea held her breath, stared intently at her laptop screen, hands frozen on the keyboard. Suddenly she missed Samuel desperately. The feeling hit her in the chest, a blow that left her winded and empty. Samuel would know what to do. Samuel would make a joke, ask Uju about her day, distract her from the airless apartment. Samuel would never have let Kaito turn the air-conditioning off in the first place.

"No," Kaito said cheerfully. "I turned it off."

Lea glanced at Uju out of the corner of her eye, without moving her head. Uju was standing in the entryway, her left shoulder weighed down by her laptop bag. She wore a light grey pant suit, a crisp white shirt under her blazer. The keys in her right hand glinted in the sunlight, like a bunch of tiny knives.

"You turned it off," she repeated, in a low voice. "I'm sorry. I don't understand."

Kaito waved a hand in her direction. "What's there to understand? It was making a noise. I turned it off. Hey, if you hadn't had the windows sealed, we'd be able to open them and get some fresh air like normal people, instead of having to have the damn air-conditioning on all the time."

Uju dropped her bag to the floor with a loud thump. "I don't believe this," she said. "I can't — are you trying to drive me insane?"

"We can just turn it on again, Mom," Lea said.

"No, Lea," Uju said. "Your father wants us to live like normal people, he says. He wishes I'd never had the windows sealed, he says."

Looking at the signs and equations on her screen, it occurred to Lea that three was an unstable number. Four was even, four was balanced, four was safe. Now that they were three, they would always be in flux, always pulling in different directions, Lea caught between the two, until — until what?

Kaito stood up from the couch. "That's not fair, Uju. You know I didn't mean it that way."

"What way did you mean it, then?"

Kaito was silent. He laced his fingers at his stomach, stared at his hands.

Uju exploded. "Why do you have to be like this? Have to thwart everything I try to do? You know it's not just the windows. First the food, you're never happy with the food —"

"How many times a week can you eat that damn sludge? It's sludge! Tasteless, soulless sludge, not fit for human consumption —"

"Oh, so you'd rather your daughter eat animal meat, even after the latest dietary directive —"

"Directives. Always with the directives. I just want my daughter to have a normal life. Is that so hard? To live like a normal human being."

"They're Nutripaks, they're *optimised* for normal human beings, I don't see why you have to be so difficult about everything —"

"You never used to mind. You never used to be like this."

"Oh? Well, you never used to be like this either. I mean, look at you. Look at you! Lying around all day, filling your body with crap, never exercising, never sleeping. What are you trying to prove? Who are you trying to spite?"

Kaito paused. And then he spoke again, in a terrible, calm voice.

"It won't bring him back."

Uju was silent, her lips a thin pale line.

Kaito went on, louder now. "It won't make any difference. All this stuff. Sealing the windows, Nutripak diets, making Lea go to fucking AquaYoga every single day. You can make her the best damn *lifer* in the world and it won't bring Samuel back, is all I'm saying."

The heat in the room seemed to expand and fill up every last bit of space until none of them could breathe any more. Lea could hear her father heaving for breath. There was a ringing in her ears, a lightness in her head. She added and subtracted, differentiated and integrated, but still all she could think about was the number three, one less than four. She saw, now, that even three was not guaranteed, that one point of the triangle could easily pull apart, detach from the other two, escape forever.

CHAPTER
EIGHT

Sometimes the silence pressed in on Anja so loudly that she was sure that she'd gone deaf. So she started playing the violin again — scales, exercises, scraps of concertos from long ago. Anything to ward off the wall of silence, broken only by the mechanical clicks and whirrs of her mother's body. Anja played for herself now.

She dug out an old, chipped metronome, sticky with dust. It still worked. She used it to keep time while playing, to lose track of it when falling asleep at night.

One morning she woke up to an icy draught flitting across her face. The streets were dusted with snow, glistening cleanly in the morning sun. That morning she played without the metronome for the first time. The notes came in a tumbling rush, like lazy acrobats whirling out of control. They seemed to have a mind of their own — yanking her fingers first this way, then the other way. They slipped and slurred and stumbled. Then Anja found herself playing a piece she thought she would never play again.

She remembered how at the audition, a tag on her dress, bought the day before on a mother-daughter shopping trip, was scratching the base of her neck. She remembered the way the serious, turtle-necked man's voice had echoed as he asked if she was ready to begin. Row upon row of plush maroon velvet sitting empty. No mother. The lump in her throat as she nodded yes. Shoes squeaking on the polished wooden stage as she shifted from one foot to the other, then lifted her bow. The familiar ache in her left shoulder, a conscious untightening.

It was the most beautifully she had ever played. Anja kept her eyes closed, at first to imagine her mother sitting there, but then forgetting to imagine, forgetting about her altogether. It was only when the final, trembling note had been wrung out of her violin that she realised she was holding her breath.

When Anja burst through the apartment door, she was so full of the news that she'd forgotten to find it odd her mother never showed up. It was only then, just as she was about to tell her she'd made it — Juilliard, finally following in her mother's footsteps — that she remembered.

Anja found her on the floor, dressed and made up, perfect except for a missing earring. That was the day her mother took to bed, her muscles no longer firm enough to hold herself up. She never left her bed again, so when the letters from Juilliard came, they were easy enough for Anja to hide.

It all came back now. As the music slipped out of her into the cold room, Anja found herself shaking, until she had to stop. An unfinished note hung high in the still air. It was then that the phone rang, as if it had been waiting for her to finish. Anja threw a blanket around her shoulders and stilled her hands. She picked up.

"Hello, Anja."

Her mother's heart clicked and whirred under the floral comforter.

"She'll be there in ten minutes," the voice on the phone said.

Her mother's cheekbones, so white under the transparent flesh.

"Are you there? Anja?"

Anja's mouth was dry. "I'm here."

"Do you still want to do it? You know you don't have to."

Her mother's windpipe, reinforced with a carbon fibre stronger than steel.

"Yes," Anja said. "It was my idea. I want to do it."

After she hung up, she put down her violin and picked up the camera.

Anja had told them she would do the second video herself. But when the knock came, when it was an actual person standing in her doorway, a woman with wheat-coloured hair not unlike Anja's own, she felt something inside her shift. Anja took in the woman's round, soft face, the dewy cheeks as full and gently furred as peaches. She scrutinised the thin rims around her pupils, saw that they were raincloud grey. She observed the faint line running across the right half of the woman's forehead, stopping abruptly in the middle, and wondered at all the things that must have led the woman to raise a single eyebrow. She wondered at all the things that must have led the woman to be standing there in front of her.

"Hello," the woman said. "You must be Anja. They said you'd be expecting me." When she broke the silence, the world seemed to get loud again, and suddenly all Anja could hear was the sound of her mother's heart. Thud, thud, thud.

"I am," Anja said, stepping out of the apartment, camera in hand. "Let's go."

Up on the roof, the woman marvelled at the view as Anja set up the camera. The tripod legs were heavy and stiff, and she struggled to get the camera balanced just right. She focused on the task at hand, ignoring the woman's attempts at small talk. Eventually the woman fell silent. It was only when Anja told her where to stand, so that she would appear in the middle of the camera frame, that she realised that she didn't know her name.

As the woman moved herself into the right spot, she tucked her hair behind her ears with two hooked fingers. The girlishness of the gesture went straight to Anja's heart. She forced herself to think of her mother, lying in her bed twenty floors beneath them, SmartBlood^{TM} pumping determinedly through her veins.

But this was different, a voice inside her cried. Look at this woman! Look at her shiny hair that won't stay behind her ears, look at her straight back, her strong legs, her bright, darting eyes. This woman was alive.

This woman was nothing like Anja's mother. This woman did not need to die.

"Ready?" the woman said. Her voice was different now. When she looked at Anja, her eyes were different too.

Anja nodded, and turned the camera on.

The woman started speaking. People might not know that the Club, she said, hadn't always been an activist group. A long time ago, they were simply a collection of disillusioned lifers who'd decided they had had enough with the maintenance sessions, the HDL competitions, the self-denial. They organised forbidden performances of live music, trad meals of the worst, most artery-clogging kind, irresponsible orgies. They called themselves the Suicide Club mockingly, in jest.

But the Ministry got worried. In spite of all the new measures, population numbers were still falling. They couldn't have people suddenly deciding they no longer wanted to live forever. It would be disastrous, the end of American global dominance as they knew it. And that was when the smear campaign started.

"What to do with us though?" the woman said, her hair whipping in the wind, her slight figure framed by the backdrop of the city, eighty floors down. "What to do with those they couldn't punish with the usual penalty — by cutting our numbers, taking away our extension treatments?"

She picked up a bottle from the floor and began to drink. When she spoke again, the bottle was empty.

"Acceleration. Fast-tracked to the Third Wave, guinea pigs for immortality. Special replacements, even more indestructible than the last. Did you know the latest SmartBlood^{TM} clots in less than a millisecond? DiamondSkin^{TM} that will withstand not just the force of a car, as yours will, but a fall of eighty floors."

The woman was backlit by the blazing sun, her eyes dark pools in the shadow of her face. She gestured behind her.

"I could jump off right now and they could put me back together again."

The woman lit a match.

"They leave us no choice." She brought the match to her face and breathed in, and the sun was no longer the only thing on fire.

CHAPTER
NINE

The first session was held on a Sunday morning, in the Outer Boroughs. It was a part of the city Lea had never been to before. There the buildings were squat and bricked, caked with dust. Their windows were great hollow yawns, large and opaque.

As she passed the ancient brownstones, she glimpsed rooms cluttered with the shapes of furniture and their owners. She'd heard of these dwellings but never actually seen one; she knew how rooms were divided and subdivided, how people lived separated by curtains in lightless spaces. This was where most of the sub-100s lived. Where Samuel would have lived, if he had been born to different parents. Lea pushed this thought out of her mind.

The streets were eerily quiet, and an invisible cold crept under her coat into the spaces between her elbows, across the small of her back. She seemed to be walking forever, past brownstone after identical brownstone, until finally, there it was. Nothing to distinguish it from its shabby neighbours, it stood just as mute and mud-coloured. Why would any clinic be here? Lea rang the bell, wincing at the loud buzz. A few seconds later, a voice of indeterminate gender came crackling through the speakerphone.

"Up the stairs, second room on the right."

The door clicked open. Lea checked the address again, one last time, before stepping into the building. But the address was correct. This was it.

Inside, the carpet was mustard and balding. Lea climbed the creaking stairs on tiptoe, trying to touch as little as she possibly could. When she reached the top, a narrow hallway extended out in front of her. She stopped in front of the second door on the right. Forget the building, she told herself, straightening her coat and smoothing down her hair. This was it, her chance to set the record straight.

The Observers had been showing up at her office almost every day. It had got so bad that Jiang had asked her to work from home, which of course, she had refused to do. Flexihours and Remotework were the fastest ways to not get promoted. Observers or no Observers, she was going to stay in her office.

They didn't really do anything, for the most part, but watch her. That was part of the feedback she wanted to give today, to the Tender who would no doubt be interested in her experience. Better to start with a tone of mild confusion — what, exactly, are they there to observe again? — than to come across as a bitter, negative sort of person. It was important to show how ridiculous this all was, that a valuable member of society such as herself would even be here, undergoing unnecessary oxidative degeneration, in a place like this.

She looked around at the hallway. The dim lights overhead gave the walls a sickly yellow hue, the colour of overripe squash. Or perhaps they actually were the colour of squash. It was impossible to tell. Not a hint of natural light, for there were no windows. Lea took one deep, restorative breath, then knocked firmly on the door.

The man who opened it was as squat and squalid as the building itself. His face was a rounded square with sagging corners, two deep lines running from the base of his nose to the corners of his lips. The pores under his eyes were sunken and glistening, and he smelled faintly of processed food.

"Lea Kirino," he said. "Yes. You're late."

Lea's lip curled involuntarily, then uncurled just as quickly as she forced a smile and nodded to the man.

Lea looked around the room for the Tender who would be leading the group. Despite a small window set in the far wall, the room was no better lit than the hallway outside. Again there was that orange light overhead, which drained the faces sitting in a circle of any colour they might otherwise have had. She counted six of them in total, slumped in plastic chairs.

The waiting room, presumably. More people here for treatment. They looked nothing alike, but they all wore the same expression, a strange mix of hope and anxiety. A quick glance around made her even more uncomfortable. Lea didn't belong here. The starched polycotton blouse that woman was wearing, the red crack in one man's lower lip, chewed to a pulp, the compulsive tapping of badly shod feet.

But then she brightened. That would make her case to the Tender clearer still. She wouldn't even have to say a word.

Lea walked over to one of the two remaining chairs and sat down. She turned to the woman next to her, trying to ignore the open scrutiny from everyone else.

"Hello," she said, extending a hand. "I'm Lea."

The other woman looked up. "Anja."

While the rest of the group tapped and twitched, the stray ends of their bodies betraying restlessness, Anja was completely still. She sat with impeccable posture, elbows tucked by her sides, shoulders relaxed, hips even.

"So how long do we have to wait?" Lea chirped, straightening her back too. "And where's the consultation room?"

Probably one of the doors out in the hallway, she imagined. It would be a room like Jessie's, bright and clean, pamphlets neatly stacked.

Anja tilted her head. But before she could say anything, a large, oozing woman sitting across from her let out a snort.

"Consultation room," she said. "Hah! What next, a paleo buffet?"

"That's enough, Sofia."

The man who'd greeted Lea at the door walked over the circle. Hitching his faded pinstriped pants up, he sat down at the last empty chair in the circle.

"Welcome to the WeCovery Group, Lea. Now, since this is your first session, I'll start with a quick intro. My name is George, and I used to be just like you," he said with a practised flourish.

Lea blinked, trying not to let the polite smile slip off her face. They could be observing her even now, it was important to appear calm, stable. So she nodded encouragingly at George, even though she sincerely doubted he had ever been anything like her.

"I know what you're thinking," he said, pushing the smudged glasses up his nose bridge. He leaned forward, looking at Lea over the tops of the frames. "You're thinking, this is a big mistake. Someone got it wrong. Misunderstanding. Am I right?" He exuded earnestness. Surely taking things so seriously had to be incredibly cortisol-generating. "I just want you to remember — you're in safe hands. We're one of the most successful groups in the tri-state area, something I have these troopers to thank for. Seven years and running."

He waved one meaty hand at a peeling wall, bare except for a row of dusty wooden plaques, their scratched gold faces glinting dully.

Everyone was nodding, except for Anja. Why were they all humouring him? Lea glanced at her watch. Where was the Tender?

"All right," he said, slapping his hands together. Out of the corner of her eye, Lea saw Anja wince.

"Let's get started. Little intro for our newest member, please. Sofia, you're up."

The woman who'd spoken earlier made an engine-like noise in her throat.

"Hi, I'm Sofia," she said. "This week I tried to drown myself in the community pool. Not seriously, just a little, and definitely less than usual. There was an AquaYoga class like, three metres away. I knew they'd see me if anything really happened."

"Good, Sofia, good. Controlled use. Leveraging others. Keep up the good work." George slapped his thighs. "Ambrose?"

The slumped figure next to Sofia unfurled. He looked like a shadow that had been separated from its owner.

"I, uh, I. Hi, hello," he said, inclining one cheek towards Lea. "I tried to do them, George. I, uh, swear. They don't work. Maybe they don't work. On everyone? Maybe they don't work for —"

"Ambrose. Hey man. Hey." George snapped his fingers.

Ambrose lifted his gaze. His eyes were two dark sparks.

George let out a long sigh. He leaned forward with his hands on his thighs, elbows splayed out. His fingernails, Lea noticed, were strangely well manicured. The gleaming squares unsettled her.

"Ambrose. You have to try, man. You know the programme only works for those who try, right? You don't want it all to go to waste, do you? Do you?"

Ambrose seemed to retreat even further into his chair at this. He shook his head.

"Good. Okay. I'm going to give you one more week. Do the exercises, lots of cruciferous vegetables, and no, I repeat, no carbs. Okay?"

As George turned to the next person, Lea tried to rationalise what was going on. Perhaps this was some kind of test. She surveyed the room for places where cameras could have been hidden. Or perhaps this was part of George's treatment. Perhaps it helped him, the poor man, to feel as if he had some sense of purpose.

It was only when she noticed George taking notes in a tablet as he went around the group, his face puffy with self-importance, that Lea began to panic.

Now a woman sitting across from Lea was telling the group, in a pleading tone, about how she'd sliced the tip of her little finger off while dicing carrots for her husband's dinner.

"A very thin slice," she said. "Barely drew any blood at all. Just to see if I can even bleed any more. Sometimes you wonder, you know, with all they put in you. Don't you? Don't you wonder?"

George was surprisingly sympathetic. Lea gathered that the woman, Susan, had already made great progress and was a testament to the efficacy of their programme. She was the pride of WeCovery, the golden girl. George expressed his certainty that this minor relapse was a mere blip in the journey of her reformation. He alluded to a certain Fateful Day, reminded her how much blood had flowed then, how it had got into the cracks between the kitchen tiles. It had been so expensive for her husband — poor old Greg, he worked so hard to get it all cleaned up, and back into her veins.

Meanwhile, Lea emptied her lungs and was counting to five in her head. A faintly dizzy sensation, not entirely unpleasant, came over her. But even so her heart continued to race.

It would be George, perspiring into his chair, who would decide when she could be taken off the list. When her life would return to normal. It would be George she would have to convince, George she would have to not tell about her father on the other side of the road.

Lea held an out-breath as she tried to think.

"Lea. Your turn, quick intro. Don't worry, we won't bite!" George guffawed.

They were all looking at her. George's face was shiny and expectant. The ceiling lights were unforgiving in their scrutiny — every liver spot and ingrown hair was clearly visible.

"I don't want to kill myself," she said at last.

A gleeful look crossed George's face. He might as well have rubbed his hands together. The others looked away.

"Now, Lea," George said, relishing every word like the charred protein-denatured animal flesh he probably poisoned himself with. "The first stage is always denial. But that's okay, we can deal with this."

"Deal with what?"

"Of course you have life-ending tendencies. By the way, please note we don't use the 'K' word at WeCovery. In any case, it's perfectly normal to feel the way you do. It's a difficult thing to accept, but trust me on this, acceptance is the most difficult step of all. Do you trust me, Lea?"

"I really think they've got it wrong," Lea said, as politely as she could manage. "With all due respect, do I seem like someone who wants to kill herself?"

Ambrose winced as she spoke, curling further into his chest.

"Please stop saying that." George's smile tightened. "And such tendencies are very deeply rooted. You're going to have to dig deep, Lea. Are you ready to dig deep?"

This was worse than talking to the Observers. Lea felt her cortisol levels rising again.

"I'm having some doubts about this — this treatment." She resisted the urge to make air quotes with her fingers. "Are you even qualified for this?"

At George's temple, a vein bulged.

"You think you're above this," he said, flinging one arm out towards the wall with the plaques. "Ms-I-Work-In-HealthFin-Capital-Management. I have your full bio and case notes. What did you think was going on here exactly?"

Lea's mouth gaped open. "How can you —" she began.

"Oh my God, George, leave her alone." It was the woman next to her, Anja.

"Anja, please, I'm only doing my job," George said, but there was something new in his tone.

"Your job? How is bullying a new, uninitiated member of the group doing your job?"

"I wasn't bullying . . . I —"

Anja examined her nails. "Can we just move on?"

George glared at Lea, but didn't say anything more. He went on to the extremely eager man next to her, who started regaling them with every thought and feeling he had experienced over the past week. The man began describing the quiet despair that the sight of a single poached egg at breakfast induced in him on Tuesday morning.

Lea glanced at Anja, tried to catch her eye to nod thank you, but Anja was staring steadfastly into the distance. Who was she?

When George clapped his hands for the last time and declared the meeting of the WeCovery Group over, Lea blinked as if coming out of a trance. Suddenly it hit her again — the mustard carpet, the artificial light, the lack of ventilation. Everyone was smiling and buoyant, even Ambrose, who in the course of the meeting had tied his long hair up into a perky ponytail. They nodded and grinned at Lea as they filed out of the room. Even George flashed her a reluctant smile.

Only Anja was left. Lea watched as she wound a scarf around her neck. Her movements were slow and deliberate, weighted down by a strange precision, as if it were of crucial importance that her outerwear be put on just so.

"Why are you here?" Anja asked.

"It's part of my treatment plan," Lea said. "I just want to go back to normal."

"Back to normal. Uh huh," Anja said. She seemed to be thinking it over, fingers tugging at her scarf. "What are you hiding?"

"What?" Lea flushed.

"It makes no sense. Someone like you shouldn't be here. What are you not telling them?"

84

Her father, her strong, young father, running thirty blocks in bedroom slippers, Samuel on his back. Her father across the street, hunched and slow. Her father in the clinic, mistaken for a sub-100.

"I don't know what you're talking about," Lea said.

Her father slipping a napkin with a phone number on it into her purse.

Anja stared at her for a long moment. Finally she shrugged. "Fine. See you next week," she said.

CHAPTER
TEN

Lea waited on the hard bench with her hands wedged under her thighs, bare palms against the smooth, worn wood, where countless others had sat before. The wind whipped her hair into her face. At first she tried to push it away, but after a while she let it flit over her eyes and nose uninhibited.

It was just starting to turn cold. The trees were aflame and the sky a proud, clear blue. The air chafed at her eyes, making them water. If her father arrived now, he would think she was crying, and that would be too embarrassing to bear, as well as entirely misleading.

Her hands were going numb. He was late. She usually hated it when anyone was late, but she didn't mind now. Her mind contained an idle blankness, filled by the brittle chill of the air and the ashy churn of the Hudson. It was one of those in-between moments, suspended in time.

"Lea."

He was standing behind her, wearing the same beige coat, but with the addition of a thick scarf that had shed wisps of dark wool all over his shoulders. He held himself tightly, like someone who had forgotten how to exist in the cold. She wondered for the first time since seeing him where he had been in the time that he was gone.

"Hi." She swallowed the word *Dad*.

Lea half rose from her seat, just as her father bent to sit. They laughed. She sat back down, and he sat next to her.

"I'm so glad you called," he said.

She'd called him after leaving the WeCovery Group. Standing outside the brownstone, she watched Anja in the distance, her grey coat flapping in the wind. Anja's words went round and round in Lea's head, like buzzing flies trapped behind a patio door. *What are you hiding?*

She watched Anja get smaller and smaller, until finally she disappeared around a corner. Lea was alone in the street now. She pulled out her tablet to call a carshare, but then found herself digging in her purse for the napkin her father had given her instead.

The silence between them now was loud, louder than when they had met in the smoothie bar with all those people around them. Lea shifted in her seat.

Her father turned to her. "What is it you do? At your job?"

"Oh, it's boring," she said automatically. "No one likes to hear about collateralised obligations and maturity rates."

"Try me," he said.

And suddenly she remembered those light-filled days, one summer nearly a hundred years ago, when

Samuel had finally got his first job. He was a clerk at a company that imported things like ball bearings and conveyor belts, and he was to fill in error reports for delays in shipments. Years later she realised it had been a dreary, mind-numbing job. But back then, when her father slapped Samuel on the shoulder so hard that his glasses slid down his nose, it had sounded like the most wonderful thing in the world. She remembered how Kaito had been endlessly interested in Samuel's work; questioning him on the minutest details of his day whenever he got home. *And Sharona did what with the W8-E11B form? No! But surely she knew that was a W8-E11F!* She remembered the love shining in her father's face as he drew the details of his day out from Samuel, how he polished each nugget of mundane information with such care and enthusiasm that it emerged as a sparkling beautiful story of success.

So Lea told him about her work. She told him about the commodity markets, the derivatives that had developed around them, the underlying drivers of supply and demand. She told him about the algorithms they used to help them trade, the clients they serviced. She told him about the kidneys, the hearts, the lungs that the traders never saw, but existed somewhere out there, some vast clearing house for the physical organs themselves. She told him about the different grades the organs were classified under. She told him about Jiang and Natalie, and her office high above the city, how much she loved sitting at her desk, how despite the recent troubles, it brought her peace like nothing else ever did.

Lea snuck sideways glances at him as she talked but otherwise stared out at the grey buildings across the Hudson. Every now and then he asked a question. They were sensible, thoughtful questions, questions that showed he was listening. Lea talked and talked, until at last she had nothing left to say.

They fell silent again. But this time it felt natural, them watching the sparse joggers and people with dogs go by. It was a thing a father and a daughter might do, Lea thought.

"Hey," he said. "What do you say we go for a walk?"

The park was a sliver of green clinging to the edge of the Central Boroughs, spanning its full length, Boroughs One to Five. Lea and her father walked along the cement pathway, the river a slow churning grey on the other side of the railing.

The official position on high impact sport changed every few years, as scientists sponsored by different corporations and Ministry bodies raced to release papers and research studies. But the latest advisory was negative, so Lea and her father had the running paths mainly to themselves. A few stubborn joggers passed every now and then, their faces pink with cold and overworked capillaries. Lea herself had given up running a decade ago, as had most people she knew, spooked by the constant vacillation within the scientific community.

Still, she felt a twinge of envy as she watched the runners go by, their mouths pinched into greedy huffing circles, eyes focused on some distant point. Bodies tense or loose, depending on the runner, but always moving with that same pounding, consuming rhythm. She missed it. The wind in her hair, the thump of blood in her ears, the hurtling feeling.

Her father walked slowly. At first it frustrated her, this ambling pace, and it was all she could do not to leave him behind. But she made a conscious effort to slow down, matching his short, uneven strides, stopping when he did, to look at some building or person.

"Amazing, isn't it?" he said, raising his palm to the buildings that dominated the length of the park. Presenting them to her for comment.

Lea nodded. She rarely thought about it, the city, but it was.

"And you. You work up there, in one of those towers!" he went on. Lea felt warm at the pride in his voice. "The most advanced financial system in the world. Kidneys. Hearts. Lungs," he went on. But then she noticed the bitter edge that tinged his words, the familiar hint of mockery.

"If you hate it so much — if you hate all of it so much — then why did you come back?" she burst out. "I have a life now, a life I spent years building, one that you know nothing about. If you hate it so much, I don't understand why you're even here."

He was silent. They kept walking. Lea's cheeks were hot, despite the cold. She already regretted what she had said, so when her father finally spoke again, remarking on an impossibly white poodle being walked nearby, Lea responded with far too much enthusiasm.

"Do you like dogs, then?" he asked, a bemused smile curling at his lips.

She'd never thought about it before, but she nodded yes.

"I used to have a dog, did you know? Before you were born; before Samuel was born even, goodness." He let out a chuckle. "When your mother and I moved into our first house, back when you could still afford a house in the Central Boroughs on a single income. His name was Peeves. He was the sweetest dog you'd ever meet. Our friend had a kid, must have been four, five years old. They used to come over for dinner on Saturdays. Peeves would let that kid sit on his back, like a horse. Can you believe it? The kid loved it, was always pulling on poor Peeves's ears. He had these long, floppy ears, some kind of golden retriever mix."

"They're meant to be good for you, you know, dogs," Lea said. "Studies have shown. Cortisol lowering. But only certain breeds, there's a list."

Her father laughed. "And the other breeds? They're what, cortisol raising?"

"I suppose so." She bristled, for he was laughing at her, but then saw, briefly, the absurdity of what she had said. She smiled too.

The story about Peeves was the first story he told her. It set something off within him, for as they walked, he started to tell her other stories too.

"Your mother was dating someone else when we first met. She had a nice Nigerian boyfriend, the son of her parents' friends, a solid guy. Engineering degree from a top school like her, destined for greatness. A good match, you know? Their families knew each other. She walked into the party with him that night, she was in this yellow dress, off-the-shoulder, I remember, and one of the sleeves kept falling down. And she'd pull it back up again like it was the most natural thing in the world, like that was part of the outfit, no self-consciousness, nothing. She was a very beautiful woman, but that wasn't it. It was the way she commanded the room, the way she listened, drew people out of themselves, the stories she told. The way she made you feel like you could be better, that there was so much *more* out there. She was one of those people everyone wanted to be around, the most brilliant woman I'd ever met."

The stories came faster as they walked, the silences between them shortening into a few breaths. There was nothing obvious connecting them — Lea's father jumped around in space and time, starting a new one as soon as the last one ended.

After a while, Lea noticed that his stories were only about the time before he left, stories from Lea's childhood or before she was born. Never about what happened after. Never about where he'd been after he'd left.

Suddenly, Kaito stopped walking. "Oh," he said.

"What is it?" Lea turned to him.

Her father was staring at the sidewalk some way ahead of them. "It's gone," he said.

Lea blinked and looked around them. There was nothing unremarkable about where they had stopped.

Her father was shaking his head, still contemplating the empty space in front of him. Slowly he removed his hand from his chin and placed it back into his pocket.

For the first time, Lea noticed how large his ears had got, the lobes stretching almost down to the scarf wound around his neck. Her own ears felt tight and small in the cold.

"Of course it is," he said. "How silly of me."

"What's gone?" Lea asked.

"You don't remember. Well, of course you don't, you must have been, what, nine? We used to come on Sunday afternoons, when your mother went to her book club. We'd get one each, one for you, one for me and one for Samuel."

And suddenly she did remember — the sticky trail dripping down the side of a cone, leaking between her fingers. Licking it off as fast as she could, while her father and Samuel cheered her on. The taste of chocolate, sweet, cold, perfect.

Memory worked in strange ways when you had lived to a hundred and beyond. For the most part, things that had happened in her early childhood were the ones which could be counted on to stay put. They were the permanent fixtures, firmly lodged into the architecture of the mind, screwed to the skirting boards.

So Lea could remember how the lump of dried gum she found stuck beneath the oak dining-room table felt wedged under her fingernails. She could remember the sweet taste of soap bubbles she tried to catch on her tongue. She remembered the way that Samuel had always smelled of trees, her mother of rain.

The feeling of a dry cough rising in her throat, the unbearable tickle that kept her awake one full night. The time she had been bitten by a fire ant at the beach in Indonesia, back when there was no advisory against travel to countries that didn't respect the Sanctity of Life Act, and her hands had swollen into paws, her face into a red-hot, itching lump. The sting of pulling off a toenail blackened from running in too small shoes.

The things she forgot were those that happened in the broad expanse of adulthood. The older she got, the faster the years sped by, and the less of an impression anything made. The facts of her adult life were couched in general truths rather than the details. She knew where she had worked, who she had dated, what she had done in the last seventy years or so. But she knew them as abstract facts, not as the acrid smell of a lover's breath or the sting of humiliation upon losing a client for the first time. She had once forgotten a friend entirely, someone she had known in university and remained close with for two decades after.

Sometimes it scared her that so much was lost, but she knew it was normal, that most people she knew forgot most of their lives too. But her childhood — that was always there, safe, neatly arranged, chronological. From her childhood she could remember a million details. So it was strange, disconcerting, to find now that there was something she had missed. The taste of chocolate — cold and perfect. With the taste came the rustling of the trees, the wind scraping her cheeks, a smooth, bony hand gripped in hers. Her brother's eyes.

Lea and her dad continued walking all the way to the southern end of the park, a full eighty blocks. When they got there, the sun was setting, and it was time for her to go home.

"Where are you staying?" Lea said. They'd talked all day, but her father still hadn't told her anything about himself.

"You haven't . . ." He paused, looking about himself as if to see if anyone was listening. "Told anyone, have you? About me?"

Lea shook her head. Todd had asked this morning where she was going, for she rarely went out on Sundays, but she had mumbled something and closed the door behind her before he could press further.

"I thought you didn't care," Lea couldn't resist saying. "You were hardly undercover when you came to the clinic, after all."

Kaito broke into a grin. "That was maybe a little — reckless of me. I wanted to talk to you so badly. But hopefully they've dismissed me as a vagrant sub-100 hankering after life extension treatments. God knows that's what they all think of sub-100s anyway."

He pressed his lips together and seemed to be thinking.

Lea shuffled her feet. She could feel a blister forming on the outer edge of her left big toe, but the soreness felt good, felt like the cold in her cheeks, the ache in her lower back, the teeming stories in her head. The sun was low in the sky now, sending violent orange streaks across the Hudson.

"I'm subletting a place in Borough Nineteen," Kaito said at last. It seemed to pain him to say. "Why don't — why don't you come by? Maybe next weekend?"

He glanced up at her. Seeing the uncertainty in his face, Lea felt something shift inside her, felt the jagged chasm that had opened up when she first saw her father again widen ever so slightly.

"Of course. I'd love to."

CHAPTER
ELEVEN

It had been three days in a row now that the Observers hadn't shown up. One would be a blip, an anomaly. Perhaps they were at an urgent Ministry-wide meeting to discuss the latest population measures; she had heard that despite everything, numbers were still falling. And when they hadn't shown up yesterday too, she went on working calmly, reassessing her client portfolio for the eleventh time that month. But today it was unmistakeable. Three days in a row.

"You look pleased. Have you found me a new account to replace the Musks?"

Lea turned. Even the sight of Jiang, standing stiffly with his morning herbal tea in hand, vapour rising from it like an acidic mist, couldn't dent her.

"Jiang, if all this . . ." she lowered her voice. "If all this is over, I'll get you ten new accounts. You'll see."

Jiang prided himself too much on setting a strong life-loving example. So he assumed a smile and puffed out his chest. Lea could almost hear him reciting in his head: healthy mind, healthy body.

"Of course," he said. "I have utmost faith in you. And then — Tier 4 benefits await." He tried a wink. It didn't suit him — he must have seen someone younger do it. When he winked his entire face spasmed like a nervous twitch.

Normally she'd be elated at the mention of Tier 4. Bigger apartment, access to subsidised firm services, non-mandatory Regen treatments. Maybe even a carshare. But ever since she'd spent the day with her father, she'd found that something had shifted. Something about her office, her desk, Jiang and his contracts, something about all of it seemed unreal.

Still, she smiled automatically. "Oh, stop," she said. "And how's the boat purchase coming along?"

Jiang was buying a sailing boat. He was still somewhat below the level at which senior executives tended to buy boats, but it was said that his latest mistress was from a powerful Ministry family.

"Okay," he said, mock wiping his brow. "You never quite realise how many *issues* can come up, until you actually try to buy one. Sounds glamorous and everything, but let me tell you, it's no walk in the park. Not for everyone, it isn't."

"Uh huh. Totally. Well, I better get back to work now," she said.

Lea worked solidly through the morning, stopping only at the polite beeps from her computer that reminded her to stretch. She hummed as she hung upside down from her chair with her eyes closed, enjoying the pressure building in her head, the weight behind her eyes, the unclenching of her spine. She would cook trad tonight, Lea decided, and have a nice evening in with Todd. Poor Todd had been tiptoeing around her the past few weeks, every gesture and word carefully calibrated so as not to offend. Ratatouille, she decided, and a nice lentil salad.

In the grocery store, Lea lifted the grapefruit up to the light like she had seen her mother do once when she was a child, back when the first directives were still being drafted. Squinting, she tried to see what her mother had seen, tried to discern the quality. But backlit by the harsh overhead lights, the grapefruit was nothing more than a dark globe, an eclipsed moon.

Lea had no idea how to buy fruit. She never ate it, of course, except on very special occasions. Today, three days since the Observers had disappeared from her office, she considered it.

Bringing the grapefruit to her nose, she breathed in its strange, air-freshener scent. It didn't stir anything; no secretion of saliva or racing pulse. She thought of the chocolate ice cream she'd had all those years ago with her father and Samuel in the park. Nothing about the grapefruit evoked the cold sweetness of dessert.

Lea put it back down on the shelf. The grapefruit were stacked furtively on a low shelf, smack in the middle of a store, between the soy milk and the nutribars. So you'd have to stoop to pick one up, and everyone would know what you were doing. *Directive 477B: Facilitation of Healthful Consumption.*

The light in the vegetable aisle was warmer, more forgiving. Brassica and other cruciferous forms lined one wall, frilly leaves neatly tucked into ventilated paper bags. Then there were the composites: artichokes, chicory, lettuce, safflower. The alliums, helpfully multi-packed, since you never needed just one bulb of garlic. Gourds hung in baskets from the ceiling, sunset colours all mixed up in pretty knobbly shapes.

Lea rifled through a pile of asparagus, their green skins silky and firm to the touch. She weighed a fat eggplant in her palm, brought a sprig of parsley to her nose, so close it tickled. Like most, she rarely cooked, so when she did, she liked to take her time choosing her ingredients.

Lea was absorbed by an overwhelmingly symmetrical, perfectly formed radish when she saw him. Standing at the far end of the store, next to a large bale of spinach. The man wasn't looking at her, but neither was he looking at the spinach. In his right hand, he held a tablet. There was nothing to suggest he was one of them, yet Lea's heart sped up. Not every man wearing a suit with a tablet was an Observer, she told herself. Don't be silly.

With his dark brown suit, the man's stocky girth meant he resembled one of the more svelte gourds in the baskets hanging from the ceiling. Lea watched as the man picked up a spinach leaf, twirling it by the stem in his large fingers. After considering it for a moment, he put it down again, picking up another leaf, and doing the exact same thing.

Just a well-heeled businessman getting ready for a trad dinner party, she told herself. Trying to impress some clients with his cultural side. In any case, no Ministry person would be allowed to walk around with a BMI like that.

Lea went back to the radish she'd put down, tried to focus on whether the crisp crunch of it would go better with lettuce or kohlrabi. Out of the corner of her eye, she saw the man put down the spinach leaf and walk out of the store.

A wave of relief washed over her. How completely paranoid she was; it definitely could not be good for her stats. She would tell Todd all about it over dinner, he would make fun of her, she would laugh it off.

The joy had gone out of shopping now, so she quickly picked out what she needed and headed to the checkout counter. The sleek display showed the total nutritional value of her purchase — well under the sugar limit, but still more than she'd usually get. It was the carrot. But they would share it between them, herself and Todd, and then it would not be quite as indulgent. She thought briefly of the grapefruit, the round weight of it in her hand, the plump smell. Maybe when she was promoted to Tier 4. Yes, maybe she would permit herself a grapefruit then.

Lea could hear it before she opened the front door. Todd was doing it again, going through her music. He thought it was funny. Some days he got serious, warned her that it really was no good for her, all those soul-stirring arias. *Directive 708A: Art, Music and Film Advisory*. He'd suggest some seaside or rainforest tracks instead. Other days he'd blast it from the speakers, giggling to himself on the sofa at how ridiculous it all was.

"Can you turn that down?" Lea yelled, going straight to the kitchen without saying hello. No response. In spite of herself, she started humming along. The *St Matthew Passion*, by one of the few remaining living virtuosos. European, of course — there were no American musicians left.

Alma, Tilda, something like that — it was a name that fired up images of long, dark winters, pickled fish and frosted windows. Lea had read about her tragic story in the news. Misalignment — when replacements and enhancements had different expiry dates — was a terrible way to go. A tremor went down her spine as the voice streaming through the apartment climbed higher, higher still. The music seemed to go right through her, slipping into crevices of her soul that she never knew existed. She closed her eyes. The image of a face floated before her, a solid, structured face, lined as tree bark, with thick pale eyebrows and colourless eyes. If not for what had happened to the opera singer, she never would have known her face.

"Lea?"

The music stopped abruptly, hanging in the air like a question mark. Lea blinked. There was something odd about Todd's voice. He stood leaning against the kitchen door, hands clasped behind his back.

"Wilma. That's what it is. Wilma Nilsson. I can't believe I forgot."

Lea gave Todd a peck on the cheek, lingering to take in his smell. It was faintly sweet, the smell of sweat masked by cologne. But under that artificial woodsy scent, he smelt like a human being. It was one of the things she loved about Todd. Something about his smell that made her feel at home, that despite the golden hair and model looks and trendy clothes, seemed to reveal a weakness. She hooked her chin over his shoulder.

It was only then that she saw them. Sitting side by side on the plush couch in the living room, each clasping a mug between their hands. The mugs said "Mr Right" and "Mrs Always Right", gifted by Jiang at the office secret Santa exchange. Their tablets lay on the coffee table — her coffee table. Todd had not given them coasters, and two faint wet rings were already forming on the carefully oiled reclaimed wood. They were still wearing their shoes.

"Hello," AJ said.

GK nodded a greeting and took a loud sip of tea.

"They were at the door when I got home. It seemed rude to just leave them there," Todd said.

Lea pulled him into the kitchen, out of the Observers' line of sight.

"It seemed rude," Lea repeated.

"They don't seem so bad. You made it sound like they were these Gestapo characters. Ajit even said he liked your music."

"Ajit?"

"Yeah. The one who talks. I haven't actually heard Greg say anything yet."

Lea massaged her inner eyebrows, pulling them apart. Blood throbbed in her ears.

"How long have they been here?" she asked.

She would breathe normally, stay calm, focus on the matter at hand. There had to be an explanation. They

103

were here to congratulate her on her release from Observation. To apologise in person for any trouble caused, offer her access to Ministry preservation services in compensation. The services would come out of AJ's — Ajit's — personal account. Perhaps he wasn't so bad after all. He liked her music. Lea stopped massaging her forehead.

"You showed them my collection?"

"Not all of it. Just some of your favourites. Ajit was very interested in them. More cultural than you'd think, these Ministry people. Surprising, isn't it?"

Lea looked away from him. Her right hand throbbed with a dull pain. Weighed down with the vegetables she had chosen so carefully, the straps of the plastic bag were cutting off circulation to the tips of her fingers.

The blood was still pounding in her ears, but Lea's movements were brisk and calm. She unpacked each leaf carefully, placed them in a colander for rinsing. She lined the squash up neatly on the counter top. She folded the plastic bag.

"Besides," Todd said. "It can't hurt to be nice to them. They seem like reasonable guys."

Lea poured some lentils into a bowl of water. Most sank to the bottom, but a few floated, tiny lily pads. She plunged her hands into the bowl and began cleaning them. The lentils were hard as pebbles, the water deliciously cold.

When Lea didn't answer, Todd left the room quietly.

"State of mind . . . high-pressure job . . . cortisol inducing." He spoke in a low murmur, but now that the music was off, fragments of conversation floated into the kitchen.

Done with the lentils, Lea began skinning an onion. Its exposed surface was taut, a tensed muscle about to spring. She pressed the blade into its midsection. The slow crunch as the pale flesh gave way was strangely satisfying. The familiar prick of her eyes as she sliced, each felled layer translucent and paper thin.

Onions were strange things. Cut open they smelled not like vegetables but of animal sweat, pungent and sweet, oddly comforting. By the time Lea was done cutting the first onion, the sound of Todd's low voice in the living room no longer bothered her.

Suddenly she was hungry. She sliced more quickly, the pieces getting thicker and less even. When she was done with the onions, she resolved, she would wash her hands, dry them on the fluffy white towel next to the sink, go outside and shake their hands calmly. She would smile, a welcoming, calm smile, containing no anger, no hysteria. Not even a hint of irritation that they were in her living room, their shoes no doubt leaving stains on the cream carpet. No, none of that.

She would even ask them how they liked the *St Matthew Passion*, compliment Todd for picking it out. It was Nilsson, she'd inform them with the grace of a dinner party hostess, the Swedish contralto. Yes, the one who'd been misaligned. This in a conspiratorial whisper, as one always used when talking about such matters. It soothes my nerves, she would say. But of course I also have the *Mandolin* album, and the entire *Sea Series*. Right here, see. She would casually pull out

105

her tablet, show them her play count so that they'd see how much more she listened to muzak than classical.

Her fingers glistened with the pungent, sticky sap. Lea marvelled at how well formed they were, precisely proportioned, slender, each trimmed nail curving into a perfect smile. Lying there on the chopping board, they were pink with life, not unlike little jointed carrots. Lea became aware of the weight of the knife in her other hand. It was a ceramic blade, newly sharpened to a fine creamy edge. There was a logic to it, bringing those two surfaces together, the tender shoot of her ring finger and that clean, objective line of the blade. Angling the sharp edge just beyond the tip of her nail, she pressed down cautiously, curiously. The knife was so sharp she didn't feel her flesh parting, not until a thin sliver lay, red and wet, on the stark white chopping board.

Then the pain came, hot and selfish and demanding. Suddenly she was nothing. Every thought and feeling rushed into that throbbing fingertip, everything wanted nothing more than to make it stop. She let out a sharp gasp. The knife loosened from her grip.

It lasted only seconds. Slowly, Lea realised she could breathe normally again. The pain melted into a soft ache. Wiping the blood off her fingertip with a dish towel, she saw that the newly grown skin was smooth and supple, just a shade lighter than the colour around it. She held her hands out in front of her, as if checking on a new manicure. While the blood had clotted and the skin regrown, the finger in question was still very slightly shorter than it should be, its tip flat and square. No one would notice. Had it even happened?

106

Todd was still talking to the Observers. The Observers — she was seized with a sudden urgency. Quickly, quietly, Lea disposed of the evidence. She rinsed the knife and chopping board, wrapped the dishtowel in a plastic bag and tossed it in the trash compacter. Soon, everything was spotless again.

It was only when she was carrying the bowl of sliced onions to the fridge that she noticed they were stained pink. The colour had seeped into their porous veins, translucent and now, almost human.

CHAPTER
TWELVE

Someone had brought him in for show and tell. Whiter than the whites of her eyes and softer than a cloud, his nose was a damp pink upside down triangle, wobbling nervously. As they passed him around, their small hands were reverent, tongues peeking out of parted lips, eyes afraid to blink. His name was Domino.

When it came to Lea's turn, she held him up to her face. He wriggled between her hands, a warm, alive thing. She felt his delicate ribs under the flesh and fur, thin bones interlocking like puzzle pieces, protecting some squirming secret within.

Lea ran one finger along the tracks of his backbone. Coccyx, sacrum, lumbar, thoracic, cervical, she recited silently. Over a hundred and twenty muscles in the human spine; how many in a rabbit's?

They had learnt about nerves and cartilage and skeletons in Biology, but this was something different. She felt where bone met tendon in his taut hind legs, the way his ribcage gave way to a sagging, tender belly. She fingered his ears, folded like leaves, and then, taking one between thumb and forefinger, she pulled gently.

"Come on, Fishy," someone whined. "Hurry up. You've had your go."

Lea passed Domino on, a sharp stab of loss prickling as the soft mass left her hands. She watched as her classmates cooed and stroked and cuddled. A tiny flame seemed to burn within her.

At recess Lea crept back into the empty classroom. She picked her way through errant backpacks strewn across aisles, chairs pushed back from their desks haphazardly, cardigans and scarves lying pooled on the floor.

When she slid the door of the cage open, her movements were silent. Cradling Domino once more, she felt again how flexible his ribs were. A birdcage in a fairytale, wrought of wispy tarnished gold, curving gracefully around an invisible treasure.

She felt the strength in her own small fingers, and she squeezed. Gently at first, as if testing the firmness of an orange. As Domino squirmed, the flame in her belly flared, purple and hot, and she pressed harder, harder still.

He was still struggling when the bones snapped, his black beady eyes bulging like tadpoles. The blood ran hot and fast in her veins, a ball of white emotion expanding in her chest. She squeezed harder and harder, even after everything was loose and crunchy and Domino was still, even after her fingernails were tipped with red.

Finally the heat subsided. Lea could hear her own breathing, the thump of blood in her ears. She could hear shouts and laughter from her classmates down the hall, where they sat in the cafeteria with their bowls of iron-enriched spinach and eggs. In a flash, Lea saw how Betty would cry, the rest of the class looking on in horror as she cradled the cold, stiff ball of fur in her arms. Maybe some of the others would cry too.

She imagined owning up to it. Waving her rust-coloured fingernails in Betty's pretty freckled face. How Betty would stop crying, her porcelain eyes wide with fear. They'd stop calling Lea Fishy, fishy fish fish fish. The rest of the class — all secretly jealous of Betty with her tight golden curls and menagerie of furry living things — would cheer, rise up and crown Lea their queen.

A door slammed somewhere in the building. The heavy thump set Lea's heart pounding again.

There would be no cheers. She would be labelled a Potential Threat, like dark-eyed Dennis Zhang, who tripped a boy while playing tag one day. Despite the mandatory protective pads, the boy had managed to scratch his shin and his parents threatened to sue. Dennis Zhang disappeared. The whispers had it that he'd been transferred to a school for sub-100s, somewhere in the Outer Boroughs.

Lea stroked Domino's matted fur, trying to take in what she had done. He is dead, she repeated to herself. I did it. I made him into this cold and sticky thing. She waited. But there was nothing.

The ceiling fans circled like birds of prey. Lea closed the door of Domino's cage. Walking over to her desk, she pulled out a brown, neatly folded lunch bag from

110

her backpack. Out went the kale chips and nutribars, in went Domino, head first.

There was no one in the hallway. The beat of her heart seemed to echo down the empty passage. She felt sure that at any moment, a teacher or classmate would come out of hiding, fingers accusing, voices raising the alarm. Her sweaty hands gripped the paper bag more tightly.

She passed like a ghost down the hallways, moisture gathering behind her knees, bangs clumping. The dumpster was out back. As she lifted the creaking lid, Lea wondered if she should say something, like she'd seen murderers do in movies. He was a good rabbit, and always liked being cuddled, something like that. But the thought of his snuffly mouth and velvety fur kindled the same feeling as before, a strange knot of heat that made her want to kick and scream. She flung the bag above her head and into the dumpster.

Because she'd left the cage door open, everyone thought that Domino had escaped. All afternoon they combed the hallways and cupboards, crawling on hands and knees to peer under desks, calling his name as if a rabbit were capable of responding.

Lea went along with it, nervously at first, sure that the deception showed on her face. But once she realised no one suspected anything other than poor Betty's carelessness, Lea went about the charade boldly, calling louder than anyone and inspecting the back of the classroom so thoroughly that her knees turned black with dust.

When her mother picked her up from school that day, Lea was in high spirits. She told her all about Domino and how mysteriously he'd disappeared, how furry and docile he'd been. She said she hoped he hadn't been run over by a car and that he'd found a nice garden to live in, one full of lettuce and tomatoes. She asked her mother if rabbits went to heaven, like dogs. She talked and talked and talked, stopping only when, on the way to the car, they passed the dumpster.

CHAPTER
THIRTEEN

Silk sleeves and skirts slipped through Anja's fingers like water. They were named colours like mink grey, iceberg pink, aurora blue — the first sign that everything in that shop, in that mall, was far beyond what she could afford.

The elegant bun sitting atop the salesgirl's head wobbled as she trailed behind Anja, rearranging hangers as soon as her fingers left them. The salesgirl's lips were pressed together in a horizontal line, her footsteps pert. Even her breathing seemed to exude disapproval.

Anja didn't take anything off the racks, content to run her hand through the flowing silks as she walked through the store. It was very relaxing, almost meditative. Even the wound-up presence of the salesgirl did nothing to disturb her peace.

"Did you want to try anything on?" Her voice sounded like anything but an invitation. Still, she maintained a minimum level of courtesy, less out of professionalism and more out of respect for Anja's shiny hair and supple skin. Even with uncut hair that reached her waist and her worn trench coat, one button missing, it was impossible to mistake Anja for anything but a lifer.

"Sure, why not?" Anja turned to face the girl.

There was a pause. The salesgirl seemed to be waiting for something, one plucked eyebrow lifted.

"What would you like to try?" she said finally.

"Oh," Anja said, turning back to the rack. "How about this one?"

She pulled out a dress at random. The salesgirl winced as its lacy edge dragged across the plush carpet.

"One of our best-selling models," she said, quickly taking the dress from Anja, cradling its long skirt like a baby. "Champagne Peony," she pronounced in a hushed tone.

The salesgirl carried it with outstretched arms to the dressing room. Drawing back a heavy curtain to reveal a mirrored room, she hung the dress up on a gilded hook in the wall. She stroked it lightly, as if it were a pet.

"Let me know if you need anything else," she said to Anja before drawing the curtain behind her.

Anja undressed slowly, letting her clothes fall to the floor in a pile. Her mother would like the dress, she thought, fingering the smooth cold fabric. It shimmered under the warm light. It wasn't the kind of thing Anja wore. This dress was far too beautiful.

Still, she slipped it on. It was so soft against her fingers that she wanted to feel it on her skin. The blushing fabric fell in soft waves around her, fluid as milk. Anja turned towards the mirror, sticking one leg forward in a mocking imitation of what she'd always

114

seen her mother do when trying on dresses before a performance.

But when she saw herself in the mirror, something began welling up inside of her. Anja found herself smoothing out wrinkles in the fabric with cold fingers, hiking her hair up in a makeshift updo. Strands of hair fell about her face, dark gold in the soft, stage-managed changing-room light.

She saw the tears in the mirror before she felt them on her face. They spilled out of her, hot and fast. Anja didn't sink to the ground or make a noise, she didn't let her face fall into her hands. She stood there, holding her hair up, cheeks shining with silent tears.

"Everything all right?" The salesgirl's prim voice cut through the thick air in the dressing room like a knife.

Anja let go of her hair.

"Fine," she said. "Very pretty. Actually, can you bring in something in a different colour? Blue, or grey maybe?"

"Of course."

A minute later, the salesgirl's arm poked through the curtain, hanger in hand. The new dress was similar in cut, but the colour of the sky. "Crepuscular Teal," she announced.

Anja wiped away her tears and changed into the blue dress. Now her gaze was critical, business-like. It would be her first public appearance. She didn't doubt that word had already got out, but this was to be the official announcement, the full shindig. There would be people, important people. There would be a band. She might perform too.

This dress wouldn't work either. The blue flattened her skin tone, made her look sickly. She didn't need to be beautiful, but she had to be presentable, she had to command respect. It was a big role she was stepping into, after all.

"No," she called out. "Can you bring me a few more?"

"Of course." She could almost hear the salesgirl's lips tightening.

Countless dresses later, Anja cast her gaze back to the first she'd tried on, which she'd hung up rather than tossing it onto the colourful pile on the ground. With its loose, cowl neckline, hip-skimming shape and low back, it was the phantom of another dress, one that as a child Anja had seen her mother carefully shake out before each performance.

A flutter of voices came from outside the changing room, cooing and gasping and giggling. Dresses rustled, and the salesgirl could be heard naming more colours ("Sea Mist Before Dawn", "Rose Silver").

Anja pulled the gold dress off the hanger and into her backpack. Balled up like that it was nothing more than a puff of fabric. Slinging the backpack across one shoulder, Anja gathered up the rest of the dresses in one messy pile that obscured most of her face and walked briskly out into the shop.

The salesgirl was now surrounded by a tittering group of coiffed, perfumed ladies. She turned to Anja with a look of simultaneous annoyance and relief.

"All done? Found anything you liked? No? Pity" She gestured towards the counter. "Could you just put them there, please? Lovely, thank you, hope to see you again soon."

And then she turned back to the group of women with a smile far more generous than she had offered to Anja before, ushering them towards the dressing room.

"Sea Mist *After* Dawn, now that's a popular bridesmaids' choice . . ."

The diner where Anja worked was a bright, boisterous place, filled with movement and shouting and the smell of stale oil. She kept her distance from the rest of the staff, content to immerse herself in the carrying of steaming plates and metal jugs, the mopping of sticky floors and wiping of crusty tabletops. All the others who worked there respected Anja's silence, automatically excluding her from the daily flow of gossip and banter, defaulting to a detached professionalism whenever they had to speak to her.

All except Branko. Branko was an Outer Boroughs native whose knotted forearms were snaked with veins and who wore singlets even in winter. He seemed to take her silence personally, and had made it his mission to harangue her out of it. Every day he scolded and flirted alternately, making jokes about her perfect posture and her lilting intonation. He made up songs about her, spent three consecutive days guessing where she was from, brought her wilted flowers.

Usually Anja smiled and bore it. But the night before she'd been thinking about the Club, had been unable to sleep. The gold dress was hung up behind the apartment door, catching the reflected headlights of passing cars in the street.

So that morning at the diner, when Branko called her "babe" for the fifth time, asked her to ditch this shift and go have themselves a party of their own, something inside her snapped. "I'd love to," she said. "But I have a dying mother to get home to."

"Don't we all, babe," he stuttered. "That's life, isn't it?" But his face was a deep purple. He turned and walked to the other end of the diner, a handful of dirty cutlery in one drooping hand.

He tiptoed around her all day. The lewd jokes stopped. All jokes stopped. She felt the atmosphere in the diner shift, become heavy. The other staff averted their eyes, throwing themselves into the demands of the lunchtime crowd.

Anja had been twelve when her father had died. The questions from neighbours, teachers, people at the grocery store were endless. What was her favourite memory of him? Had they travelled much together? Did he take his morning coffee black or white? The questions had made her cry. She remembered breaking down in public places, convulsing in embarrassing sobs. She had felt aggrieved, attacked even. It seemed a cruel thing to do to a twelve-year-old girl who had just lost her father.

But here, in this country, where there was only silence around death, Anja finally understood the purpose of those questions. Back home they would have asked about her mother, kind yet direct. They would have posed questions about her illness, bedsores, siblings, favourite food, all unabashedly. Perhaps they would have made Anja cry. But at least her mother would exist, would be a human being once again. She would be more than an inconvenient body to hide or handle, more than a statistic warning against the dangers of black market extensions, more than Anja's responsibility, Anja's burden, Anja's life.

At the end of the day, Anja asked Branko if he could give her a lift to the ferry terminal.

"Sure, of course," he mumbled, still not meeting her gaze.

She got into the car. Branko started the engine, shifting gears with rough ease.

"Where did you get this?" she asked, looking around. She couldn't remember the last time she had been in a driver-controlled car. These days, only eccentric hobbyists or men like Branko owned them any more. They were relics from a different time, carefully maintained over the years.

"Had it since I was a teenager," he said gruffly. "Couldn't buy one today with all the money in the world."

"Is it quite valuable then?" she asked, looking doubtfully at the balding seats and scratched windscreen.

"Who knows. Could probably sell it in the Markets, they've got a big vehicle section. But who'd buy it? You like R&B?" he said. He pressed a button on the panel in front of him and music jerked through the speakers.

"No, not really," Anja said.

"So what do you like?" He kept switching stations. Most of it was that terrible mandolin and ukelele strumming that people now called music.

"My mother is being kept alive by a heart replacement that won't stop for another fifty years," Anja said.

Branko's fingers stopped moving. An upbeat pop song came on.

"I thought you said she was dying."

"She is. I mean, she should be."

He fiddled with the control panel. "Your mother's not really dying, then," he said.

"Of course she is." Anja's eyes flashed.

"My brother had a heart attack, five years ago. He was forty-three. I never had the chance to say goodbye. His eight-year-old daughter lives with me now. She looks just like him."

"Oh," Anja said. "I'm sorry."

It had never occurred to her before that Branko, and probably everyone else who worked at the diner, was a sub-100, as the Americans called them. She'd never thought before what that meant, what that must be like in a place like this. She wanted to tell him that back home, in her town, there was no such thing as a sub-100, but she didn't know how to say it without sounding pitying or patronising.

"What kind of music did he like?" she asked.

He paused. Then, reaching out, he turned off the radio.

"Old stuff. R&B, hip hop, drum and bass."

Anja smiled politely.

120

"You don't know what I'm talking about, do you?" Branko said. "Man, Milan would flip out if he were here right now. He'd talk your ear off for like, five hours. It would become his thing, his personal mission, to educate you. Trust me, you're lucky he's not here."

"Is that his name? Milan?"

"Yeah. Milan."

She watched the dark streets roll past. Scattered among the homogeneous apartment blocks were low houses, sandwiched in on either side by towering concrete. Once, she had heard, Staten Island had been all houses like that. Surrounded by water, it would not have felt too different from home, she imagined.

"So, what's your mother like?"

"She was an opera singer. That's why we came here. She sang at Carnegie Hall."

Branko's eyebrows shot up.

"Carnegie Hall? That's a big deal, right? So she's some kind of celebrity."

"Some kind, yes."

He turned the radio back on. *Baby, you should have come over*, a deep voice crooned.

"So what's the daughter of a famous opera singer doing waiting tables at New York's finest eatery?" Branko grinned.

"She doesn't sing any more."

His smile faded. "Oh. Yeah. Sorry," he mumbled. "What's wrong with her?"

"She had some replacements. Now she's almost a hundred and fifty, things are breaking down, but she can't, you know, die."

"You're a lifer," he said, turning to look at her as if they'd just met. He squinted in the dark, as if trying to make out the telltale signs on her face. "How old are you?"

"Just over a hundred."

"Holy shit."

"I know. I think that all the time."

"Why? I mean, that seems strange. All the lifers I've met seem to think, you know, we're the fucked up ones. Not them. We're the damaged goods."

Anja laughed. "Where I'm from, we're all damaged goods."

"And where's that?" he asked. There was no mockery in his tone now.

"Sweden." The word escaped her like a sigh.

"Sweden, right. Winter, pancakes, universal healthcare. Why'd you leave?"

"I don't know," Anja said.

Baby, won't you come over. Branko stopped the car. "Well, here we are," he said.

They were pulled up by the terminal. Ahead of them, the lights of Manhattan and Brooklyn twinkled like wildfire, sending specks of gold dancing across the dark water. Somewhere in that forest of buildings was the room she shared with her mother, that damp, silent room. Even as she sat there with Branko, the sharp beauty of the night sky spread out before them, Anja felt the walls of the apartment closing in.

CHAPTER
FOURTEEN

The problem with visiting her father was that Lea would have to take the subway.

"No carshares," he'd said before they parted ways. "Anyone could track where you go."

"Who would want to track me?" Lea laughed, but then remembered the Observers. She hadn't told her father about any of it, not the Observers, not WeCovery. She was afraid it would scare him off, that he would disappear again, now that he seemed to care about getting found by the Ministry. So she agreed to take the subway.

Lea hadn't been on the subway in decades. Part of it was wealth and status — as she rose in her job, she began taking expensive carshares wherever she went. Part of it was the advisory against being sedentary, which meant she, like most lifers, walked wherever she could. But the other part was simply that, without really noticing, the radius of her life had shrunk over the years, become confined to the most central of the Central Boroughs, so most days she was able to get where she needed just by walking.

As she descended into the subway station, Lea wondered where the people who thronged the staircase were going. She scrutinised the chiselled chin of a smooth-shaven man carrying a duffel bag larger than his torso, the filmy coral eyes of an elderly woman with dark crepe paper skin, the stubby fingers of a businessman gripping his tablet. She wondered if they, too, had secrets. If they, too, did not want to be tracked.

The station was brighter than she'd imagined, floodlit with fluorescent light. Lea bought her ticket from an ageing machine, one that still had a disused slot for cash.

Suddenly, her neck prickled. Lea turned away from the machine, looking about herself wildly.

"Lady, you done yet? In case you haven't noticed, there's a line," a man behind her said.

Lea ignored him, eyes still scanning the crowd. She'd felt, with sudden certainty, that she was being watched. But there was no one — only a fluid crowd of strangers, streaming in and out of the station.

"Um, excuse me?" the man said again. Lea shot him a look, and he fell silent.

There was no one. No one was following her. Lea shook herself, grabbed the ticket and headed down the escalators. In the train, she plugged her headphones into her ears and pulled out her tab to go through her emails.

The train had pulled out of the station when a new email appeared, slipping in unread above the rest. It was from an unknown sender. Her father, perhaps. She tapped it open.

The video started playing right away. Her first thought was *ad*, and she moved to close it. But something about the man's face seemed familiar, so she paused, brought the screen closer to her face.

124

"I did my best," the man in the video said. "I have a diversified portfolio of organs, dutifully invested, enough to last me several lifetimes. But try as I might, I couldn't ignore it. It just doesn't seem right. It's not right that these — these *numbers* are assigned at birth, that an algorithm decides who lives and who doesn't."

A portfolio of organs.

Suddenly, his face resolved into focus. It was one of the Musks, the client that Lea had supposedly caused LTCP to lose because of the Observers.

"Do you think sub-100s truly are, as we say, sub-100? Who decides who gets the SmartBlood™, the replacements, the maintenance sessions?"

Her mind raced. Why would he send her this? Was this because they'd lost the account?

"We think that if we can find the lifers with the right genetic predispositions, we can crack the population problem. Immortality. No need to worry about birth rates any more. Maybe though, maybe the solution is already here, right under our noses."

The man took a long sip from a bottle in his hand. Lea's heart sped up, her hands grew cold and clammy. But she couldn't look away. She realised now that the video hadn't just been sent to her, but the way he stared into the camera, the way his eyes locked with hers, it felt as if it had been. She realised that the man in the video was, in all likelihood, already dead.

"But if we don't fight for it, no one will. We are complicit. All lifers are complicit. You are complicit."

He lit a match and stared into the camera, at the millions of invisible viewers watching with suspended breath.

"I'm not a member of the Suicide Club. I don't always agree with their agenda. But we are united behind a common cause."

He brought the match to his face.

"We leave ourselves no choice."

Her father lived at the end of the subway line. Lived — a strange word, as if he had always been there, when really it was temporary lodgings he had taken up. Though how could she know? Perhaps he had always been there, a two-hour subway ride away from her mother's apartment in Borough Three, pretending to be missing but really sharing the same water system, the same public transport, the same night sky. Perhaps he had been hiding right under their noses, for eighty-eight years.

Lea raced up the closest staircase. She wanted to leave the memory of the video she'd watched underground, wanted to get as far away as possible from the image of the Musk heir bringing a lit match to his alcohol-soaked tongue.

When she emerged from the subway station, the sky above was pale and bright, the distant sea a shimmering mirror suffused with sunlight. She was on the boardwalk. The wind licked her cheeks and impulsively, Lea stuck out her tongue to lick it back. For a moment, she forgot the video, forgot even the father she was here to meet. She wanted to taste the salt on the air, but there was nothing, only a scraping cold. She closed her mouth again.

"Beautiful, isn't it?"

Lea turned. Her father was standing by the exit, wearing dark glasses whose bottom rims bumped his cheeks when he smiled.

"Dad," she said. And then, without thinking, she rushed towards him and grabbed his waist, burying her face in his chest.

He smelled of dry, crackling twigs. Of smoke and mould, of something kept in a closet all winter. He smelled different, but also, even after all those years, he still smelled the same.

He placed his hands tentatively on her shoulders, not quite embracing her back. Eventually, Lea pulled away, embarrassed.

"Trip here okay?" he asked.

She started to nod, but then shook her head. "I got this — video in my email. One of those Suicide Club ones."

"Oh?" He raised his eyebrows.

"You might not have seen them. They call themselves an activist group, but they're really just terrorists. What they do — well. It's exactly what the name sounds like." Lea shivered, pulling her coat tighter around her shoulders.

"Suicides," her father said drily. He squinted into the sun.

Lea nodded. "The thing is, the guy in the latest video. I — I knew him. He was a Musk."

Kaito was still looking into the distance. He showed no sign of recognition at the name.

"Surely you remember. One of the founding Healthtech families? Anyway, we were pitching to him at work. For a while it looked like he might switch over to us. It would have been a huge win for LTCP." Not that it would have mattered, given the video.

"Shall we take a walk?" her father asked. He had a strange, closed expression on his face.

"I thought we were going to your apartment," Lea said, even though the wind whipping through her hair meant there was nothing she wanted more than to take a walk. But she had to see where he lived. She had to tie him to something, to see his furniture, his wardrobe, his toothbrush on a bathroom counter. She wanted to know how he arranged his shirts, whether he made his bed, if his fridge was full or empty.

"We will," he said. "There's something I want to show you first."

He started down the boardwalk, Lea by his side.

"I didn't know . . ." Lea stretched one hand out towards the sea. "I didn't know this was part of the city."

"Not many people do, I suspect. No one comes out here any more," her father said. "No idea why."

"I suppose — I suppose it's not what you think of, when you think of the Outer Boroughs," she said.

When had it happened? When had her life become so tightly circumscribed within the limits of her office, her home, Boroughs One through Three? They all did it, all of them, her, Todd, Jiang. That was why it always felt so crowded everywhere, even as the population numbers

128

kept falling. It was as if the fewer of them there were, the greater need they felt to cling together. Lea looked at the wide open space, the empty boardwalk, the large dome of luminescent blue overhead.

"It's so empty," she said.

Her father nodded. "Outside the city, it's even emptier than you can imagine."

"Outside the city?" Lea said.

Her father paused.

Finally he spoke again. "Outside the city, you can travel for tens of miles, hundreds of miles, without seeing another person. Empty shells of entire neighbourhoods, towns, the old buildings left to crumble. And then there are other big lifer cities, of course, Boston, LA, Chicago. Identical to New York. Where all the clinics are. I couldn't avoid them entirely."

Lea kept walking, but otherwise was very still. The last time they met, she had learnt to let the silence hang between them so that her father would tell his stories.

"When I left — absconded — all those years ago. At first, I made sure to hide my tracks. I got a fake passport — paid a small fortune for it — grew my hair out, never stayed in one town for too long. I found a new clinic, a small one, in a strip mall in the middle of nowhere. My new passport seemed to work — I was no longer Kaito Kirino, but I could still get the basic extensions and treatments, all my bio-data seemed to match up just fine to my new identity.

"I couldn't believe it. Couldn't believe that in our world of hyperconnectivity and biometric scans, I'd actually got away with it.

"Until one day, I happened to glance at the screen of a Tender I was seeing. A lovely young man, well, likely older than me, but you know what I mean. Anyway, I looked at his screen, and all its numbers and scatter plots and trend lines, random alphabets and code. You know how it is. But then I see it — I see it in the bottom of the screen, in tiny font . . . Kaito Kirino, that's what it said."

He let out a low laugh. It was an unpleasant sound.

"They knew who I was. They knew where I was, all along. The whole time I'd thought I'd pulled off this great escape, but they'd let me go. Then it hit me. No one cared. I wasn't a fugitive. They never wanted me back at all. Sure, I'd been labelled antisanct, but as long as I stayed out of their cities, their great citadels of life and longevity, no one cared. The problem was solved. As long as I stayed away, as long as I wasn't here, infecting the Ministry's precious investments with my so-called antisanct mindset, no one cared."

They stopped walking. Lea's thoughts were spinning. She didn't understand. If that were the case, then why had he come back? Surely coming back meant he would get caught, put on trial for the crime he'd committed all those years ago?

"Look," he said, pointing.

Lea blinked. At first she didn't understand what she was looking at. The shapes were dark against the sky, their dips and loops tessellating madly, extravagant sculptures set by the sea. Her eyes adjusted to the light and she took in the faded big top, the rusting roller-coaster rails, the stationary bumper cars.

130

"When you were a girl, I always wanted to take you here," he said, turning to Lea. He pushed his sunglasses up onto his forehead, squinting in the sun. "Uju — she never let me. Said it was crazy, dangerous, that the place should be shut down. Sure enough, it was shut down a couple of years later. But they never demolished it or built anything new. The population kept shrinking, lifers started to cluster closer and closer to the centre, land prices fell. No one wanted to buy it."

Her father was silent. When he spoke again, it was in a low voice. "Can you believe it? They never tore it down."

"If no one was looking for you, why did you come back? Surely — surely it's dangerous for you," Lea asked. "What are you doing here?"

He contemplated the abandoned theme park in front of them. Finally he turned to her. His brow was furrowed, his eyes urgent. "I can't tell you yet, Lea. Not yet. But it's important that no one knows I'm here, only you. Can you promise you won't tell anyone?"

Lea thought about the Observers sitting on her couch, looking through her music collection, drinking tea from her mugs. She thought of Jiang, who had recently implemented a new open-door policy in the office, that she knew was meant for her. She thought about Todd, who wouldn't stop asking her where she was going whenever she left the house.

The sky was so pale it was almost white, rather than blue. She thought of her father, all those years ago, persuading her mother to let them go to the theme park.

"Of course," Lea said. "I promise."

The studio apartment he had rented was the size of Lea's bedroom. It was small, but thanks to a large window that overlooked the boardwalk, was also very bright. A narrow single bed was pushed against the far wall, a desk covered in papers against the window. A kitchenette containing a sink and microwave, a mini fridge under the counter. The room was dominated by the dining table, an oversized glass-top affair that could comfortably seat four people. There was no sofa. Nothing on the walls except a poster in a black plastic frame of some bland pastoral countryside scene, the kind of thing you'd see in clinics or hairdressers.

"Have a seat," her father gestured at the dining table. He hovered awkwardly by the sink, his hands crossed over his stomach. "Sorry there's nowhere more comfortable. The landlord refuses to move this monstrosity of a table."

Lea pulled out one of the plastic chairs and sat down.

"Would you like some water? I don't have anything else to drink, I'm sorry"

She nodded distractedly, still casting her gaze about the room, hungry for details. The apartment was clean, almost bare. No piles of clothes lying around, no half-read books left open on the bed, no packs of crisps or half-smoked cigarettes. There was nothing in the apartment to indicate what kind of life her father lived.

He filled a glass with water from the tap and set it down in front of Lea.

"Just tap water," he said.

Lea sensed another apology in his voice, so she made a show of drinking thirstily. She wanted to tell him to stop saying he was sorry, but she didn't know how.

"Be right back." Her father flicked a switch and opened a door she hadn't noticed before, behind which lay a modest bathroom. He closed the door behind him.

The air in the apartment was still now. Lea looked around again, more carefully this time. It was small and bare, yes, but not completely characterless. His bed was made, corners tightly tucked in, pillow plumped. On the kitchen counter was an empty beer bottle with a plastic sunflower in it. She wondered if her father had put it there himself. She wondered if he drank beer. It would not be unlike the Kaito she had known when she was a girl.

She got up from the dining table and walked over to the desk. The papers she'd noticed earlier were mainly bills, utilities from the past six months, addressed to a name she didn't recognise. Likely the landlord, she thought. Lea began to sort the bills chronologically, as she did with her own paperwork. She was stacking them into a pile, enjoying the neat alignment of folds and corners, when she noticed a different sort of envelope underneath the papers.

The envelope was small, about the size of a business card. It almost fitted into the palm of her hand. The powder-blue paper was fresh, child-like, a colour you rarely saw in the city except on certain mornings in the spring. For something so small, the envelope was heavy.

Lea glanced behind her. The tap was still running in the bathroom.

She flicked open the envelope's unsealed flap. The card inside was the same colour as the envelope. It was luxuriously thick, the kind of card that might be used for a wedding invitation. Perhaps that was what this was. Except it was far too small, and only printed with a date, time and address. The date was next Saturday, and the address was somewhere in a wealthy part of Borough Five. She traced the embossed text with her fingernail, memorising the street and building number. Then she placed the card back into the envelope, slipping it under the pile of bills. When her father came out of the bathroom, Lea was still standing by the desk, staring out the window.

"Great view, isn't it?" he said. "I got really lucky."

Lea nodded. "Beautiful," she said.

Her father's eyes lit up. "Hey," he said. "I have something for you."

She wondered if it was the card, hidden under the pile of bills. Perhaps there was a simple explanation for it. Perhaps he had been invited to a party of some kind, and he wanted her to come with him. But instead he turned, walking over to the kitchenette. He opened the mini fridge, dug around inside, pulled something out.

"Here," he said. "It was hard to find. Turns out the stand on Riverside Park wasn't the only one to shut down."

He pressed it into her hands. It was an ice-cream cone, wrapped in cheap colourful paper, wet and cold to touch. She could tell already that the mini fridge

134

hadn't been cold enough, that when she tore the paper open the melted ice cream would drip down the sides, would make her hands sticky and sweet.

"Thank you," she said, staring at the cone. Where had he got it? She hadn't seen one in years.

"What are you doing next Saturday?" Lea asked. "I thought maybe we could do something again. Maybe at my place."

She wanted him to remember the invitation card on his desk, for his face to open up and for him to say: *There's this party. I was hoping you would come.*

But instead, something else crossed his face, his eyes seemed to shut down. He looked away.

"Saturday's no good," he said. "How about Sunday?"

"Why?" she pressed, trying to keep her tone light. "What are you doing on Saturday?"

"Oh, nothing," he said vaguely. He picked her empty glass up from the dining table and began to rinse it. "Just some errands. Sunday works better for me."

Lea was silent as she absorbed his answer.

"Aren't you going to eat that?" her father said.

She was still holding the ice-cream cone. Her fingers had grown numb with cold. "Yes," Lea nodded, tearing at the paper.

It was only when the cold sweet fluid touched her lips that she remembered she was eating sugar, synthetic sugar, non-fruit sugar. And dairy, preservatives, additives, food colouring. She thought of the days she would lose from eating that ice cream, the spike in insulin levels that so much sugar would trigger. She thought of the cravings that would come later, the potential addiction that would set in.

It was too late, for she had already gulped half of it down. It was delicious. She stared at the ice cream, melting in her hands, dripping between her fingers, and took another greedy bite. The cloying sweetness was almost too much to bear, almost sour in its intensity, like a forgotten secret.

Lea got home late that night, on purpose, so that she wouldn't have to explain herself to Todd yet again. He normally went to sleep early, sometimes before sunset, so as to ensure optimal circadian rhythm compliance. She was still thinking about her father — his shoebox apartment, his spartan life — when she stepped into the living room, so she didn't immediately find it strange to see Todd sitting on the sofa in the dark.

"Hey," she said. "What are you doing up?"

"Where have you been?" he said.

"Office," Lea answered. The lie slipped out of her casually. She shrugged her coat off and stretched. "I'm exhausted. Why aren't you asleep?"

"Office," Todd said. "Which account are you working on? I thought the Musk account got pulled."

She turned to him. Todd was doing something with his feet she'd never seen before. He was tapping his heel, jerking his knee up and down, in an erratic, nervous motion. He wasn't looking at her. He was looking at his tablet.

"What are you doing?" Lea said.

"What?" Todd lowered his hand and met her eyes.

"Your tab. You're looking at it."

"Oh, yes. Just emails, you know how it is."

Lea narrowed her eyes. "No, Todd, I don't know how it is. Why don't you tell me?" she said calmly.

"You said you were in the office?" he said again.

"What's this about, Todd?"

She could tell him the truth, Lea thought. She could tell her partner of twenty years the reason why she had been slipping out of work early, why she disappeared for long hours on weekends.

Todd was looking at his tab again. "I tried calling your office line, you never picked up."

No, she couldn't tell Todd.

"I called several times through the day. Finally, Natalie picked up."

Her hands turned cold.

"She said you weren't there. She said she hadn't seen you all day."

Todd was typing. He was typing something into his tablet as he spoke to her.

"What are you doing, Todd?"

"I should be the one asking you that, Lea. What are you doing? Where have you been?"

Before she could stop herself, Lea had walked over to him and grabbed his tablet out of his hands.

He didn't protest, only folded his arms and pursed his lips.

On screen was an app that Lea had never seen before. Its interface was gloomy, though the font was clean and modern. Todd had "checked in" and a small, red dot showed their position on a map. Under "mood", a green circle blinked. It was recording. At the corner of the screen was a stylised heart.

"What is this?" Lea demanded.

"I had a long conversation with Natalie. We're worried, Lea."

Her insides churned. "Oh. *Natalie*'s concerned. Of course she is. How convenient for her to be concerned."

Todd frowned. "Jesus, Lea. It's got nothing to do with your — competition at work. Why do you always assume —"

"Why do I always assume the worst?" Lea stuck Todd's tablet in his face. "Clearly I wasn't assuming anything close to the worst, or it wouldn't come as such a surprise to me that my fiancé would be trying to get me stuck on the Observation List forever."

"Don't be like that, Lea."

"I'm sorry, *clearly* the fault is mine here."

"Anyway, talking to Natalie — it cleared my head. I realised I had to do something, that I wasn't helping you by staying silent about all your disappearances, your moodiness, your strange behaviour. I mean look at you — creeping about late at night, lying about where you've been — where *have* you been? I don't know what's going on, Lea."

"So, what? You're reporting on me to the Ministry? Please explain to me how this is *helping*, Todd. Because I really don't see how this is making anything better."

"I just don't know what else to do. I don't want things to get worse. Especially with the rumours about the Third Wave coming — I want what's best for you, what's best for us."

What's best for us. Something clicked.

"You're afraid," Lea said flatly. "You're afraid that me being on the List will affect your chances if the Third Wave happens. You're not worried about me at all, you only care about your goddamn self."

His silence told her everything she needed to know.

Lea gave Todd a week to move out. He didn't argue, it wasn't in his nature. That week, he tiptoed around the apartment as if it were made of porcelain, his footsteps soft and attentive. He started talking to her in a considerate, hushed voice, his eyebrows permanently raised in solicitude. He began leaving the toilet seat down.

That week she spotted it. Her first wrinkle, a clean fold extending out from the inner corner of her right eye. Looking closely, she saw that while the most obvious, it was not the only one. A delicate web radiated outwards from the tear ducts, minuscule rays of lined flesh, barely perceptible but nevertheless there. Along with the wrinkles came a tightness in her abdomen. It felt like a ball of rubber bands, stretched over one another, each more taut than the last. Everything Todd did — the way he placed a fork on the kitchen table, the splayed ivory bristles of his designer toothbrush in the bathroom, an ironed shirt hanging on a window frame. All of it she kept inside, wound more and more tightly around that ball of slow rage.

On the third day of silence, as Todd crept past her with a glass of water, Lea reached out and grabbed his wrist. He stopped at her touch.

"How long have you been doing it?" she asked.

Todd's eyes were bloodshot, unhappy, but still had that new, unfamiliar edge to them.

"Not long," he said quickly, as if he had been waiting for her to ask. "The Observers came to me right after it happened. Said I would be helping speed things along, since you had nothing to hide. They said it was better not to tell you. Then you could prove you were fine, and you could come off the List."

His words made sense to her, but something in his voice was different. Beneath the pleading tone was a certain care; a planned thoughtfulness. His words seemed carefully chosen, too carefully chosen.

"So what have you told them?" Lea said, her tone even.

"Nothing, really. I don't see why . . ." He ran one hand through his hair, boyishly, pleading innocence. "Trivial things, like what you ate, how long you were in the bathroom, the number of times you scratched that mole on your neck this morning. I don't know why they even want to know any of it at all."

"What else," Lea said. *Did you tell them about my father?* But of course he hadn't. He didn't know about Kaito.

"Nothing!" Todd said. "Well, when you get home. When you come home late at night. When . . ." He paused.

"Go on," Lea said tersely.

He cast his eyes to the ground.

"Go on, Todd," she said again.

"You might not like it," he said slowly, as if she was hard of hearing. "But I think, to some extent, maybe, there's no harm in getting, you know, help."

As he spoke, Todd's face changed. It had a serene, evangelical quality to it, all lifted chin and wide eyes and flushed cheeks.

It was only then that Lea noticed how clear his skin was. Fairer than usual, almost translucent. His freckles glowed a faded pink.

"What have you done to your face?" Lea said.

Todd winced and glanced down. Lea's fingers were wrapped, vice-like, around his wrist. Her fingernails left half moons in his soft skin when she let go.

"They're experts, you know," Todd went on as if he hadn't heard. "I mean, what do we know about being at risk? What experience do we have with safeguarding? And it's, I guess, my responsibility. It's all our responsibility, I mean, if you did hurt yourself, I would be responsible. I mean —"

"Todd, listen to yourself. This is insane."

He stared back blankly. Then, worse still, a look of soft concern came over his face.

"Lea, what I'm saying is maybe you should give it a shot. Stop sneaking around, come clean. Take them seriously. Take this whole thing seriously."

Her cheeks burned. He was telling *her* to take it seriously? What else had she been doing, schlepping down to WeCovery, tolerating the Observers, even working with Natalie on her accounts, and here was

Todd, Todd with his perfect skin and HealthFin trust fund and spying ways, here he was telling her to take it all seriously. As if that was the problem.

"I think you should leave now. Take a bag. I'll send you the rest of your stuff by courier."

Todd's lip twitched. "I can't leave. Even if I wanted to, I can't. You can't be unaccompanied. It's for your own safety, you know."

There was that strange gleam again. The tip of Todd's alpine nose was shiny and pink, his cheeks impossibly rosy. She wondered about the tiny blood vessels beneath his skin, wondered how easily they would break should she strike him. Again, there it was, the old feeling humming underneath the surface.

Bringing the glass of water to his lips, Todd took one long sip, eyes never leaving hers.

There was a split-second where something flashed before her, a split-second filled with possibilities, but then that moment was over and Lea was raising her hand, slapping the glass away from his lips.

The noise of shattering against the floorboards was louder than she'd expected. It was a rude, disorderly sound, a sound she had only heard once before, as a child in a restaurant. Then, the noise had cut through the mundane hum of conversation, inciting craned necks and quiet murmurs, the harsh words from an invisible chef to the unfortunate culprit. It wasn't often, these days, that things broke any more. Everything was toughened, reinforced, enhanced. You really had to try to break something.

Pieces of glass were puddled in the spilt water. It had not shattered; rather, broken into large pieces, four or five of them in total, jagged and twinkling at the edges. Strewn across the floor, they looked like an incomplete jigsaw, an art installation. Lea knelt and picked up the largest piece. It had been the base of the glass, a heavy crown that shone like ice. As she turned it in her hand, the light caught its clean, jagged edges, winking and sparkling. A ghostly fragment of her face, her mother's nose and her father's eyes, gazed up from the glass.

She flung her hand hard against the wall. There was that noise again, but this time she was expecting it. The sound of shattering seemed to cut through her skin in some way, seemed to slit the thin protective coating that surrounded everything up till then. Blood rushed to her cheeks. The feeling that swelled up within her, something alive and vital, was something she had not felt since she was a child, before she learned to stop breaking things.

Todd had not moved. The hand that was holding the glass remained outstretched, fingers wrapped dumbly around air. After the initial shock, his face had grown calm, serene even. He watched Lea smash each piece of glass into smaller and smaller fragments, watched her grind the shattered pieces into powder with the heel of her shiny patent leather shoes, watched her pick out the small shards embedded in the fleshy base of her hand.

Then, when she was done at last, as she looked at him with a defiant, insane exhilaration, he pulled out

143

his tablet from his pocket. He would do what was right. He would help Lea. Todd pressed his lips together as he prepared to write it all down.

CHAPTER
FIFTEEN

Lea had expected the Observers to show up at her apartment after she kicked Todd out, but so far, they hadn't. Still, she had been on edge all week.

So when George clapped his meaty paw on her shoulder in greeting at WeCovery, she shrank away in visible irritation. His hand was left hanging in mid-air, a look of awkward confusion clouding his features.

"Hi," Lea said with a bright smile. "Hi," she gave a stiff wave to the rest of the group.

They nodded and mumbled greetings. No one met her eye except for the bread-faced woman, the one with the husband. Greg. Susan — that was her name. The bandage on her little finger was gone now, and her toothy smile seemed to suggest she was in high spirits.

George took his place in the circle. Lea noticed for the first time that he had a different chair — while theirs were white folding chairs, his was made of polished pine. "So." He straightened up, clapped his hands together. "Gratitude session."

Silence. Only Susan was nodding furiously, her lips parted as if the words were on the tip of her tongue.

"You guys know the drill," George went on scanning their faces. He caught Lea's eye. "Don't worry, Lea, it's

145

exactly what it sounds like. We talk about something we're grateful for this week, to remind ourselves why we are here. Simple, really. But the hardest things to do are the simple ones."

Susan had leaned forward so much that she was practically falling off her seat. Without waiting for George to call on her, she started going on in a high, breathless voice: "I am grateful for so many things, so many, really! But of course the main thing, if I had to pick just one thing, of course, that would be Greg. Not that I'm saying he's a thing, of course," she let out a high-pitched giggle that made Ambrose wince.

"Uh huh. Greg, yes, great." Lea wondered if she was imagining it or was there a hint of impatience in George's voice? She shot him a quick glance. But no — he looked as earnest and well meaning as ever.

"He's just an angel, really. I guess you all know that already, since you all know about my Fateful Day. How he got down on his hands and knees to clean it all up. Took him hours. But I don't want to bore you with the details again. You've all heard this so many times. There are other things, though, like how he always remembers to charge my tablet when I'm asleep, so he can send me sweet text messages through the day. Or how he installed that location tracker on my tab, just in case it got stolen. You never know, these days. He jokes it's in case I get kidnapped. Ha, ha. Who'd ever kidnap a big old lump like me? Ha. But that's Greg. Always kidding around . . ."

Susan went on for another five minutes, her nostrils flaring, barely pausing for a breath. Her face grew more and more animated as she spoke, until it was contorted into an ecstatic, fevered mask. A slow revulsion began to build in Lea's stomach. But she couldn't look away. Something pulled her gaze irrevocably towards Susan. Lea tried not to think about what they shared.

Then all of a sudden, Susan was done. Her mouth was still open, but she had run out of words. A strange look crossed her face as she pressed her lips together slowly. A long breath escaped her like the air from a balloon.

After a moment of heavy silence, George seemed to come to, saying briskly: "Great, perfect, thank you, Susan. Shall we keep going? Lots to do today, lots to do."

A small dark man with a trim moustache went next. His name was Archie, he was grateful for sunrises, the way they always surprised you, bleeding out into the sky in that wild, uncontrolled way.

"Very good, Archie. Natural beauty, that's a big one. But please remember, for next time, the 'B' word." George inclined his eyebrows towards Archie.

They kept going. Family was a common theme ("Heartening, truly heartening, in this day and age," George beamed), beauty again, and then some other epithets like hope, choice, the future. When it came around to Lea's turn, she bit down on her lower lip and mumbled something about her fiancé, and their future offspring. She tried not to look as George typed something into his tablet.

"Pair work?" George announced, gleefully pushing up his glasses, leaving a fat fingerprint on the left lens. He didn't seem to notice. "All right, guys. I've heard you. We've all heard you. Now, talk to each other. Ready, set, go."

The two on either side of Lea, Ambrose and another man who always spoke with a stuffed nose, turned away from her. She sat awkwardly, hands clasped in her lap. George was preoccupied with Susan, who was now whispering furiously at him, stabbing one finger into the empty air.

No one was looking at Lea. They all seemed absorbed in the activity. She shifted, trying to ignore the feeling of being left out. She wanted to be left out, she reminded herself. The WeCovery Group was hardly the kind of club she was dying to be a part of.

The 'D word'. Lea let out a small snort.

"Lea. Glad to see you smiling again. It must be all those grateful feelings," George boomed at her. Susan was still whispering behind him, apparently deaf to all else. He ignored her, instead watching Lea, a satisfied, cat-like grin on his face. His eyes were flinty behind the glasses.

She looked away from him, the laugh freezing on her face. Her gaze flitted from the mustard carpet, to the chipped wooden plaques hanging stubbornly on the walls, to that small, clouded window in the far side of the room. The room felt smaller all of a sudden, despite all that empty space.

"Just reflecting, George," Lea said, flashing him a measured smile. "Friends, mainly, companionship like what we have. That's what I'm grateful for. The WeCovery Group."

"Of course. And you have lots of friends watching out for you, don't you?"

There was no mistaking the note of warning in his voice. Did he know about Todd?

Suddenly her nerves seemed to light up; her vision narrowed, a white-hot sensation, her fist clenched in her lap. An old, familiar anger. She paused, forced herself to exhale silently, counting to ten. It was that, rather than anything George could possibly say, that made Lea afraid. She exhaled silently, counting to ten.

Susan was still muttering pitifully. Lea could just about make out something about a puppy, poor puppy was sick, Greg was upset about the puppy, so it was important that she, Susan, was there for them all. The glue that held them together.

"Of course," Lea said. "Friends." She looked around. Anja too was sitting silently on the other side of the circle, the two beside her having turned away, their hunched form symmetrical as wings.

Lea dragged her chair across the musty carpet towards Anja. She thought of all the lung-clogging particles and microorganisms being roused from the ground. Salmonella, Campylobacter, Listeria, Shigella, she recited mentally.

"So, how do we do this? What are you grateful for?" Lea was aware of George's eyes on them, watching and assessing. She strained for the right words, hoping Anja would play along. But her eyes gave nothing away. The way she breathed was unsettling — long pauses between each breath, sudden, slow intakes of air like she had suddenly remembered to do so.

"Yes," Anja said. "Gratitude."

"I know exactly what you mean," Lea cut in. "As in, you never know when it's going to hit you. Since there are always so many things to be grateful for."

Anja narrowed her eyes. She seemed to shake herself, imperceptibly, and her gaze settled on Lea as if noticing her there for the first time.

"Music, I guess," Anja said. She stopped.

Lea nodded, chin pressed against the heel of her hand. She had no idea what Anja was talking about, but she was acutely aware of George's eyes on them. The fluorescent lights seemed to shine straight through the skin pulled taut over Anja's cheekbones.

"That's what I'm grateful for. Music."

"What instruments do you play?" Lea asked.

"I play the violin," Anja said. She had a way of looking at things as if they gave off a glaring light; that was how she looked at Lea now.

"And?" Lea asked.

"Don't you know? Oh, of course you don't," George said.

Anja seemed to solidify. As if the cells that made up her body suddenly drew together, eliminating the empty, misty spaces between them.

"Our Anja here is famous. A celebrity."

"I am not," Anja said. Her voice was calm, but the air around her seemed to grow heavy.

"Her mother too," George said. "Even more famous. Used to sing at Carnegie Hall."

He pronounced Carnegie like it was a French word, his thick wet lips curling grotesquely around the last syllable. Anja was silent.

150

"I don't know why you're so shy about it. Not the healthiest profession, of course. Probably why you're here now. We get a lot of 'artistic' types. Used to have a painter, now he was a lost cause, ended up in a detention centre, takes all his nutrition intravenously. At least he's alive."

George pressed the tips of his fingers together thoughtfully. Then he turned back to Susan, who had spent the last minute tapping his elbow.

Anja didn't move. On impulse, Lea reached out and placed her hand over Anja's. She never usually touched strangers, but there was something about the look on Anja's face that made her do it. Despite their icy pale appearance, Anja's hands were warm, almost hot, trembling invisibly.

"She was actually famous," Anja said, so softly that Lea wasn't sure she'd heard.

"Does she still perform?" Lea asked. A thousand other questions raced through her mind — what kind of singer, were there even live performances any more, why would anyone knowingly choose to be a musician, given the stats?

"No. She doesn't."

Lea shot a sideways glance at George. He sat with his head close to Susan's, nodding seriously every now and then. The solid trunk of his thigh was pressed up against her knee.

"What is it with him?" Lea asked in a low voice. Lea wasn't sure exactly what she meant, but Anja cocked her head to the side as if she did. She shrugged.

"Some people have callings, I suppose," she answered. "I don't think he means harm."

Lea looked around again. Everyone else was still deep in conversation.

"It got worse. After the last session. The Observers — they showed up at my apartment, in my living room. Can you believe it?"

Anja's expression didn't change. There was a calm, blank quality about her features, a kind of emptiness that Lea felt compelled to fill. Maybe that was why she was still talking.

"And then I found out my fiancé was reporting on me. I think it was him — George," Lea went on, glancing at George. "Who else would it be? And the way he talked to you. He's out of line. He has too much power."

Anja turned to look at George. She looked at him as if appraising a piece of furniture. George dispensed words to Susan with a grave air, making deliberate hand gestures that looked like he was screwing in a lightbulb.

Suddenly Lea saw him through Anja's eyes: a bespectacled, crumbling man. When he spoke, his lips were thick and fleshy. A small rust-coloured stain marked the collar of his carefully ironed shirt.

"George is just like us. He gets visits from them too. It's not George. It's everyone."

It made no sense. Lea realised her hand was still pressed over Anja's; the pale translucence of Anja's fingers stark against Lea's tan skin. She drew away.

"So what's the point of this? All the talking, the meetings, this?" Lea waved one hand at the plaques on the wall, their gold surfaces glaring in the harsh light.

152

Anja shrugged again. The grey woollen shawl she wore slipped down one thin shoulder. "What about you?" she asked.

"Me?"

"What are you, you know, grateful for?"

"Why are we even talking about this? Does any of it matter?" Lea crossed her arms, wrapping each hand around her torso. Through the fabric of her blouse, she felt out her ribs with her fingers and began counting them in her head.

Anja let out a long, hissing sigh.

"I paint," Lea said in a low voice. She paused.

"Is that what you're grateful for, then?" Anja looked up.

"No! I mean, they came to my house. Where I keep my paintings. And they saw my music collection."

No reaction from Anja. If she was shocked, she didn't show it. Though, if she herself were a musician, Lea thought, this would hardly shock her.

"I'll never get off the List if they find out," Lea went on, almost to herself now.

Anja looked up. "What list?"

"The Observation List?"

Anja's lips parted to release a high, hacking noise, like a cat trying to get rid of a fur ball caught in its throat. It was only when she glanced at Lea, her eyes crinkled and wiry, that Lea realised she was in fact laughing.

"Do you like music, then?" Anja asked at last.

"Music?"

"You said you had a collection."

Lea scrutinised Anja's face, but it was as blank as before, without the slightest trace of laughter.

"What kind? Pop? Rock? Jazz? Funk? R&B? Classical?" Anja persisted.

"Classical," Lea said, just above a whisper. She looked around — everyone was still wrapped up in their rapturous confessional states. No one seemed to have heard. "Bach's Passions, you know," Lea mumbled, a hot flush warming her cheeks.

Anja nodded approvingly. She brought one fingernail to her front teeth, and bit down. She seemed to be thinking.

"But, back to gratitude," Lea said. "My boss, too, he's a great guy. Never gives us too hard a time, not even when —"

"Can I come listen to it?"

Lea stopped. "What?"

"Your collection. You said you had the Passions. Can I come listen to them? At your place?"

Lea shook her head. Was Anja crazy?

"Please," Anja said. "I haven't heard music, proper music, in such a long time."

Lea was about to shake her head again when she remembered what Anja had said. *It's not George. It's everyone.* The way she had laughed when Lea talked about getting off the Observation List. Perhaps Lea could talk to her. Perhaps Anja knew something.

CHAPTER
SIXTEEN

It was only when they were standing awkwardly in her living room that Lea wondered what she had done. Anja's gaze darted about, dwelling on the high, white ceiling, the full-length window, the spotless linen curtains hanging straight and just so.

Lea cleared her throat. "Would you like a drink?" she said.

Anja shook her head. Now she was examining the bookshelves at the far end of the living room, reaching out one hand to touch the matt grey rectangles that emitted soft chirps and gurgles.

"Rainforest medley #235," Lea said. "I can change it, if you like. It's automatic. The latest technology. Detects our moods as we walk in through the door, and then picks the right track for optimal oxidative replenishment." What was she saying?

Anja walked over to the window, standing so close that her nose touched the spotless glass. Usually Lea would be thinking about the smudge it would leave, obsessing about the moment when she would be alone again and could go at it with a clean lintless cloth. But this time she didn't mind. She wondered what Anja was looking at.

"Where do you live?" Lea said. She sat down on the sofa. Perhaps if she pretended this were a perfectly normal visit, it would be.

Anja pointed down. "Somewhere there," she said. "Behind one of those buildings, the dark brown ones."

The last remaining projects. The ones that they couldn't knock down because so many tenants had been on the First Wave of experimental Replacement programmes, so many that had gone wrong in some way or another. The buildings were stolid, all dark brick and stingy windows.

Anja turned to face Lea. Backlit against the window she was a shadow, the outline of her head silver in the diffused rays, loose strands of hair catching the light like sparks.

"So," Anja said. "What are you doing in WeCovery?" As she said it she threw her hand out at the window, as if it was Lea's doing, as if she was responsible for the city that lay beneath.

Lea ignored the implication behind Anja's gesture. "Well," she said. "I was in an accident, of sorts. And then they started following me around, Observers, they came to my office, my apartment. They sat here," she pointed to the cream sofa, trying to convey what it meant, how it felt, to have them appear in her home. "They talked to Todd. He showed them my music."

"Todd?"

"My fiancé. Ex," she corrected herself. "He doesn't live here any more."

156

"So you live alone?" Anja asked, lifting her head to stare at the ceiling, taking in the far corners of the room.

"Yes," Lea said. "It's a company apartment, part of my package. I wouldn't rent a place like this on my own. Well, you wouldn't be able to. They're all held by corporations, anyway." Why was she justifying herself to Anja? "How about you?" she asked.

"I live with my mother," Anja said.

"Oh, that must be nice."

Anja only nodded. Then she smiled, but it was a small, hard smile.

"Does your mother know that you're under Observation?" Lea asked.

"No," Anja said. "She doesn't."

"Of course, she must be pretty busy."

Again, silence from Anja. Suddenly, she perked up. "Do you have a swimming pool here?" she asked.

Lea turned to follow her gaze. Anja was staring at Lea's navy swimsuit that lay draped over a radiator.

"Yes, on the top floor," Lea said. And then, something in her face made Lea ask: "Would you like to go for a swim? I have an extra bathing suit." She regretted it as soon as she asked. Anja would say no, Lea was sure of it.

But then Anja smiled. It was a smile that lit up her eyes and lifted her shoulders, that seemed to draw her whole body up to stand.

"Could we really? I'd love to," she said, a quick delight curling at the edges of her voice. "Can we go now?"

The pool level was empty when they arrived. Lea placed the tote bag down onto a deckchair and turned, uncertain, to Anja.

Anja's head was hidden in a cloud of white as she struggled with the T-shirt. Finally it came off, and she was grinning underneath.

"Wow," she said, surveying the length of sparkling blue, still as glass. Above them, sunlight streamed in through a vast skylight. Anja dipped one toe in. "It's warm," she said, sounding almost disappointed.

Then, in one smooth arc, she launched herself into the air. There was barely a splash as her body sliced into the glassy surface, hands outstretched in a prayer above her head. She swam fast but silently, as if afraid to disturb the water. Lea watched as Anja went back and forth, back and forth again. Wearing Lea's blue swimsuit, her light hair in a dark wet slick at the base of her neck, she almost looked like a paler, fainter version of Lea.

Outside, the sun was beginning to set, salmon rays filtering through the floor-to-ceiling windows. The skyline glowed orange, and Anja swam, back and forth, back and forth. When Anja stopped, Lea could hear her breathing. She paused, staring out at the city.

"It's beautiful," she said, still slightly breathless. "I never thought the city could be this beautiful."

"It is. The view's even better from my office. We're further downtown, and higher up."

Her office. Lea's insides contracted, and the softness disappeared. GK and AJ were still visiting her at work, but now when they came, they sat with Jiang in his

158

office for long hours at a stretch, laughing and patting each other on the back when they emerged. Jiang barely talked to her any more.

"Aren't you coming in?" Anja asked, wiping the water from her face.

Lea nodded and eased herself into the pool. The water was cool to her skin. It slipped under her knees and between her thighs and into the small spaces between her fingernails and flesh. Lea dipped her head beneath the surface, then emerged, pushing her hair back into a wet helmet. Goosebumps prickled her skin.

"Warm?" Lea gasped at Anja, who was still hanging on to the side of the pool.

Anja shrugged one shoulder. "It's a lot colder back home."

"Sounds awful," Lea said, shivering.

"It does, doesn't it?" Anja's face cracked into a smile. "We used to go in the morning, just after waking up. It was so cold you couldn't feel your legs. But somehow they keep moving, even if you can't feel them. My mother loved swimming."

Loved. Anja's use of past tense hit Lea in the gut. Suddenly she thought of her own mother, now long gone. Uju had not loved swimming. She had not seemed to love many things after Lea's father left.

But more than that, Lea heard the loss in Anja's words. Suddenly she saw the fine lines under Anja's eyes, the red rims that were perhaps caused by the pool water, but made her look like she had been crying. There was something vulnerable in the pallor of Anja's skin, the thin, bony shelf of her collarbone, the wisps of

159

wet yellow hair that stuck to her forehead. Suddenly, Lea saw her pain. Perhaps they had more in common than she'd thought.

"I lost someone too," Lea said quietly, into the water. Her feet, rippling and shifting through the water's surface, seemed to belong to someone else.

Anja was looking at Lea now, her face flushed orange in the evening light. Drops of water sat in the alcoves of her clavicle and on the smooth bridge of her nose. Lea's swimsuit was too small for her lanky frame, and the straps cut into her thin shoulders. Lea saw the red marks they would leave when Anja took the swimsuit off later that evening.

"Tell me," Anja said.

So Lea did. She told Anja about her own mother, Uju. How she'd had beautiful, delicate hands that were also wiry and strong, how those hands could build a mail order sofa or take apart a broken dishwasher so deftly it was as if she was playing an instrument, how those same hands could turn into hard paddles when Lea disobeyed her as a girl. How when she'd met Lea's father, she had been working for a social enterprise, a mechanical engineer designing portable toilet systems for informal settlements. They always said it was her father who had changed after the Second Wave, but her mother had changed too. She left her engineering job to join a human resources firm. It didn't matter that it was human resources, that it had nothing to do with her experience or interests, all that mattered was that it was Ministry-linked.

160

Lea told Anja about Samuel's death. How it drove a wedge into the crack that had already appeared between her parents, how it solidified her mother's new convictions, her father's disillusionment. How Kaito began to eat more and more, avoided physical activity, seemed to want to spite the world that was getting on with the business of immortality. How Lea found him once, standing shock-still in the doorway of Samuel's room, how he didn't move for a full hour.

She alluded to her father disappearing, but she didn't tell Anja why he'd left. She didn't tell her about how her father had come back, how she was afraid the Observers would find him.

Anja didn't say very much in response, only nodded and made soft noises of encouragement as she bobbed in the water. At times she'd ask a question, but mostly, she listened.

When Lea finished talking the sun had set, and a cool artificial light was now flooding the room. The sky outside was a purple bruise, the last rays of the sun vanishing between thin streaks of clouds.

They stayed like this, hanging on to the edge of the pool in silence for a while. Now Lea no longer felt compelled to fill the quiet, she felt comfortable in it, like all her words had been spent.

"You haven't even swum yet," Anja said finally.

"No, I haven't." Lea's fingertips were rough raisins to touch.

Anja dunked her head underwater. She emerged with a rush, grinning.

"Race me?" she said.

"What?"

"You heard me."

Lea started to shake her head, but then she found herself smiling too.

"Sure," she said. "There and back?"

"There and back," Anja nodded.

On the count of three they set off. The sound of the water roared in Lea's ears. She swam faster, harder than she normally did. She didn't look to see where Anja was, which of them was ahead, but she wanted to win. She focused on her form, made sure her kicks were clean, her arm strokes deliberate, precisely angled. When she reached the other side, she caught a glimpse of Anja as she turned. They were neck and neck. So Lea swam faster, pushing herself even more on the lap back. It didn't even occur to her to think about the risk of micro tears or tendon strain, it didn't occur to her to think. For those few minutes, she lived in the burn of her calves and the swell of her lungs, the pounding of her still organic heart in the cage of her chest.

She touched the edge of the pool and turned to look at Anja triumphantly, sure that she had won. But Anja was right next to her, panting heavily, one arm slung over the concrete edge.

"Who won?" Lea asked.

"I don't know," Anja said cheerfully.

"So me, then," Lea said, massaging a calf muscle.

"I was trying to be tactful," Anja laughed.

Lea didn't want to leave the pool. Everything seemed easier in the last few hours, and she felt like it would change once she got out of the water and dried herself off. But Anja was already hoisting herself up onto the cold tiles. Water sluiced down her legs, slowed in places by tiny light hairs.

So Lea got out as well. As they towelled themselves dry, slipping into robe and T-shirt respectively, Anja asked if she could stay the night. She said it so quietly that Lea wasn't sure that she'd heard, but when she turned to look at Anja she was so busy adjusting the strap on her swimsuit and avoiding Lea's eyes, that Lea knew she'd heard right.

"Of course," she said, a strange, budding warmth in her chest. "I'll make up the guest room for you."

The guest room was also her studio. When Lea remembered this, she felt an instinctive nervousness but then laughed inwardly. Anja was hardly the sort of lifer to care. So when they got back downstairs, Lea stacked her paintings in a neat pile in a corner and set up the sofa bed for the first time in years.

Sure enough, Anja didn't seem to find the paintings strange at all. She didn't even comment on them, though her gaze lingered on the paint-splattered mirror and the unfinished streaks on the canvas still occupying the easel. Walking over to the window, she ran her fingers along the bottom of the glass pane, where sealed rubber joined glass to cement.

"How do you open this?" Anja asked.

Lea stared at her. Was she serious? When her expression didn't change, Lea replied incredulously: "You don't. Directive 7077A."

"Oh," Anja said. "What a pity. You'd get such a breeze up here." She pulled her fingers away from the window.

"All done," Lea said as she finished plumping the last pillow.

"Thank you," Anja said, smiling, as if Lea had done her a great favour.

Lea knew she should say goodnight now, leave the room and go to bed. But she didn't want to. Instead, she said: "The music! You said you wanted to see the music. Listen to the music. We haven't even done that yet."

"Yes," Anja said. "The music." Suddenly she looked tired, and something about her expression made her look very young, almost child-like. Lea wondered for the first time what her number was. She realised all she had done that day was talk about herself.

Lea led Anja back into the living room. She felt the foolish urge to please her, so she started with the most controversial items she owned. Sliding a cabinet door open, she revealed shelf after shelf of plastic covers housing compact discs, each procured at great expense and effort over the years. The advisory on classical music meant that you couldn't stream it through the ordinary channels, that you couldn't stream it at all, really. The only way to listen to it was physical copies, which in turn were difficult to procure, rare and expensive.

Anja ran her fingers over the plastic spines. Lea stared at her eagerly, hoping her face would light up with joy or excitement or wonder, that she would turn to Lea and share her enthusiasm for her shameful, secret hobby.

But Anja was frowning in concentration. She moved her hands over the discs from left to right, first one shelf, then the next, tilting her head to the side so she could read their titles. She was looking for something, Lea realised.

Finally Anja stopped. Her index finger rested on one title, which she stared at, unblinking. Lea waited for Anja to pull it out, to hold it in her hands, ask if they could listen to it. But she didn't. She was completely still, the only movement in her body a slight flexing of the tendons in her neck.

"Do you want to listen to it?" Lea said at last.

Her question seemed to break the spell. Anja swallowed and nodded, but made no move to pull the disc out from the shelf.

Lea bent down to see what Anja had picked. It was the *St Matthew Passion*; the recording Todd had been playing just weeks earlier, featuring the famous Swedish contralto. She wondered momentarily if Anja had known her from back home. Lea placed her hand gently on Anja's and moved it aside, noting with surprise how cold Anja's fingers were. She opened the plastic housing, taking pleasure in the satisfying click as she popped the disc from the catch that held it in place.

Lea slid open another cabinet, where the antique CD player was hidden. It had taken her decades to find one — she'd had to go to the Outer Markets to get it, and it was her most prized possession.

Lea hit the play button. The melancholy voice of a single violin streamed from the speakers, filling the room. Her chest felt full and warm from the day — the fatigue of swimming, the sharing of confidences, the swell of music that entered her bloodstream now. She turned to Anja smiling, wanting to share the moment with her.

Anja was sitting on the sofa, very still. Her feet were flat on the floor and her spine was straight. Her knees were pressed together, each hand resting on one knee. Her eyes were closed.

Lea sat down at the other end of the sofa. Anja didn't move.

After the first song ended, Lea saw that tears were trailing slowly down Anja's cheeks, from beneath her closed eyelids. She still hadn't moved. On a sudden impulse, Lea moved towards her, close enough that their legs were touching, and very gently placed an arm around Anja's shoulder. She felt an imperceptible sigh pass through Anja's body, a slight tremble of the soul.

They sat like that through one song, and then the next, and then the one after.

CHAPTER
SEVENTEEN

Anja walked small circles over the plush carpet, nerves jangling. As she passed the large bay window for the twelfth time that morning, she caught a glimpse of the guests starting to arrive downstairs. Women with their shoulders naked and heads piled high with hair; men straight-shouldered and slickly sideburned.

The pictures on the wall didn't help. One face in particular, portrayed in a series of portraits, peered out from beneath polished glass panes. Anja had never met the woman in the gilt frame, but she was strangely familiar. She had a high, straight nose that bisected her face, cheekbones carved in improbable angles. Her hair was dark and her lips were darker still, as if stained by wine. She looked happy in the pictures, smiling in a cautious but genuine way, here receiving a trophy, there holding up a fish. The pictures only spanned her girlhood. She must have moved out after that, her parents keeping this room just the way it had been. Anja wondered what she had grown into, whether her features had sharpened or dulled with time, if she had kept her childhood haircut. Then, Anja realised, she would soon be able to see for herself.

Her violin lay unopened in its case. She had told them she needed somewhere quiet to prepare, and they had looked at her with knowing eyes and hushed tones, showing her swiftly to this room.

But there was nothing to prepare. She'd done the preparation three days earlier, sitting on Lea's sofa, letting the music flow through her. Now she remembered every crescendo and decrescendo, every rest and fermata. More than that, she remembered how the music felt in her gut, in her nerves, in her bones.

What she had really wanted was to avoid the crowd downstairs. It had just started to fill up when she'd arrived, but already she could smell the thick, heady scent of all those bodies simmering in the summer heat.

Anja sat down on the bed and opened the case in her lap. Nestled against dark velvet, the violin's polished wood seemed to give off an invisible light. She picked it up, held it to her chin and closed her eyes. She touched the bow to its strings, feeling the music trapped within, the tension of contact. Without playing a note, Anja began running through the piece in her head.

She was still sitting like this when the door clicked open, so quiet that at first she didn't notice.

"What a lovely dress."

Anja opened her eyes. The figure in the doorway was tall and slim, her hair gathered atop her head so that she appeared even taller.

"Mrs Jackman," Anja said, rising and stretching out her hand. "I'm sorry for —" She stopped. A warm flush spread across her cheeks. Was it a loss? Could she call it that?

But Mrs Jackman was unfazed. She flashed a broad smile, revealing a set of blindingly white teeth. Her hands grasped Anja's, warm and soft as her mother's once were.

"None of that around here," Mrs Jackman said. "I don't mind, but there are people who will, as you know."

She cupped Anja's waist. Her grip was warm and firm through the thin fabric.

"Such lovely material. Where did you get this?" she went on.

Anja flushed. "Oh. A shop back home. Sweden. I've had it a long time," she lied.

Mrs Jackman nodded, as if Anja had said something of grave importance. "And if you don't mind me asking, what will you be playing later?"

"Bach," Anja said. "Like we discussed."

"Of course," Mrs Jackman said. She seemed to want to say more, but fell silent instead, turning to the pictures on the wall.

"It's an honour —" Anja started to say.

"Shush. You've done great work for the Club. The videos — that was the best idea anyone could have come up with, worthy of Dominique herself. It's too bad she didn't live to see them, she would have been so impressed. But it's really increased our reach. Public opinion seems to be changing, in earnest this time. It's bifurcated, of course, since we've really riled some evangelicals. But even among the so-called life-loving, there are whispers that the tide is turning. And it's all thanks to your idea."

Anja nodded. She wondered what her mother would have thought of the videos, but then pushed the thought out of her mind.

"So. It's an honour for us that you've agreed, really. There's no one better placed to take over from Dominique." Mrs Jackman paused, reaching out to touch one of the photo frames. "I think she would agree."

The woman in the photos watched from the walls, a younger, chubbier version of Mrs Jackman. Given the opportunity, would her cheekbones have shifted beneath her flesh, to match the angles in Mrs Jackman's face? Or perhaps she would take after Mr Jackman, who was softer, rounder, darker skinned. They would never know, Anja realised. She gripped the neck of her violin and followed Mrs Jackman through the door.

CHAPTER
EIGHTEEN

Lea knew she shouldn't go to the party. Who knew what antisanct business her father was mixed up in? Given the events of the past few months, she should be lying low, attending WeCovery, apologising to Todd, cooperating with Observers. Attending a shady event her father was eager to hide from her was the last thing she should be doing. It was reckless, foolish, very likely contrary to the life-loving behaviour she was meant to be exhibiting right now.

Quite right. She could imagine her mother's accusing gaze, her lips pressed into a thin line.

But that Saturday afternoon, she found herself standing in front of a beautiful stucco house with its doors and windows thrown wide open. The people milling about on the lawn were dressed in their best and brightest, the overall effect a violent bouquet of primary colours that ebbed and flowed. Silk hems rustled, streamers fluttered in the wind, glasses kissed with melodious clinks. Her father was nowhere to be seen.

It was no sleazy underground smoking den, no alcohol-purveying dive bar, no rundown greasy diner. It was like none of the places her mother had told her about, the places she'd had to fetch Lea's father from late at night in the weeks towards the end, before he vanished. It looked exactly like the kind of party her mother would have taken her to as a girl, the kind of party filled with Ministry officials and top-decile lifers.

Lea felt a faint flutter of hope, a surge of lightness. Perhaps her father had changed. But then what was he hiding?

Lea stepped onto the lawn. The autumn-dry grass rustled under her pumps. She looked about her; people were still arriving and she blended right in.

All of a sudden, Lea noticed the smell. It threaded its way through the haze of floral perfumes laced with a not unpleasant trace of perspiration (the sort of people at the party were, after all, the sort to perspire sparingly and sweetly). It was a nutty, burnt odour, and yet strangely appealing. It was achingly familiar, yet difficult to place, like a memory from a previous life.

A tall man in a tux stood at a grill. He flashed Lea a grin full of white, square teeth as she approached, then turned his attention back to the sizzling food.

When she saw what was on the grill, a bitter taste rose in her throat and her stomach clenched. Great slabs of oozing meat dripped red blood onto the coals, thick and marbled with milky white. She couldn't tell what it was — pork, beef, lamb or something else altogether — having only ever seen red meat in the Ministry posters that warned against colorectal damage.

"How would you like yours?" the man said to her. She saw that his white shirt, unbuttoned at the neck, was splattered in oil.

"Excuse me?" Lea choked, stepping backwards. She brought a hand to her nose in an attempt to block out the fumes, stomach-turning now that she saw where they came from.

"Medium rare?" he said. "That's what I'd recommend, with a cut like this. But you look more like a well done kind of lady."

He was broad-shouldered and smooth-cheeked, with no sign of premature degeneration that she could spot. He was the kind of man that her mother had invited to dinner parties, a fine specimen who could even be Ministry. Yet here he was, at a party like this, grilling contraband animal flesh.

The steaks were slowly turning reddish-brown, a rich, earthy colour. How could anyone bear to put something so bloody into their systems? Lea tugged at the hem of her dress, suddenly wishing she had worn something looser. Sweat gathered at the backs of her knees and under her arms.

The man was still looking at her.

"I — uh — no, thank you," she said.

"Suit yourself." He turned back to the grill.

She imagined him sinking his perfect, white incisors into the soft red flesh, juices coating his tongue, the charred animal scent filling his nose. Her stomach lurched again, but this time, it wasn't revulsion that she felt. It was, unmistakably, a kind of desire, so powerful that it scared her. Her mouth filled with warm saliva, her jaw clenched. She imagined running her hands over the man's chest as he bit into a steak, as the juices slid down his throat. She imagined him sliding greasy fingers through her hair, touching the nape of her neck with filthy, animal-scented hands. She imagined slipping her tongue between his lips, tasting the blood, the salt, the scent of barbecued meat.

Lea turned away from the grill, backing away slowly. She would leave. It had been a terrible idea to come.

But then she heard the music, pouring out of the house to a wave of cheers and whistling. Notes tumbled after one another, rolling and somersaulting through the air. Sometimes they'd pause, suspended somewhere up above, before plunging again, joyfully, chaotically. It was unlike anything she had ever heard before.

Lea was well versed in classical music, but that was not what this was, though something of the same tense energy ran through its core, an electrified vein of urgency that swept you along with its irregular thumps and squeals. Tiptoeing, Lea saw four men on a stage inside the house. The instruments were large and shiny; she recognised the curve of a bass, the flashing movement of a saxophone. It was a live performance. Given the rarity of musicians, Lea had never seen one before, let alone one that played music like this. She stood transfixed, the melody flowing through her, pulling her this way and that, thumping through her veins.

"Great, aren't they? They played at her wedding. She would have been so pleased we managed to book them for today."

Lea started and turned. It was the man from the grill, who now stood next to her holding a bloody hunk of meat between two slices of bread. A single rivulet of juice inched down the side of his hand towards a spotless white cuff. Lea pointed at it.

"Oh, thanks." When the man twisted his arm around, the fabric of his suit stretched to reveal a hard forearm. Lea watched as he extended his tongue, an alien, pink thing, to catch the drops of animal oil dripping down his wrist.

She nodded, hand still pinching her nose closed. The smell was stronger now that he stood right next to her, but it didn't bother her as much any more. There was something sweet and primal about it, the smell of meat, that wasn't entirely unpleasant.

"You like jazz?" the man asked. His smile was familiar, as if alluding to an inside joke. He talked to her like she was an old friend.

"Is that what this is?" Lea said.

"Miles Davis," he said. "You've probably never heard of him."

"No," she said. "It's meant to be . . ."

A sudden pause. Classical music already occupied a grey area; there were still some experts who claimed positive, calming benefits, but jazz was a different matter altogether. And here she was, listening to it, not a recording but a live performance. It would almost certainly show up in her next maintenance review. For a second, Lea considered clapping her hands over her ears and running out the gate.

But she stayed right where she was. As if it would make a difference, after what had happened with Todd, as if she was ever getting off the List. What mattered now was that she found her father.

Suddenly she missed him desperately. Being here, being in this place, she felt strangely close to him. Were these the people he had aligned himself with? Was this the lifestyle Uju had been so against? Now that she was here, it didn't seem that bad. Yes, there was meat, live music, and very likely alcohol, but Lea felt herself drawn in, felt the glamour sweep over her like a wave pulling her under. It did not feel unnatural, no, quite the opposite.

The man was still eating his sandwich; a fresh trail of juice snaking down his other hand now, but this time she didn't say anything. She watched it gather momentum, the heavy brown droplet catching in the hairs of his wrist, seeming to come to a stop before breaking free again and continuing on its downward path.

The music continued, as loud and full of life as before, but now the roar of conversation had started up again. People had turned back to one another, bored already, and were carrying on with their conversations as if a live four-piece band was nothing unusual at all. They clinked glasses filled with a shimmering golden liquid, laughing and shouting, their eyes glinting in the evening sun.

Everyone on the grass was moving into the house. Lea watched one woman's heels sink into the soft ground. When she reached the wooden patio, Lea observed sadly that the cornflower blue stilettos were stained with mud, a clean line marking how far she had sunk as she walked.

176

Lea felt herself giving in. She felt intoxicated by the smell of meat, the white flash of the attractive man's teeth, the pulse-racing beat of the sultry music. Yet everything else — the smooth, poised people, the elegant surroundings — was just like any other party of lifers. This world was so familiar, yet so completely different.

Where was her father?

She allowed herself to be carried along by the crowd of chattering people. Soon she was tightly wedged between a group of women in matching dresses, who would every now and then let out a ribbon of shrieking laughter, and a large, rather squat man whom she suspected would have heart problems within the next two decades. Sunlight flooded in through a large skylight overhead, bouncing off shiny foreheads. The room was dense with breath and conversation.

Then, without warning, the noise drained away, the crowd stilled. Even the matching, loud-mouthed ladies next to Lea turned to face in the same direction, faces alert as meerkats. Lea turned too.

It was only then that she noticed the box. It lay on the stage where the musicians had been set up before, propped up on a table dressed with leaves and small wildflowers. The box was approximately as long as Lea was tall, and as wide as a coffee table. It appeared to be made entirely out of glass.

"Doesn't she look just beautiful?" one of the ladies whispered. The others murmured assent.

They were talking about the woman who lay inside the box, arms arranged neatly on her stomach, feet pointing up. She was beautiful. From where she stood, Lea had a clear view of her profile: the small rounded nose, full lips, skin the colour of autumn leaves. Her eyes, Lea thought, would be dark when she opened them.

"I heard it wasn't easy," the whispering went on.

The whispering grew quieter now, but they were jammed so tightly together that Lea could still make out what they were saying.

"They — did — it — themselves. She did it, herself," said the first whisperer. "That's what I heard."

The gasp that followed was so loud that Lea wasn't the only one to turn and look.

The women mumbled apologies and went back to whispering, now huddling together so that Lea could no longer hear them.

Just then, a woman in a long red dress, glittering and sequinned, stepped up to the stage.

"Hello, everyone, and thank you so much for being here today," she said.

A hush descended.

"I see many familiar faces in the room, many faces dear to me and of course, to Dominique." The woman paused, setting her wine glass down onto the surface of the box, glass base clinking prettily. "But I also see new faces, unfamiliar faces, curious faces. And even though I do not know you, I am glad that you are here. Dominique too, would have been glad. Some of you will know that she planned all this herself, right down to the font on the invitations you would have received. The music, the decor, the food — she wanted it to be the best party she'd ever thrown, and you know that she's thrown plenty in her role at the Club."

The crowd murmured its agreement. A few claps broke out, but most were quiet. A contemplative mood had descended, respectful, almost. Overhead, the electric fans hummed softly.

"Dominique represents the best of us. She was a dedicated veterinarian, Club member, daughter. As you know, her number placed her first in line for the new experimental phase of mandatory extension treatments, the ones which the 'life-loving' fight to receive. Only once all the kinks have been ironed out, of course, and it would be guinea pigs like Dominique who would help the Ministry do that. The Third Wave, they call it. She would have had to receive them today. Who knows what side effects she'd have suffered — misalignment at best, physical impairment at worst. And even if there were no side effects, well, then she would've been sentenced to thousands — maybe more — years of enforced living, carefully guarded and maintained as a potential so-called Immortal."

Around Lea, people shook their heads and folded their arms.

Suddenly she couldn't breathe. The heat of the room slammed into her with a vengeance, oppressive and heavy. She looked around for an exit, but the room was jam packed and she was right in the middle. The panic within her grew.

"Who's Dominique?" she asked one of the ladies next to her.

"That's not funny," the woman whispered sharply. "It may be a party, but we're still here to pay our respects." She turned pointedly away from Lea.

Pay our respects. Despite the sun pounding down through the skylight, Lea's hands were suddenly cold.

"Dominique's brief existence was more meaningful than any of the so-called Immortals who wanted to suck the best out of her. Someone once said death was the best invention life had to offer, and I know I'm preaching to the choir here, but I think it always bears remembering."

Applause. The woman in the box — Dominique — did not clap. She didn't do anything at all.

Was that what death looked like? So peaceful, so alive? Maybe she was alive, the whole thing a sick joke, an antisanct protest taken too far. Lea could see from where she stood that Dominique's cheeks were dewy and plump, her fingers gently curled at her side.

But when the man got up onto the stage, Lea knew it was true. The man in the tux was no longer smiling.

"Dominique," he said. "My darling. I wish it didn't have to be this way."

The woman in the dress shot him an embarrassed look, but then she took his hand. He leaned into her.

"Your mother and I will miss you. But today we celebrate your decision, the inspiration you will provide to all others who live life and seek death on their own terms."

The crowd seemed to shift uneasily. Lea got the impression that they were not used to such shows of melancholy; they had come expecting a good time.

180

After a long pause, he took his hand away. His expression was jovial again, eyes crinkling, dimples pinching. Then he gave a faint nod and there was a click. Water began to fill the box, submerging the body.

"What are they doing? What are they going to do?" Lea realised she was gripping the arm of the lady who had told her off earlier. The lady was looking at Lea again, the same annoyance on her face, but then her expression softened.

"Oh honey. Is this your first time? Who invited you?" Her eyes were sympathetic now. She placed one hand over Lea's trembling fingers. "It's all very clean, the whole thing. A chemical of some kind. It won't do anything till he activates it and you won't see a thing."

Dominique's mother was speaking again. "As Club leader, Dominique has left big shoes to fill. But we are happy, no, *honoured*, that someone very special, very competent, will be stepping into them. That someone, as many of you already know, is also a talented musician. And here she is now."

Lea didn't recognise her at first when she stepped onto the stage. Her face was bone-white, and it appeared even whiter in the light gold dress she wore. She was clutching the violin like a newborn baby. It was only when she touched her bow to the strings, sounding the opening notes of a piece they had listened to together three days ago, that Lea realised it was her.

Dominique's mother held her wine glass above the open box. She stared down at her daughter's body, then, as if as an afterthought, reached out with her free hand to stroke her face. There was no grief in her

181

expression, only something Lea thought might have been pride. With a flick of the wrist, she emptied the contents of her glass into the box. The dark purple drops floated in clear fluid for a split-second, then dissipated. The fluid in the box turned darker and darker, until the girl — the girl's body — was no longer visible.

You won't see a thing. The woman's words rang in Lea's head.

The mist began to rise from the box just as Anja finished her piece, a fine, red cloud, like a tiny ecosystem storing up rain. The last note hung in the air. Silence. Then the thunderous roar of applause, pressing in from all sides.

CHAPTER
NINETEEN

After the ceremony was over, the band started up again. People began to dance. The music was just as electrifying as before, but Lea was no longer listening. The notes that had made her spine tingle just an hour ago now sounded flat and jarring to her ears.

She felt as though the blood had been drained from her body. Stupid. It had been so stupid to come here, even stupider to be drawn in by the flash and glamour. She was at a Suicide Club party. Lea thought of the videos, the large anonymous man, the wheat-haired woman, the Musk she had met. She looked around at the people milling about. Was it one of them who had organised those deaths? Who had filmed them? She shuddered.

But still, Lea didn't leave.

Anja stepped down from the platform. There was something different about her — though her face was still pale, her posture was straighter somehow, her stride more purposeful. She held her violin by the neck, like a weapon. Lea noticed how sharp her collarbones were, how they held the straps of her gown away from the skin of her chest, how deep shadows gathered beneath them.

People were talking to Anja. Lea watched as they closed in around her, shaking her hand, patting her shoulder, placing their hands on the small of her back. Anja didn't seem to be saying much, but she was smiling, smiling and nodding. Pride shone from her face.

Eventually the well-wishers melted away, floating off with their long glasses in hand, drawn away by the music or the sunny day outside. Lea continued to watch Anja from a distance. At first Anja stood alone, surveying the crowd. But she wasn't alone for long. Soon, she was approached by a tall woman, dark-haired, sleek and garish all at the same time. She was very pale, with green veins running down her neck. Her eyes were a watery blue, lacking definition. Her lips were a gash of deep purple. When she spoke, Lea saw that though dazzlingly white, her teeth were abnormally large, and seemed to be desperately pushing their way out of her otherwise quite dainty mouth.

The woman lowered her head to speak to Anja. From where she was standing, Lea could see her mouth moving rapidly, feverishly, without pause, but she couldn't hear what was being said. Anja had her head tilted to the side and seemed to be listening. From time to time she nodded, or appeared to ask a question. The other woman's torrent of speech didn't end; now she was speaking with her hands, her long fingers tense and insistent, clawing the air between them. Finally, she fell silent and still. Anja too was silent. She was staring at the empty space above the woman's head, and seemed to be thinking. After a few seconds, she turned back to the woman and shook her head. It was a quick, firm rejection. Lea half expected the tall woman to start talking again, but she didn't. Instead she pressed her dainty lips together, flexed her fingers and balled them into a fist. Then she reached out, shook Anja's hand, and walked away.

No sooner had the tall woman left when someone else approached, this time a man, rather portly, tawny-skinned and with scalp so shiny that it looked as if it had been oiled. The same thing happened with this newcomer — him talking, Anja listening, asking the occasional question, then pausing, thinking. This time, however, after a long pause, she looked back at him and nodded. The man nodded too, slowly, repeatedly, grasped her hand and then walked away, still nodding.

Lea watched as the scene repeated itself again and again, as different people approached Anja, one at a time. She watched as they talked, as Anja listened, as they waited, as Anja nodded or shook her head. Soon it became a kind of game for Lea, predicting whether the person talking to Anja would get a yes or a no. She realised it had little to do with the way the petitioner looked — there was no pattern linking the yeses to the nos, but that the clues lay in Anja's face. Something about the way she held her lips as she listened, the way she tilted her head to the side, the long pause she took as she stared blankly into space — all of these pointed to a yes.

Lea was so absorbed in watching Anja that she didn't notice the familiar slouch of the man as he approached her. It was only when the man started talking that Lea

185

turned her attention to his face and she saw that he was her father.

He spoke to Anja like any of the others had before him. Watching Kaito now, Lea noticed for the first time that the way he moved his hands as he spoke was like a sculptor shaping invisible clay. Again Anja listened, again she asked questions, again she paused.

And even before Anja reacted, Lea knew. She saw from the softening of Anja's shoulders, the knitting of her brows, the cast of her mouth that whatever her father had said, Anja would agree to it, to whatever he was asking. But even so, when Anja finally nodded at him, Lea still wasn't prepared for the sick feeling that started in her stomach and travelled up her spine, expanding into her lungs and tightening her throat, a parasite burrowing deep into her heart.

After speaking to Anja, her father moved to a corner to stand by himself and watch the band. No one spoke to him; he spoke to no one.

It was an unusually hot day for so late in the year and the room was packed to the brim. Everywhere, brows were shiny and necks sticky. But even so, Lea's hands were ice. She felt herself move, as if in a dream, through the crowd.

He didn't see her at first. And then even when he did, his eyes slipped right across her face without recognition. It was, after all, the last place he'd expect to see his daughter.

But when she stopped in front of him he started, blinked, shook his head. The space between his eyes grew pinched and sad.

"So that's it then, this is why you've come back," she said.

"Lea," he said, looking around. "What are you doing here?"

She shook her head. "I can't believe —" Lea swallowed and stopped. She felt the pressure behind her eyes building, the heat in her throat rising.

"You shouldn't be here, Lea," he said in a low voice.

"You came back to kill yourself," she said flatly. Said aloud, the words lost their power, became pathetic, cowardly. But her feet were still cold, her hands still shaking.

"Look, Lea —"

"You came back to kill yourself," she repeated.

Her father fell silent. They stood facing each other in that crowded room, two still islands in a sea of movement and noise. When Kaito spoke again, his words came in a rush.

"They stopped my benefits decades ago. Of course they would, I was a fugitive, non-life-loving, low priority. Low probability. I got replacements on the black market, non-sanctioned parts." He spoke fast. He brought his hand to his lower abdomen. "First, my kidney. Which wasn't the problem. Won't be a problem, that is. No, the problem is this . . ." He grabbed Lea's wrist. His fingers were bony but strong. He brought her hand to his chest. "My heart. I had it replaced without getting the right advice, without thinking. Later I found out there's a reason why heart replacements aren't granted to anyone over a hundred and fifty."

Lea felt the warm thump of his heart in the palm of her hand. She felt the hair on his chest through the crisp white shirt that was now slightly damp in the heat.

"I'm misaligned," he said, still in that low, urgent voice. "Do you know what that means?"

Lea pulled her hand away.

"Everything will go, but my body will stay alive. My heart will keep pumping, my body will survive. I'll be a shell. Brain dead, but maybe not. Maybe trapped. Who knows?" Her father still had his hand over his own heart. "I'll be sent to a farm, in all likelihood. My body will be slowly drained for nutrients, recycled into new synthetic parts. And my mind — who knows? They say you're unconscious in that state, but what if they're wrong? What if you're trapped there, blind and deaf, unable to speak, for another hundred years?"

Lea balled her hands into fists. "Medtech is advancing every single day. You don't know that that will happen."

He blinked. "But they won't —"

"What are you doing to help yourself? What are you doing to show that you're worth the resources? Why are you slinking around in secret, why are you getting messed up with, with this —" Lea flung her hand out towards the crowd, towards the platform where Anja had stood, where the box in which Dominique had lain was now empty.

"And besides," she said, with the sick feeling of being about to shatter something. "If you really wanted to die, you could have done it without coming back. If you can get black market replacements, you can get black

188

market T-pills. Why bother with all this? No, I know why you're here. You like the spectacle, you want to feel important. Like your death has some kind of . . . purpose. Like it's anything other than any of the hundreds and thousands and millions of deaths before. Like it's anything unlike Samuel's."

Her blood ran quick and hot in her veins. She was breathing heavily, her head hurt. She thought her father would get angry, would storm away, would disappear once again from her life. Perhaps that was what she wanted.

But all he did was shake his head, slowly and sadly.

"Yes. Maybe you're right, Lea," he said. "Purpose. No one comes here, comes to the Club, just to die. All of us want to feel like we're fighting for something, something bigger than ourselves. And maybe you're right. Maybe we just want to feel important."

He paused, dropping his hand from his chest to his side.

"But when Samuel died, when I left, I promise you that I tried. I tried to live life to what they call the fullest. I travelled, I met people, I worked in bakeries and construction sites and offices. I tried to believe in it, in immortality. I really did. That's why I got the replacements even after they cut my benefits. I thought, maybe, if I could only get myself to believe in it, then I could come back to you and your mother, then maybe we'd live together, forever, happily ever after. But the years kept going by, and one day, it was too late."

Lea could feel her heart wringing itself into a knot.

"And you understand. I know you do."

Lea shook her head. "I don't understand. I don't get any of this. It's unnatural and selfish. Antisanct."

Her father stared at her sadly. "And Dwight?" he said, so quietly that she wasn't sure he'd said anything at all. "The hospital?"

It was difficult to breathe. The crowd seemed to be hemming her in from all sides, the music deafeningly loud.

"You understand, Lea. Underneath it all, you're just like me."

CHAPTER
TWENTY

"Dwight. Oh Dwight, Dwight, Dwight." Opal's eyes were glittering as she said his name.

Dwight looked up from where he sat, bony ankles slung together under the desk. His eyes, Lea noticed for the first time, were not actually blue, but an icy, pale grey, frosted by eyelashes that were so faint they appeared to be transparent. Freckles clumped together on his cheekbones, little red dots that on first glance, could be mistaken for pimples.

The class watched in anticipation. What would Opal do today? Sometimes her insults were finely honed darts, sharpened to kill, other times they were like the edge of a blank sheet of paper, innocuous until wielded at just the right angle.

"Dwight, you have a girlfriend? Huh, Dwight?" she went on.

The atmosphere deflated. This was an old joke, one they had made many times before.

Dwight shook his head politely, as if it were the first time he'd been asked the question. Under the table, his fingers gripped the khaki fabric stretched tight over oddly shaped knees. The pants were fastened with a brown leather belt that looked like something Lea's father wore to work. They were folded at the cuff, revealing running socks covered in lint.

"But you want a girlfriend, don't you, Dwight? I can tell you do. You're a romantic at heart. You'd treat a lady well."

Maybe because the others were no longer paying attention, maybe because of Opal's pretty black eyes, so pretty they could almost be mistaken for being kind, maybe because he just wasn't thinking, Dwight said in a small voice: "Yes."

"Of course you do." A slow smile curled at the edges of her lips. "You know who I think would love to be your girlfriend?"

Dwight shook his head, his eyes watery. His lips hung apart, revealing a set of large clunky teeth that had not yet been forced into braces.

"I can't believe you don't know. It's okay, boys are pretty oblivious, I guess," Opal let out a tinkle. The others broke off their conversations now, looking again to the spectacle.

"I've seen her staring at you in class, practically drooling. It's a wonder you haven't noticed."

Dwight could have looked down at his neatly completed homework. He could have excused himself, gone to the toilet until the teacher arrived, one of his most-used escape routes. Or he could have just stayed silent. But maybe he saw the greed in Opal's eyes, sensed that for once, he wasn't her real target, not this time. Maybe it was that note of sly complicity in her voice, the way she was looking at him, as if he was a friend. He wanted to please her.

192

"Who?" he said, boldly now. "Who is it?"

"She's very shy. You'd be perfect for each other like that."

She was no longer looking at Dwight. Her gaze cut right past him.

He turned, together with the rest of the class. Now they were all looking at Lea, who sat, still as salt, at her desk.

She looked back at them with mild interest, as if through a screen. When Lea was a child, sometimes the things and people around her felt part of an elaborate show, put on for someone else's benefit, with an invisible logic that she could not quite grasp. This was one of those moments.

"Isn't that right, Lea?" Opal said, her voice stronger now, crackling at the edges. "You've been pining for Dwight all this while. No need to thank me, I know you lovebirds would never have done anything on your own."

Lea gave no sign of hearing what Opal was saying. Dwight's gaze flickered back and forth between the two girls.

"Why don't you show her, Dwight?" Opal stood up suddenly, the metal legs of her chair screeching against the polished floor. Opal glanced around at her classmates. They tittered obediently. Someone obliged with a wolf whistle. "Give her a kiss. A little peck on the cheek."

Dwight was leaning back in his seat as Opal advanced. He no longer looked bold. His thin, white fingers gripped the edge of the desk. His fingernails,

Lea noticed, were as long as hers. They were grey with dirt.

Opal stopped in front of him.

Dwight wasn't looking at Opal any more. He stared at Lea, lips still parted like a stupid fish. His face was paler than normal, if that was even possible.

"I'm not in love with Dwight," Lea said.

It came out more scornfully than she'd intended. As if the whole scene was ridiculous, childish. It was how she always talked, and maybe why she had no friends.

Opal whipped around. "Of course you are," she said gleefully. Turned to the rest of the class. "We've all seen you making eyes at him. Come on, don't disappoint everyone now."

Her supporters nodded in agreement, giggling and shuffling. Opal turned back to Lea. "Besides, what with your dead sub-100 brother, we all know you could use some support."

Dwight remained motionless. Opal grabbed his hand. He stood up obediently, letting himself be led like a farm animal towards Lea. The class was hooting now, whooping like he had never heard them whoop before. Not when they were looking at him. They never made sounds like that for him.

They were standing in front of Lea. Dwight fixed his eyes on where her shoulder broke the fall of her thick hair. They were close enough for him to smell her.

"Are you just going to stand there?" Opal hissed.

Dwight leaned forward obediently, his face drawing towards the smooth plane of Lea's cheek, lips pushed together as he had seen in the movies. He closed his

194

eyes, perhaps waiting for the moment of contact, anticipating the whoops and cheers that would surround them, the warm embrace that Lea would draw him into.

But then, instead of the warm touch of skin against his pursed lips, there was a loud crack.

The sound reminded Lea of a river she had once seen melting in the spring, great sheets of ice tearing away and rushing downstream. Then Dwight was falling backwards, backwards still, his legs tangling with metal legs, his elbow thudding into wood. He was on the floor, something wet sliding down his face.

Lea stood over the boy on the floor, her fist still clenched. The world had slowed down, as if rushing at her through the screen, pulling her into this fictional universe complete with the jeers of classmates and the hot, pungent breath of a white boy in her face. The pilot light within her, that small flame that was always threatening to flare up, filled her with heat.

And suddenly it was not enough that the boy was on the floor, blood streaked across his lips. Lea fell on him, one hand gripping a scrawny shoulder, the other held in a ball that she brought firmly into his straight freckled nose. It was as if she could see his skeleton within him, all those intricately shaped bones joined up together, so perfect that it made her angry. She swung again and again and again. It was only when the teachers pulled her off him that she heard the shrieks and crying of her classmates, felt the wet slick of blood and tissue on her knuckles, the hard bruises on her knees.

The others shrank away from her as she was led away. Some were crying, others, silent and pale. No one would meet her gaze, no one except Opal, who was sitting back in her chair, as if calmly waiting for class to begin. Opal's eyes met hers straight on, a satisfied smile twitching at the corners of her lips, as if something had been confirmed. As if she had always known.

The Incident — that was what Lea's mother called it. You wouldn't know Uju's power just by looking at her. It was from Uju that Lea got her wiry frame and narrow shoulders, her mild, canine eyes. Uju walked lightly, as if on eggshells or water, and her movements were always measured and careful. She gave the impression of being breakable, particularly when standing in the shade of her stocky, strong-limbed husband.

But when she started talking, people turned to watch and listen. They couldn't help it. It was something to do with her voice, deeper and slower than you'd expect, a voice that compelled the world to bend to her will. She imbued individual units of speech with whatever meaning she wished. So when she used the word "incident", tongue tripping around the three syllables like an obstacle course, her listeners barely registered the first syllable. Accident it sounded like. An accident for poor, dear Lea.

While Uju did not have a Ministry job, she had the next best thing (the word *next* nullified by her intonation — it was the best thing, really). Senior Vice President at Talent Global, a human resources agency and one of the Ministry's few preferred suppliers.

It was only years later that Lea would link the sudden slew of dinner guests and lavish parties with what had happened. She never found out exactly how Uju managed it, but somehow enough people in the Ministry agreed with her definition of the Incident for nothing to go onto Lea's permanent record.

She said all the right things at the interviews. It was easy. Her mother had laid the groundwork. Lea said it over and over, the same story in different gleaming offices, their walls lined with the same Ministry posters and their desks stacked with the same leaflets, the doctors' faces blurred into one solicitous, concerned blur. She told them about the bullying. She told them she felt trapped, intimidated, in danger. She told them about her brother's death, about how she still woke up in the middle of the night calling out for him only to realise he was no longer there.

From her mother's warnings, she had expected the doctors to be stern-faced women with stark, window-less offices, women who would interrogate her mercilessly. But instead they were chatty young men, curly-haired and with startling eye colours and bookcases filled with potted plants. They listened to her with rapt expressions, heads attentively cocked, occasionally writing down something particularly salient she had said with old-fashioned ballpoint pens. They pulled her chair out for her when she entered the room, enquired after her mother and her pet goldfish, offered her jasmine green tea.

Reactive Explosive Episode — these were the words offered up after months of diagnosis. When she heard,

197

Uju clapped her hands together and raised her gaze upwards, as if to thank some being that she did not believe existed.

"A Class C illness," her mother told her with her usual manner, now that everything had gone according to plan. "That means incidental, not chronic, or worse still genetic. Treatable, and most importantly, it won't affect your record."

"Took them that long to figure it out?" Kaito remarked from the couch. "Lea beat up a kid trying to lay hands on her, big deal. Sure, it's bad luck he hit his head on the floor the way he did. I still think she was well within her rights."

"Lea put a boy in hospital," Uju said testily. "Severe head injury, fractures, plastic surgery. He'll need replacements at the age of eleven. He's in a coma, they say he might be brain dead. She could have been charged with something far worse, could have been considered — antisanct. I don't see how this is just a big joke to you."

Antisanct. Lea rolled the unfamiliar word around in her head. She had heard it whispered in recent years, had seen women in sharp skirt suits — not unlike the ones Uju wore — discussing the rise of antisanct behaviour on morning talk shows. It was a serious, adult word, one which frightened her. Antisanct, antisanct, antisanct. Lea had heard what was unsaid in her mother's words, the shape of what could have been, if not for her connections and coaching. This alternate version of events loomed darkly at the edges of Lea's imagination.

The doctors would monitor her for the next year, just to confirm the diagnosis. During that time she buried the memory of her mother's ominous words, ignored her tense optimism, reinvented her own story. She said it so many times she came to believe it — it was their fault, not hers. Her classmates were cruel, ignorant, thoughtless. She had merely been lashing out like a trapped animal. A fluffy white rabbit, fur softer than air, came to mind. There was nothing wrong with her, nothing wrong with her at all.

It seemed that everything had been taken care of, that Uju had made the problem go away. But one evening, as Lea sat with her parents around the dining table sipping their Nutripaks, Uju said she thought Lea should pay Dwight a visit in hospital. It had been six months and while his condition had stabilised, he was still in a coma.

Lea stopped sipping. Her hands went cold. The boy's face, pale and smeared with blood, his nose at a crooked angle, flashed before her eyes. She did not want to see him again.

"It would be good if you brought him something, maybe a decorative fruit basket of some kind. Something you could leave behind," Uju was saying.

"What, aren't we done with this PR bullshit yet?" Kaito demanded. He ate with a spoon from a bowl, into which Uju had poured the Nutripak contents. Ever since the Incident, he had been trying to cooperate with Uju, perhaps because one of the reasons given for Lea's outburst had been what the doctors called a "dysfunctional home environment". Still, he could not bear to sip the Nutripaks from their built-in straws. Made him feel like a child drinking from a juicebox, he said. He would eat with utensils like a regular human being, thank you very much.

"It would help," Uju said, steely-eyed. "Remember, the diagnosis is conditional. She's still being monitored."

"The diagnosis was bull to begin with, and I don't see why —"

"I'll go," Lea said, cutting her father off. "I want to go," she lied, swallowing hard.

Kaito looked at her. "You sure, Lea? Don't let them pressure you into jumping through any hoops, now. You don't have to prove anything to anyone."

She knew from the past few months that her father was wrong. After the Incident, she had to prove herself to everyone. She would have to keep proving herself, over and over, for a very long time.

"I know," Lea said. "I just want to go. I want to see him — Dwight." Saying his name made her feel slightly ill.

Her father studied her face. She felt he could see right through her.

"Okay then," he said slowly. "I'll go with you. We can go tomorrow morning."

"Wonderful," Uju said.

They forgot the fruit basket, so they picked up an oversized bouquet of lilies in the hospital. The flowers were white and waxy — "To signal we come in peace," Kaito joked — spitting tongues daubed with bright yellow pollen. They were beautiful and extravagant, but there was something aggressive about their cloying smell. Lea didn't like them, but the only other option was a bunch of wilting roses, so they went with the lilies.

Lea had been to the hospital once before, to visit Samuel close to the end. So she wasn't surprised that it looked nothing like the maintenance clinics she normally visited, did not find the stark lights and chemical smells alarming. It was the largest, most reputable hospital in the Central Boroughs, so it was no surprise that Dwight's parents had checked him in here, just like Lea's parents had checked Samuel in all those years ago.

It had been seven years. Lea still knew where the cafeteria was, still remembered that the toilet doors swung out instead of in. She scrutinised the faces of men and women in white coats passing urgently down the hallways, wondering if she would recognise Samuel's doctor if she saw her again. But Dwight was housed in a different wing of the cavernous hospital. After consulting with a candy-coloured map, Kaito and Lea headed to the elevator that would take them to the right ward.

Lea was holding the flowers. They were half her size and towered over her head. Strangers in the hallway stopped to smile at her, to ask her kindly if she was visiting someone. She nodded and smiled back tightly, while her hands grew cold and slippery, and her arms ached with the weight of the bouquet. Still, she would carry them, she would not ask for Kaito's help. She did not deserve the strangers' kindness, Lea thought to herself. If they knew why she was here, if they knew what she'd done, no one would smile at her in the hallways.

She was antisanct.

Uju may have smoothed things over and the doctors may have been fooled, but Lea knew what she had felt when she broke Dwight's nose, when she pushed him to the floor and heard his head crack against the hard wood and yet, still, she did not stop. She alone knew about the tiny light that burned within her each and every day, a light that threatened to flare up at any moment, to scorch the unblemished surfaces of things and people around her. She alone knew that the feeling had not gone away after hurting Dwight, but had only grown stronger.

The elevator pinged open at the twelfth floor.

"Here we are," Kaito chirped. He was being unnaturally cheerful. Lea knew he was doing it for her. She was transparent to him, so she knew he could sense the heaviness she felt. But the converse was also true, and his attempts to buoy her up were painfully obvious to her as well.

Dwight was in Room 1212. Lea counted the numbers as they walked down the busy hallway, nurses with tabs and visitors with styrofoam beverages lining the walls. Kaito and Lea looked like anyone else, a father and daughter, flowers in hand. There to visit family or perhaps a close friend. There was nothing to mark Lea out as the perpetrator, the reason for the visit itself. Nothing telling the world that it was the very fist that grasped the wet stems of white lilies which had also slammed into Dwight's white face; no telling anyone that her dainty pre-pubescent feet shod in spotless sneakers were the same feet that were still driving into Dwight's ribs even as they dragged her off him. There was nothing to say that Dwight was innocent, that he was harmless, a mere unfortunate passer-by.

1202, 1204, 1206, 1208, 1210. And then they were there. They stopped outside Dwight's room.

Kaito crouched down so they were at eye-level. "We can still go home," he said. "Leave the flowers with a nurse. You don't have to go in if you don't want to."

Did he know? Did he have a premonition, a sense of foreboding, did he read it in Lea's face? Lea shook her head, but she didn't trust herself to speak. The lights in the hallway hurt her eyes when she looked up at her father. His familiar face, soft with concern, filled her with loneliness. She did not have the words to tell him about the feeling Dwight induced in her, about the violence that bubbled up unbidden, the pleasure and relief of giving in to it, the shame after. Antisanct.

She opened the door with resolve. She would go in, look at Dwight in the eye, apologise, leave the flowers next to the bed.

But there would be no looking at Dwight in the eye, for his face was wrapped in gauze. A large plastic tube protruded from his mouth, two smaller ones from his nose. His chest was bare, bandaged in some places, tiny wires stuck to bare skin in others. His arms were the worst. Speckled with bruises, Lea counted seven different IVs on each arm, hooked up to separate hanging bags of colourless fluid arranged around his bed.

"Jesus Christ," Kaito muttered.

He'll need replacements at the age of eleven. They say he might be brain dead.

Kaito pinched the base of his nose, squeezing his eyes shut. He looked like he was counting to ten. When he opened his eyes again, they were dry, but filled with resolve.

"What's the point?" he said in a low voice. "Are they going to keep him on a machine forever?"

He was still talking to himself when Lea went up to the bed and placed her hand on Dwight's arm. His skin was cold and faintly moist to touch, the purple bruises blooming across its pale expanse. Those bruises had not been caused by her, she realised. They were dotted with scabs. She lifted her gaze to the various IVs protruding from his arm, the ventilator protruding from his mouth, keeping him alive.

"Replace every part of his body? Replace his brain?" Kaito was still muttering behind her, his hand over his face.

He had said the same thing when Samuel was in hospital. Samuel had hated the cold white room filled with machines and only plastic chairs to sit on. In his brief windows of lucidity, he'd asked Lea where he was, told her he wanted to go home. She remembered Kaito tentatively suggesting that they should indeed bring him home. But Uju had insisted on keeping him in hospital, where doctors were on call around the clock in case anything happened. *The boy is dying. What else could happen?* Kaito had asked. But he had given in, Samuel stayed in hospital. Lea wondered if he regretted it now.

Suddenly it became clear to her what had to be done.

Lea began pulling the needles out of Dwight's arm, gently but firmly. She placed them in a neat pile by his side, then leaned across and began doing the other arm. Kaito was still muttering to himself with his hands over his face, and didn't seem to notice what she was doing.

The ventilator would be more difficult, she gathered. She could pull it out, but she knew from when Samuel slipped into his coma, when they finally took it out, that it was deeply wedged in his throat and required a doctor's expertise to remove. She did not want to hurt Dwight.

No, she did not want to hurt him now. The flame inside her was gone, the violence she feared replaced by a sense of peace. She was saving Dwight. She had hurt him, yes, but what the doctors and the family and the world could not see was that they were hurting him more now. Dwight was no longer there.

Her gaze followed the plastic tube from Dwight's pale lips to the machine it was connected to. The machine, in turn, had a long grey cord leading from it to the power socket in the wall. When she removed the plug from the socket, all she was thinking of was Samuel. Samuel didn't get a chance to lie in his own bed one last time, didn't get a chance to feel the curtain-fluttering breeze from his window, to hear the noise of cars and conversations floating up from the street below, to see the faces of his family around him in his home. Dwight wouldn't either, she thought, but at least he wouldn't have to suffer for another six months in this cruel white room.

But to Lea's dismay, the low rumble of the machine kept going even after she disconnected it, incessant and unforgiving. Even worse, a loud beeping noise began emitting from somewhere in the room. She stood up and backed away from Dwight.

"What did you do, Lea?" Kaito said, his voice quick and urgent. He stepped towards the bed, taking in the piles of bloodied needles removed from Dwight's arm, staining the white sheets. "Oh Jesus," he said. "Oh, Lea."

He looked down and saw the disconnected plug. Lea heard his sharp intake of breath. Time seemed to slow down as Kaito bent to pick up the plug, but it was not enough. It did not slow down enough to stop altogether, to keep her in the time before everything changed forever.

The doctors burst in through the door.

CHAPTER
TWENTY-ONE

They were in Branko's car, on their way to the ferry terminal after their shifts had ended, when Anja grabbed Branko's hand. She couldn't go home to her mother that night. The image of Dominique's face had haunted her all week. Dominique, peering out from the photo frames in the bedroom. Dominique, lying in the glass box. Dominique, reduced to mist and air.

Anja had never met her. Dominique had been leading the Club when Anja joined, but by then, she had already been lying low. She'd thought that if she distanced herself from the Club, they wouldn't follow through on their threat to force experimental Third Wave treatments upon her, but the Ministry was persistent. Anja's main source of direction came from Mrs Jackman, who, at a hundred and seventy, was unafraid of anything the Ministry could threaten. But even so.

She'd known Dominique remotely, mainly through secondhand accounts. After Anja had the idea for the first video, after she executed the second, she'd received bottles of expensive Argentinian wine in the mail, with long handwritten notes from Dominique thanking her for her work. The handwriting had been looping and girly, old-fashioned, that of a bygone era where children were trained to write cursive in schools. She'd signed off with a large "D", followed by "XOXO", as if they were teenage pen pals and not antisanct activists running a criminal organisation. Anja had always wondered what Dominique was like in person. She'd always assumed she would meet her one day, but now she never would.

She felt the tendons in the back of Branko's hand stiffen at her touch, sensed him glancing at her surreptitiously, while still pretending to look at the road. She ran her fingers up his forearm. It was warm and solid, comforting. She slid her hand around his bicep, to feel the inside of his upper arm, where the skin was smooth and soft as a baby's. She squeezed gently, felt him flex imperceptibly under her touch, smiled at the vanity that this betrayed.

Branko didn't speak. She could hear his breathing grow slow and shallow. He didn't move, either, except to gently steer the car to the side of the road. When they had come to a stop, he folded his hands in his lap and looked at her.

His lips were rough and chapped when she brought her mouth to his, but when he parted them his tongue was warm. He let himself be kissed, shyly. Anja was struck by the thought that Branko was at least thirty years younger than her, despite his thinning hair and crinkled skin. There was no bravado in the way he brought his hand to rest gently on her knee, the way he kept his tongue behind his teeth as she probed his mouth. There was something chaste in it, something hesitant.

She wasn't the only one who hadn't touched another person's skin in years, Anja realised. The thought made her soften inside, made her warm towards loud, crude Branko, who made braying jokes in the diner but secretly pined for his long-gone brother, who spent his days and nights working to support the niece he had left behind.

Branko's apartment was not much larger than hers, but the air inside was fresh and cool, and she could tell that in the day, it would be a bright, airy space. She imagined waking up in the rumpled futon by the window, a breeze caressing her bare skin, the room lit up by the early-morning silence. She would stay the night, Anja decided.

The thought made her turn to the man standing next to her, turning his keys in his palm. The crunching metallic noise stopped when she placed her hand on the small of his back. As the soft slugs of their tongues curled around each other, she wondered what it would be like to run away with a man, leave the small, cramped apartment, the diner job, the Club. Give her mother's body up to one of the farms. She would live with someone in an apartment like this, one where the living room was separate from the bedroom, one with its own modest toilet and shower. She would give violin lessons to neighbourhood brats, spoilt in the way that only kids from slightly deprived families were, where guilty parents overcompensated by giving in to their every request.

Branko pulled away from her. He rested his thumbs in the hollows of her collarbone.

"What are you thinking?" he asked.

It was dark enough that Anja couldn't see his face, but still she could feel his gaze on her.

"How do you ever know . . ." She paused.

"Know what?"

"How do you ever know — anything. How to do the right thing."

Branko was silent. His hands were warm and heavy on her shoulders. She felt the sturdy solidity of him, the opaqueness of his skin, the stale heat of his breath. She felt him as a weight, anchoring her, binding her to the earth.

"Never mind," she said hastily. "I was just thinking out loud." She pulled him towards her again, pressing her thighs against his, resting one foot gently on his toes, claiming him for her own.

He led her over to the futon, lifting and swinging her to the ground as if she weighed nothing. Then he knelt over her in the dark, stroking her hair, thumbing her cheek. She waited for him to climb on top of her, to press his mouth against hers again. But instead, he lay down next to her, pulling a thin sheet over their bodies. They lay side by side in the dark, staring up at the ceiling in silence for a long while. His breathing was deep and steady. She relished the sound of it, the sound of those long, robust breaths travelling in and out of his lungs, no wheezing, no rattling, no uneven starting and

210

stopping. She thought he was asleep until he spoke again.

"I think," he said slowly, kindly. "Whatever you decide to do, your mother would understand."

Then he turned, and gently kissed her clothed shoulder.

"Goodnight, Anja," he said into her skin.

"Goodnight," she answered, closing her eyes.

CHAPTER
TWENTY-TWO

In the weeks that followed, Lea didn't hear from her father, nor did she try to contact him. Now that Todd was gone from her apartment, she lived a solitary life. After the initial rage and confusion she'd felt at the party, all the feeling seemed to have been drained out of her body. It was a problem so large, so impossibly sad, that she found herself doing what she'd learned to do when her father left the first time. She would not think about it. She would ignore it, pretend it wasn't there. It was as if she'd flicked a switch in her heart. She blocked out all thoughts to do with her father, or the Club, or Anja, throwing herself into her work, going into the office before sunrise and staying till the Max Work alarms sounded in the evenings.

One morning she came to work even earlier than usual. At that time of the morning, the lobby was a vast and empty set, robotic floor cleaners whirring in smooth circles. Through the glass walls, the sky was a weak, ashy grey. There was no rain yet, only a violent wind that squealed and moaned across the windows and walls.

Upstairs, the lights flickered on when she tapped her security code into the panel at the door. Lea stood still, listening to the silence. She remembered the early years of her job when Jiang had first hired her as a junior analyst. Those long days and nights of reading reports, building programs, writing recommendations. She didn't have any clients of her own then, nor a private office. She sat in the middle of the floor with the other analysts, their four desks arranged together making one large island. Hired around the same time, all of them were meek and eager to please, in awe of their sleek surroundings, of the serious women and men behind closed glass doors, with the city at their feet.

Lea was the only one left of those four analysts. That was how they did it at LTCP — *Up or out*, as Jiang liked to pronounce, as if it weren't another corporate cliché and he had come up with the term himself. It wasn't an easy life, not at the beginning at least, back when cortisol-generation indices were still regarded with suspicion and disdain, when dark circles and frown lines were still unofficially a badge of honour, a sign of ambition. Those were the days before the Max Work directives and the mindset shift that came years after the Second Wave, when the HealthFin industry still ran on the same heady fuel as the rest of the alternative finance world. Lea had done the all-nighters, the day-long flights to and from Asia, the chain drinking of coffees and energy drinks. She'd spent hours labouring over logos and colour-coding for presentation to clients, ran painstaking simulations in the clunky, glitching spreadsheets that predated the intelligent programs they had today.

She remembered the time she'd left at four in the morning for a third day in a row, her mind simultaneously buzzing with numbers and foggy with sleep, only to receive a call from one of the partners just as the taxi reached her apartment. She remembered the numb resignation of taking a shower and changing into a fresh suit, heading straight to the airport with a stack of presentations once she was done.

There were no analysts in sight now. Working any staff member that hard today was deeply counter to the new order of things, the culture of careful preservation and upbeat life-loving behaviour that ran through every successful company's veins.

Things were much better today, by any measure.

Still. There was something to be said for it, the way things used to be. Lea remembered the thrill of a model coming together on screen in the still of the night, after everyone had gone home except for her and the other analysts. She remembered the easy silence that flowed between them, the pattering of fingers across keyboards as soothing as the sound of rain. She remembered the coffee runs and the Nutripak orders, the gossip they'd exchange while sipping from their cartons.

Lea crossed the office floor silently, heading not for her room but for the analysts'. There were three of them these days, fresh from their post-doc programmes. They sat in an office together, but as far as Lea could tell there was no camaraderie between them. They were odd, tense things, exuding the unique mix of confidence and the fear of failure that only thirty-five years of elite schooling could breed.

Their room was empty now. Lea sat down at one of the research terminals and logged in.

What was she looking for? She didn't know, but now she knew why she was here. It was something Dominique's mother had said at the party: *Her number placed her first in line for the new experimental phase of mandatory extension treatments, the ones which the "life-loving" fight to receive. The Third Wave, they call it.*

It was something that had niggled at the back of Lea's mind in the past few weeks, a question beneath all the other questions. She would tackle this first.

The interface had changed, but the keyboard shortcuts were still the same. Slowly, her fingers found their old reassuring rhythm. Lea examined reams of market data and metrics for every day of the last year, alert for any anomalies or spikes. It was an immersive, hypnotic business. She worked quickly and silently, the satisfying rush of productivity sending her spine straight and her feet tapping.

An hour passed, and then two. Lea stood up abruptly. There was nothing. Nothing irregular at all, nothing that suggested even a hint of the Third Wave.

Lea was still standing at the window, staring out at the dappled grey sky, when she heard Jiang's voice out in the lobby. She turned to look. The top of his balding head was just visible above the partition wall that separated the receptionist's desk from the rest of the office. Lea couldn't hear what he was saying. But something about the tone of his voice made her crack open the door of the analysts' room, and then, without knowing why, slip behind a filing cabinet where Jiang couldn't see her.

". . . But it's hard to say for sure. It all depends on the actual resource efficiency projections, and those haven't been released yet," Jiang was saying. Was he on the phone?

"Well, yes. But my husband . . ." A second voice faded into a murmur.

Lea peeked out from behind the cabinet. Jiang and Natalie stood, heads huddled, by the reception desk. Natalie was speaking now, in a low, urgent voice that Lea couldn't make out. As she spoke, she chopped the air with her hands. Jiang was nodding, slowly, pinching his chin between thumb and forefinger. Then, he clapped one arm around her shoulder.

"Exciting times," he said. "The Third Wave. Who knows, we might be about to witness a historic moment," he boomed.

Natalie smiled. It was a smug, self-satisfied smile, but it was also more than that. Suddenly Lea realised what it was — Jiang was deferring to her.

As they went into Jiang's office, Lea crossed her arms across her chest and leaned her cheek against the cool grey metal of the filing cabinet. She remembered now — Natalie's husband was a politician, high up in the Ministry.

The Third Wave. So it was true.

She squeezed her eyes shut, trying to drive Uju's voice out of her head, trying to think straight. She would not make it, she knew. Not while she was on the Observation List; not while Todd was reporting on her strange disappearances; not after she threatened Todd with a broken glass. Not while she was hiding her father.

CHAPTER
TWENTY-THREE

"Wonderful of you to join us," George said, tapping a note into his tab.

Lea nodded curtly. She had already missed one WeCovery session, citing work as a reason. The next day, the Observers showed up again at her office, where they spent the entire day interviewing her colleagues about whether Lea was contravening Max Work guidelines. Jiang had been furious, and ordered her to abide by a strict nine to five schedule.

Lea was exhausted. She hadn't been sleeping well since the party, and after she'd overheard Jiang and Natalie talking about the Third Wave, it had got even worse.

But most of all, she hadn't wanted to come because of Anja. Lea wanted to hate her. She wanted to feel angry for having let Anja into her home, for having told her about her past. She wanted to feel that Anja had used her, for the music, maybe for a place to stay, for who knew what kind of trouble she was mixed up in? Perhaps she too was on the run, perhaps she had lied, didn't really have a place of her own, but spent her days hopping from one oblivious soul's couch to the next.

She wanted to hate Anja for agreeing to help her father kill himself.

But when Lea finally looked at her, all she felt was the same hollowness she'd been carrying around with her ever since the party. She was sitting next to George, her hair tucked neatly behind her ears. Lea studied her face, but her eyes were as mute as ever, her cheeks as drawn and sallow. She did not look like the newly crowned leader of an underground activist group. She did not look like the woman who would be responsible for the death of Lea's father.

The WeCovery sessions had got repetitive. Lea realised, by now, that George had a limited arsenal of "exercises" and would cycle through them as the weeks went by. That week, they were doing "Gratitude" yet again, George typing away on his tab, giving little imperious grunts from time to time as the group spoke. Most of them said the same things they had said last time.

Lea studied their faces. Under her gaze, George's self-importance resolved itself into self-preservation, Susan's chirpiness into obscene parody. Lea began to feel a prickling of sympathy for the members of the group. Perhaps, like Anja, they were only people trying their best.

"And you, Lea?" George asked. It was her turn.

They were all looking at her. Something in her was churning, tumbling, flipping over.

"Can I ask you a question, George?" she said. She went on, without waiting for an answer: "Why do you do this? WeCovery, reporting, why do you do any of it?"

George froze. A chill spread across his features, closing him off, withdrawing into the large, meaty hunk of his body.

"Do you think they'll take you off the List?" Lea pressed on. "Does anyone know anything about this List? Who decides who goes on it? The same algorithms that dispense lifespan adjustments?" She glanced around the room. No one would meet her eye, not even Anja.

"Now, Lea," George said, a warning in his voice. "I know you're going through a difficult time. Everyone here is. But there's no point being petulant about it, is there?"

Lea locked eyes with George. This time she didn't see the sagging cheeks, the oily pores, the rounded shoulders under loosening seams of a badly cut jacket. She saw the aggressive glint in his eyes behind the tortoiseshell glasses, the faint tremor of his fleshy lip, the sweat stains in the creases of his shirtsleeves. She heard the threat behind the entreaty in his voice. But what was it really? What did he have to threaten her with?

Lea felt a sudden rush of recklessness. "What do you think? That if we keep doing this, keep meeting here every week, talk about the same things over and over again, we'll somehow be different people? We'll be given our lives back?"

"Lea —" George started.

"She has a point," Ambrose said, so quietly that Lea thought she had imagined it. But the others were all looking at him too.

George snapped around to face Ambrose, flushing a deep purple.

"What was that, Ambrose?" George said. The tremor in his lip was gone, and his eyes were hard and cold.

"It's not completely wrong, is — is all I'm saying," Ambrose said in an even quieter voice. He looked around the circle, seeking support, but no one said anything.

"Right," George said, shifting in his seat. "Right, right, right. You know what? Forget Gratitude. Let's do one we haven't done in a while, shall we? Shake things up a little?" He cracked his knuckles at his side.

Lea noticed that Susan was blinking rapidly, her mouth hanging open.

"Fateful Days, shall we do that instead? Tell you what, let's do that instead," George went on, staring at each one of them in turn, his gaze finally landing on Ambrose.

"N — no, man, no," Ambrose said, drawing his knees up to his chest. His shoes, Lea noticed, were strangely formal, polished to a high shine.

"Come on, Ambrose," George said in a new voice, one that Lea hadn't heard before. "You don't want to talk about Yasmin? The look on her face when she found you on that chair, when she found her own silk scarf, an anniversary present from you — so thoughtful, really, so sweet — when she found that scarf knotted in a loop, hanging from a hook in the ceiling?"

Ambrose's face was in his knees now. His shoulders were shaking, a movement that seemed to come from deep within him, spreading through his entire body. Everyone else was silent.

"Ambrose," George went on. "Hey, man —"

"Stop it," Lea said. "Leave him alone."

George turned to her. "Oh? Did you have something to add, Lea?"

Lea's fists were balled at her sides. A hot rage flickered at the base of her stomach. She pressed her feet into the ground, feeling the world pushing back up against her.

"Why don't we move on to you, Lea? Your Fateful Day. Tell the group, come on, you don't want Ambrose to feel like he's being singled out, do you?" George smacked his lips together. A bubble of spit gathered in the corner of his mouth.

"What, the car accident? Big deal, I jaywalked. God forbid. Traumatised for life," she said.

"Oh Lea," George said. "You really don't get it, do you? You still think you're exceptional, above all this."

"Who's the one who thinks they're above it? You're just a sad little man, lording it over your poor —" She looked around at the group. Suddenly she hated them all — Ambrose, the weak curve of his spine, Susan and her flat, bluntly cut hair, Sofia and her spreading thighs that spilled over the plastic chair.

Anja and her thin wrists, her violin, her serious nods. Anja nodding at Lea's father. Lea hated her too.

"Dwight. That was his name, wasn't it?"

Lea froze.

"Yes, that was definitely it." George said it evenly, a small smile curling at the corners of his lips.

222

"What did you say?" Lea whispered.

"Dwight," he said again, matter-of-factly. "Your Fateful Day."

"How —"

George looked down at his tab, scrolling and tapping. "Did you actually think that it wouldn't be in your file?"

"Who's Dwight?" Susan said. "Tell us, Lea. Tell us about your Fateful Day."

They were all staring at her. She seemed to hear her heart pounding in her chest. Even Anja was staring at her.

Lea stood up.

"Session's not over," George said. "Where are you going? Hey. Hey!"

CHAPTER
TWENTY-FOUR

Lea rushed out of the room and down the stairs, taking them two at a time. Even in her haste, she was careful to keep one hand on the banister, so as not to fall. She praised herself for her self-control, until a sharp pain in the heel of her palm stopped her at the bottom of the staircase. She examined her hand. A shard of dark wood, barely visible, had pierced her skin. As Lea watched, the splinter was already being pushed out of her flesh. Soon it sat, harmless and inert as a fallen eyelash, in the palm of her hand.

"Lea. Wait."

It was Anja, coming down the staircase. Lea felt an unbidden rush of warmth at the concern in her voice and the worry etched on her face. Lea wanted, for a brief moment, to fall into her arms, to band together against George's tyranny, to spill the rest of her childhood darkness. Anja would understand, Lea felt. She thought of the rush of chlorinated water in her ears, the burn of exertion in her calves.

But as Anja drew closer, the memory of their swim together was replaced with the ominous discord of jazz notes and the smell of burnt animal flesh. Lea recognised in the knitting of Anja's brow the same look of attentiveness that she had given her father, right before she said yes.

"What do you want?" Lea said.

Anja shrugged. Her sweater was too large for her and the sagging shoulders flapped like wings.

"I just wanted to see if you were okay," she said. "George can be — well, he has his own problems, you know? Don't take it to heart."

When Lea didn't answer, Anja reached out and touched her elbow.

"We all have Fateful Days, as he calls them." A small smile curled at the corners of her mouth.

She didn't understand, Lea thought. Anja didn't understand that Lea wasn't like her, wasn't like any of them. Up till that moment, the Incident had not been mentioned for almost ninety years. There was no official record of it anywhere.

Kaito had taken the blame for what happened at the hospital. It was easy enough to pin on him when he already had a reputation of being not quite life-loving enough, with his hefty bulk and rebellious lifestyle. To label him antisanct was a step further, but a logical one. And he was already disillusioned, unhappy, older. He wasn't precious like Lea. Everyone had accepted the lie without questioning it, for why would they? How could a twelve-year-old child, even one with a history of violence, have the sickness and presence of mind to try to unplug a brain injury victim from life support? No, it had all the hallmarks of a closet antisanct trying to upend the system. Even Uju believed it, or if she didn't, she never let on.

When Kaito disappeared while out on bail, no one was surprised. It made things even easier for Uju, who used her Talent Global connections to make sure everything was attributed to Kaito, even the Incident at school. Lea was a susceptible child, she expounded, living under the same roof as a maladjusted, antisanct father whom she loved dearly. The Ministry swallowed it all, so Lea kept her perfect record. She remained a prime candidate for the Third Wave, for immortality.

Would have been a prime candidate for the Third Wave, she corrected herself.

"You weren't here last week, but I wanted to thank you for letting me stay that night, and for sharing your music with me," Anja said.

Lea suddenly realised that Anja hadn't seen her at the party. She had no idea that Lea knew who she was, had no idea that the tall hunched man in the worn blazer was Lea's father.

Anja didn't understand that Lea wasn't like her, she thought again. An idea began to form in her mind.

"I'm fine," Lea said. "It's just — I don't understand what I'm meant to do. What do they want me to do?"

Anja nodded. Her hand was still on Lea's elbow.

"I've been thinking," Lea lowered her voice. "I saw one of those videos lately. The antisanct ones. What do they call themselves? The Club?"

Anja's expression didn't change, but Lea felt her fingers tense.

"I wish I could get in touch with them somehow," she went on, her heart thudding in her chest.

"Why?" Anja said. She had a clear, curious look on her face now, that attentive gaze she'd had at the party.

Lea shrugged, mirroring Anja's earlier gesture. "I don't know. It's stupid, maybe, but . . ." She paused. "I feel like maybe they'd understand."

Anja was studying her face. Lea tried to keep her expression neutral, but her palms were damp and her pulse quick in her throat. Surely Anja would see right through her, she thought.

After a long pause, Anja cleared her throat. "Not here," she said in a low voice. She dipped her hand into the large purse she had slung over her shoulder and rummaged about. Glancing behind her, she turned back to Lea and pressed something into her hand. "If you want someone to talk to, I'm here. I'd like to return the favour," she said.

Muffled clapping came from upstairs.

"I'd better go back," Anja said. "I'll say that I couldn't find you, you'd already left."

Lea nodded, her fingers closing around the card that Anja had given her. "Thanks," she said.

Anja smiled and for a moment, her eyes lit up, her sallow cheeks seemed to brighten. Lea almost felt guilty.

CHAPTER
TWENTY-FIVE

Lea counted fifty floors at least, so a reasonable height. But the building's steel bones were grey and dull, its windows tinted purple with low-tech UV protection. The building was in a part of the city that had once been billed as the new downtown, the fringe between the Inner and Outer Boroughs, when lifespans first began to lengthen and the pharma boom was in full swing. More space was needed for the unretired who wanted to stay in the city, the proliferation of Healthtech companies, to reap the demographic dividend that was ripe for reaping. They'd built and built, pushing further and further towards the sea, but the infrastructure couldn't keep up. Soon the roads were choked with even more cars than before, traffic moved at a measly five miles an hour at most times of day. You were almost always better off walking, people realised, especially since the subway was so jammed that gloved handlers were hired to stuff commuters in. The greatest city planning oversight in history, it was called, but by then it was too late. They could hardly knock the skyscrapers down to widen the roads, and any major overhaul of the subway would require lengthy track closures that would bring the city to a halt.

So walking became the preferred mode of commuting and the buildings in the Central Boroughs grew ever taller. The new downtown — now named mockingly — still did fine, since there was a limit as to how quickly they could elongate the already four-hundred-storey-high skyscrapers in the Central Boroughs, but it never fulfilled city planners' early ambitions.

Lea had always pictured the top Ministry divisions in a building like her office, something soaring and see-through, in Borough One or Two. Still, this was the address she had been given.

The receptionist was a taut brunette, impeccably dressed. The sharp creases in her pant legs seemed out of place in that echoing lobby with its laminate faux-marble floor. She brightened as Lea approached, sitting up straighter in her plastic chair.

"Hello," she said, flashing a smile.

"Good morning," Lea said. "I'm here to see AJ. Or GK. I'm sorry, I don't have their full names."

"Of course. And you are?"

"Lea Kirino."

"Of course. Fifteenth floor, Ms Kirino. Just follow the signs."

It was astonishing how she maintained her smile even as she spoke.

As Lea waited for the elevator, the lobby began to fill up. Lea shuffled her feet. It wasn't too late. She could still leave. Make up an excuse for coming here — to check on her case status, for instance.

Her phone rang. When she pulled it out, she recognised the number immediately. Kaito. She turned the sound off, and shoved her tablet back into her purse.

She remembered the hard satisfaction in George's eyes as he said Dwight's name, the fearful fluttering of Susan's hands. She would not end up like one of them. Not now, not after all she had worked for.

Before the first interview, Uju had put Lea's hair into two thick, heavy braids. They rested like docile snakes on her shoulders.

"I don't like them," Lea said, pulling at a tufted tip. "They look stupid. They make me look stupid."

Uju gave her a look in the mirror. Lea folded her hands in her lap automatically. It was a look that Lea would describe to Todd many years later as business-like, something clicking into place as she finally found the right word. Uju had always felt more like an employer than a mother, and that look — a tight dip of the chin, a gentle lift of the eyebrows — exemplified their relationship. Lea was an employee in the corporation of their family, subject to regular performance reviews that determined her worth.

"Why did you do it?"

It was different when her mother asked. Lea thought about trying to tell her. *Fishy fishy fish fish fish.* That feeling of being behind an invisible screen, apart from the things and people around her that moved with a logic she couldn't quite grasp. The hot embers that smouldered inside of her, that flared up unexpectedly and made her want to reach out and grab and smash and feel. The rotten soft feeling that always came after, a feeling that she did not know yet to call shame. That the only thing to do was to go out and get more of the feeling, because if she stopped then that meant whatever she was doing was wrong.

She thought about trying to tell her. But looking at her mother's perfect heart-shaped face, the walnut frizz rising from her scalp golden in the lamplight, Lea felt the words turn spongey in her throat. She saw how, even if she could get the words out, her mother would pretend not to understand. How she would re-say them so they came out her way.

So Lea shrugged and said: "I don't know."

Uju's face took on a satisfied sheen. *I don't know* she could work with.

"Well," she said carefully. "They were bullying you, weren't they, those horrible delinquent girls? Not that physical retaliation is ever the answer. But anyone would break under such a prolonged period of psychological torment."

Lea nodded.

"Try and remember, darling. Don't leave anything out. And don't you worry about a thing."

She felt the force of her mother's will washing around her as she always had, the invisible tides nibbling away at the edges of herself.

"It started last year," Lea said. "Small things at first. Whispering. Giggling. Pulling out my chair."

Uju nodded, squeezed her shoulder.

"Eventually it was happening all the time. My eyes didn't match my skin. My hair stank. They said it was — greasy. Why was it always so greasy."

Lea kept going, drawing on Dwight for inspiration. She talked and she talked and she talked. Uju began stroking her hair in a rare show of affection. It was easy now that she had begun.

When she got to the Incident, Lea paused. She suddenly recalled Dwight's eyebrows pulled tightly together, the weak curve of his cheekbone, the soft pink flap of his lower lip. A faint, purplish blood vessel criss-crossing beneath translucent skin. She wondered, for the first time, what was wrong with her.

The elevator finally arrived. They piled in, every last one of them. It clanked upwards slowly, stopping at each and every floor. When they reached the fifteenth, Lea wriggled out from between suited shoulders.

White plastic signs tacked to the wall matched names to office numbers. AJ's was the fifth from the top, sandwiched between AG and AJB. Lea walked along the brightly lit hallway, heels clicking on the same veined maroon marble, past door after identical door. The hallway was empty, but a buzz of activity seeped out from the cracks under the black doors. The ringing of phones, urgent voices, scraping of chair legs and tapping of keyboards. Above it all, a tinkling tune — "Triangle and Bluebird Calls", Lea recognised — streamed out from invisible speakers. When she reached AJ's office, Lea paused, listening. She couldn't hear anything from behind the door. Perhaps he wasn't there. Perhaps she should go home.

"Come in," a voice called.

Lea opened the door. Two large desks, facing each other, took up nearly all the space in the room. Behind one was AJ, behind the other, GK. AJ appeared to have grown, his toned bulk filling out his small desk chair, his jacket tight at the elbows. Or was it the smallness of the room that emphasised his size? GK, on the other hand, looked skinnier and paler than before, hunched over his keyboard, long fingers pattering across the black squares. Neither AJ nor GK looked up as Lea entered the room.

Lea waited. Still they said nothing. They continued to type, staring fixedly at the multitude of screens that crowded their desks.

She cleared her throat. One would think they'd be pleased to have her just turn up at their doorstep like that, given the amount of time and effort they spent following her around.

AJ glanced up. "Lea Kirino," he said. "What are you doing here? Wait. Before you answer that. What were you wearing last Tuesday?"

"What?" she said.

"The sweater. Was it orange, or was it yellow? We know it was a crew neck. Tangerine sort of shade. But can you be more specific?"

"Why are you —"

AJ sighed. "Fine, orange it is."

He typed harder now, banging on his keyboard so that his screens shook.

Against the window pane was a single photo in a silver frame. She recognised AJ, still in the same dark suit, standing next to a forty-year-old in a mortarboard.

"Is that your son?" she asked. It was strange to think of him as a family man.

AJ stopped typing and looked up. He looked at Lea, then he looked at the picture. Slowly he stood up and took one step towards the window. He turned the picture around so that it faced out.

"So," he said. "What brings you here then, Lea Kirino?"

Lea cleared her throat. GK's typing clattered on.

"I have a complaint to make," she said.

"Go on," AJ said. He was still looking at her, but had picked a ball of rubber bands off his desk behind him that he began turning in his hands.

"It's about George. The . . . leader, I suppose, of my group. The WeCovery Group."

"We don't deal with complaints," AJ said, putting the rubber band ball back down onto his desk.

"He's out of control. What he's doing — it's emotionally abusive, cortisol-generating. Completely unacceptable," Lea said, her voice growing louder.

"Like I said, we don't deal with complaints. Therapy and rehabilitation — T&R — they're a different department altogether." AJ turned back to his screen.

"But he threatened me. He brought up —" Lea stopped.

AJ looked up again. "Dwight Rose?" he said.

So they knew. So everyone knew.

"Is that it then? Goodbye then, Lea, I'm sure we'll be seeing you soon," AJ said with a smirk.

"Wait. There's something else. Someone else in the group. Anja — I don't know her last name. She's foreign."

"Nilsson," GK said, still typing.

"I think she's part of — of an illegal group, of some kind. Antisanct. Non-life-loving for sure. Some kind of murder cult. The ones who do the videos." Lea squeezed her eyes together as she said this, but Anja's face appeared, silent and reproachful, so she opened her eyes again.

"Suicide Club," GK said. He didn't look up, but slowed down his typing.

"GK," AJ said, a warning note in his voice. "Thank you for your time, Lea. Was there anything else?"

"I don't understand. I thought that's all you wanted, information. If you already know about the Club, then why aren't you doing anything about them?" Lea asked again.

AJ pinched his nose bridge.

"We're very busy," he said. "If there's nothing else, I'm going to have to ask you to leave."

He stepped back behind his desk. They both went back to ignoring her, and started typing again.

Swiftly, Lea rounded the corner of GK's desk and slipped behind him.

Verbal: I don't understand, I thought that's all you wanted. Information. If you already know about the Club, then why aren't you doing anything about them. Physical: Habitual gesture #7, pinching left elbow.

Nails painted, light nude brown, hiding something? Ring finger appears freshly bitten.

The screen went black. Silence filled the room.

"Are you trying to ensure a lifetime of Observation?" AJ said.

"Where does all this information go? What's the point of it all?"

"That's none of your business. Classified Ministry information," AJ said.

Lea suddenly noticed a faint liver spot spreading across the base of his left cheek, coin-sized.

"Actually," GK piped up. "Under the last FIA —"

"GK!" AJ shot him a look. GK stopped.

"FIA?" Lea asked.

"Freedom of Information Act. You'll have to file a request, of course," AJ said, grudgingly. He began removing rubber bands from the ball on his desk. *Snap.*

"And how do I do that?"

"The forms are on our website. You'll get an official answer within twenty business days."

"I don't want to wait twenty business days," Lea said.

They stared at her silently, the same blank look on both their faces.

"Look, I just want to give some information on the Suicide Club. And maybe you can take that into account at my hearing."

They looked at each other.

"You'll have to download the official reporting app," AJ said. "We're not authorised to take oral testimony."

"Well then who is?" Lea asked. "I want to speak to whoever's in charge." She drew herself up to her full height.

They looked at each other again.

"I'd have to check," AJ said. "There's been a lot of turnover lately."

He waved one hand at their desks, so closely pushed together, Lea saw now, that it was clear they were never meant to be in the same room.

"But they killed her. Dominique," Lea burst out. She fixed her gaze on AJ's serene face, but there was no shock or glee, nothing to indicate he had heard her revelation, that it was a revelation at all. He glanced at his watch.

"Fine, don't leave," he said, turning away. He squeezed past her, heading for the door.

"Where are you going?" Lea asked.

"Lunch," AJ called over his shoulder as the door shut behind him.

GK had his screen back on and was typing furiously once again.

"Look," he said. "We've got a lot on our plates. More than we can handle. The Suicide Club — they're old news. Been on record for decades now. Can't ever pin anything on them; besides, it's not our case. Someone else looks after them."

"Because they're wealthy and powerful," Lea said. "Of course. So, what, you're not even going to try? They're allowed to get away with it, just like that?"

GK shrugged.

"They killed a girl, got rid of her body in some sick public ritual. And you're sitting there typing up the colour and fabric of my blouse."

GK stopped typing. He looked up at Lea, suddenly alert.

"What did you say?"

"It's ridiculous, I should go to the press with this, people need to know where their tax dollars are going."

"No — what did you say about the body?"

Lea paused. She remembered the tip of the girl's nose, peeking above the liquid level before it was submerged.

"They had it laid out on stage," she said in a low voice. "In this — this box — made out of glass."

"The body?" GK said, his voice excited now. "As in you saw her physical, non-living, body? With Club members in the room? You're sure?"

"Of course I'm sure. Do you want to listen to what I have to say now?" Lea narrowed her eyes.

GK stood up, pacing in the narrow sliver of space between his desk and the wall behind him. He could only take about four steps before he came to the end of the room and had to turn around again.

"And AJ out for lunch," he said. "Actual body. And you there — a witness. But how is that possible?"

He turned to her.

"You're lying," he said coldly. "They would never take a risk like that. How did you get there, anyway?"

"Anja. She invited me." The lie to protect Kaito slipped out of her like a dropped marble, thudding heavily in the room.

Suddenly Lea realised that if she got the Club shut down, maybe she could stop Kaito from killing himself. Yes, he could still obtain black market T-pills on his own, but he could have done that years ago, and he hadn't. No, he wanted the spectacle the Club could give him. But maybe she could stop it.

GK's upper lip was pursed, a deep line ran between his eyebrows. Lea noticed, for the first time, that his skin was much duller than AJ's.

"What's this cost-cutting AJ mentioned?" Lea asked.

"It's awful. Started with the move here — what was it — ten years ago now? I'd just joined then, fresh out of grad school, pretty pleased with myself. Entry-level Ministry jobs weren't exactly common back then, you know. And I'd thought, wow, new office, this is going to be great, but then we moved out here."

Lea nodded sympathetically.

"And then there was the meal reduction, benefits reduction, supplemental shift schedule, space consolidation . . . Who knows where this is going to end?"

"I didn't realise it was quite so bad from what's been in the news," Lea said.

"The news," GK wrinkled his nose, "Fat Ministry Gets Long Overdue Revamp makes for a headline and that's all they care about, isn't it? You know, I have a triple-post-doctorate in forensic science. Yet here I am," he gestured towards his screen.

"Paperwork," Lea said.

"Yeah." GK looked down at his feet.

"You know, they know me now. The Club. And Anja — she trusts me."

"What are you saying?" GK's hands hovered over the keyboard, but he didn't start typing again.

"I'm saying," Lea weighed her words carefully. "Maybe I could help you. You said you can't ever pin anything on them. I could go to their meetings, gather information. Get you what you need."

"You want to report on them," GK said. "Report on Suicide Club."

Lea swallowed.

"Would that help?" she said. "Would that get me off the List?"

"Do you realise who they are?" GK said.

Lea blinked. "Of course I do. I was there. I saw what they do, I heard them speak. They're a bunch of antisanct criminals."

GK pinched the bridge of his nose, squeezing his eyes shut.

"It's not that easy," he said. "The Jackmans — they're, well, let's say they're well connected."

"What do you mean?"

GK removed his hand from his face. His nose was red, and his eyes bloodshot. He looked like he hadn't slept in weeks.

"Don't you know who Mrs Jackman is?"

Lea shook her head.

"She comes from one of the largest Healthtech families. Ministry folk throughout the family tree. She's — well, different, clearly. Has her issues, caused lots of problems for the family. But that doesn't mean they won't do anything to protect her."

"But how can that be —"

"You know what, AJ will be back soon, and I still have a full day's report to type up." He struck his keyboard, bringing the screen back to life. "You'll have to leave. We'll take note of this visit, incorporate it into your case notes."

"You didn't answer my question," Lea said. She placed both hands on the desk, leaning in towards him. He smelled faintly of antiseptic. "Would it help?"

"I can't condone any such activity," GK said. "Reporting on the Club — the Ministry would never ask that of anyone. And we don't do — deals, as it were." He glanced at the door nervously. Outside, the muffled ringing of telephones and the clattering of footsteps continued.

"But say you were to receive such information. Say you were to get such testimony, recordings, even. Hard evidence you could use, linking Anja to the actual videos. Linking the Jackmans. That would be useful to you, wouldn't it?"

GK blinked rapidly. He began running his fingers along the surface of his keyboard, nervously caressing the worn black keys with their faded letters. He looked around the room, his gaze flitting from the towering stacks of paper, the yellowing stained walls, the sliver of space between his desk and AJ's.

"We might be able to act on it, were we to get such information. It would have to be a recording, of course, and some sort of eyewitness testimony," he said. "Quite impossible," he added hurriedly. "And it would have no bearing on any other open cases. All cases are considered in isolation, with full objectivity. Particularly," he went on. "With the latest developments."

"Developments?" Lea asked. "You mean the Third Wave?"

The door clicked open.

"I couldn't possibly comment," GK said, avoiding her gaze.

"Still here?" AJ said. "You know, this really isn't going to help your case."

Lea straightened up. "I was just leaving," she said, calmly now. Glancing at GK, she saw that a deep red flush was spreading across his neck.

"Great. Lots to do, you know, not much time to do it all. You're not the only one we have to keep track of, after all," AJ added.

Lea thought of the hallway of doors. How many like GK and AJ were there, how many like her?

CHAPTER
TWENTY-SIX

"Three vegburgs, two nutrishakes, four sides of boiled chips," the chef shouted. "Three vegburgs, two nutrishakes —"

"Got it, got it, I'm here," Anja said, wincing. She balanced the plates nimbly on her forearms, one shake in each hand.

"I'll be back for the chips," she said.

"Better hurry, hun, we're running out of counter space. And where the hell is Branko?"

"No idea," she said.

"Of all the shifts to miss," Rosalie muttered, flipping a row of cabbage patties deftly.

Anja dashed back out. The diner was full, and Branko was still nowhere to be seen. The place was noisy most peak hours, but today it was absolutely chaotic. Anja set the burgers down in front of an arguing family who barely acknowledged her presence.

As she walked back to the kitchen, a braying voice cut across the noise.

"Excuse me! Ma'am. Ma'am."

She turned around. The woman she'd just delivered the burger to had plucked the bun off and was waving it at her. Her pearl earrings glinted under the fluorescent light.

"Um, I think we ordered these with carb-free buns? These just look like regular gluten-free ones to me?" Also we've been waiting for at least forty minutes now, and no one's wiped down this table." She pressed one manicured finger on the vinyl surface and grimaced.

"Let me just check on that for you." Anja turned to go.

"Aren't you going to take these back?" The woman's voice rose an octave.

"I was just going to check the order first," Anja said through a tight smile.

"Check? What do you need to check? Just get us what we ordered."

"Of course." Anja swept the dishes off the table again, the smile on her face unwavering.

"I got four bowls of kale wafers wilting in their own juices," Rosalie said as Anja re-entered the kitchen. "Why are you bringing food back in? No no no. Food goes out the kitchen. Not in. Wrong way. Turn around."

"They said they ordered the buns carb-free."

"Carb-free? We don't do carb-free. What will they want next, premium-flavoured Nutripaks? Tell them we're a diner, honey, not some zero nutrient bar on the Upper West Side. Carb-free. I'll give them carb-free." Roasalie pushed beans violently around the pan.

Anja went back out, burgers still in hand. As she stood there contemplating whether to tell the lady that the buns were a new composite that perfectly simulated the texture of carbs, the door clattered open and in came Branko.

"Where the hell have you been?" Anja hissed as he approached.

"I had an appointment," he said, taking his puffer jacket off slowly.

"Halimah is out sick. It's been manic here. What appointment?"

"I'll tell you later."

He took his scarf off with the same slow deliberation, carefully hanging both items of clothing up on the hook by the door.

"Hurry, won't you? Ros is going crazy," Anja snapped.

Branko nodded wordlessly, then headed to the kitchen.

Anja brought the burgers back to the family. She was in the middle of explaining that the carb-free supplier had been in an unfortunate accident when she felt a tap at her elbow.

"I need to talk to you," Branko said. Anja noticed with a frisson of irritation that he was empty-handed.

"Why aren't you serving?" she said in a low voice.

"It's important."

"Um, excuse me?" the lady was waving a leaf at them. "Your menu also says baby wild rocket? This looks like regular rocket to me."

Anja turned back to Branko.

"Fine," she said.

They went behind the bar. Branko pulled out some glasses and began pouring drinks at random.

"What is it?" she said. Now that she was standing next to him she realised his hands were shaking and there was a strange, shiny cast to his face.

"I have a guy," he said. "I can hook you up with him."

Anja could barely hear him over the noise of the diner and the clinking of glasses as he moved them about the counter.

"What are you talking about? Hook me up for what?" She laughed. Surely Branko wasn't trying to matchmake her with someone.

He shot her a sideways glance. "Your mother," he said, quietly.

Something clicked. "Are you offering to get me —" Anja started.

"Not me. I have a guy, like I said. It'll cost you. But he could get hold of what you need. T-pills, other variants, you know."

Before she could stop herself, Anja started to laugh.

T-pills. If only it were that easy. If only that were the problem, the simple mechanics of it. Buy some black market drugs, crush them up, mix with water, dribble down her mother's reinforced throat.

That was not the problem. The problem was her.

"What?" Branko said. His face closed up. "I'm just trying to help."

Anja saw the hurt on Branko's face but she couldn't stop laughing. She hated the sound of it, bitter and mocking. Suddenly she saw the person she had become, saw the person she would become if she went on like this.

246

CHAPTER
TWENTY-SEVEN

Kaito had been calling her ever since the party. One call every morning, before she went to work and one at night, when he thought Lea would be home. Each time the phone rang, Lea stopped whatever she was doing and stared at the lit screen, her father's name flashing at regular intervals. She'd saved his number under Kaito Kirino. "Dad" had seemed too intimate. She longed to pick up, to hear his voice, to pretend that she had never been at the party, that she knew nothing of his plans. But each time she let the phone ring until it came to rest.

The day Jiang told Lea she was suspended from work, he walked into her office with an odd spring in his step, with a greater sense of purpose than she was used to. He wore a salmon-pink shirt underneath a pressed blue blazer, and shiny leather shoes. More flamboyant than his usual work attire. His thin hair was combed back into some approximation of a trendy pouf, the sides slicked up but already sagging.

He delivered the message with a note of superiority she had never heard before. She took it calmly, observing the steadiness of his hands. Clearly handling her "case" as Jiang now called it had given him a new lease of life. He used words like "unfortunate", "temporary" and "monitoring". Unfit, reputation, treatment. He handed her an official letter, typed out by Joo Lee, the secretary who always asked Lea where she got her shoes. She read the letter, quickly, under Jiang's watchful gaze. It said nothing that he hadn't already told her. When she looked up, Natalie was standing outside.

"She'll be taking over your clients," Jiang said. He blinked, and for the first time, appeared apologetic.

Lea nodded. There was no point in fighting back. She sensed it from Jiang's eerie good cheer, his detached calm. They had decided, Jiang and the other partners, that she had become a liability. They hadn't said it, of course, couched the suspension in terms of her own wellbeing rather than the reputation of the firm, but she knew better.

She didn't ask when she could come back. She knew that Jiang didn't have an answer for her, that he was just the messenger. But as he closed the door behind himself to "give her a moment", as she packed up her pens and powered off her computer, as her fingertips grazed the cool polished surface of her glass desk, the hard knot in her chest grew.

Her belongings fitted into a small box, which she left in the corner of the office. She looked around one more time, taking in the view from the floor-to-ceiling windows, the skylight, the planters lining the walls. She was surprised to feel no anger, no pang of loss, now that a plan was forming in her mind, its edges solidifying like the shape of a person approaching through a fog.

The morning after she was suspended, Lea ran herself a bath. She lit a soy candle, scrubbed her legs luxuriously, tried to take her time. Then she made herself a trad salad, her favourite, kale and sunflower seeds. She ate it with her hands, picking one leaf after another into her mouth, staring into space. But then, once she had washed and dried the bowl, once she had wiped off the sink and dried her hands, the apartment was so quiet she couldn't bear it. Lea longed for the soft patter of feet on glass ceilings, for the ringing of phones and the chattering of voices.

She walked out into the living room. It too was quiet. The linen curtains hung straight and limp on either side of the large window, cold white columns guarding the outside world. Lea wondered, briefly, what it must be like to live in a place where the curtains fluttered, lifted by the breeze coming in through an open window.

The curtains didn't move. Neither did the house plant sitting in the corner of the living room, or the grey-cushioned sofa. Looking around the living room, Lea decided that the furniture needed to be reconfigured. That was probably why it felt so stale and quiet, she realised, it was all just a matter of interior design. She set to work immediately, dragging the sofa one way, the side table the other. She carefully removed glass framed prints of harbours and cities from the bookshelves on the far end of the wall, then slowly pushed it across the room. She reoriented the cream rug underfoot. Placed diagonally it did look better, she thought. Finally she picked up the plant, and surveyed the room for the right spot. Next to the sofa, she thought, where the side table had once been. She put it down.

Lea straightened her back and looked around at the living room again. Better, she thought, far more dynamic an arrangement. Previously everything had been all parallel lines and right angles; things pushed up against walls and aligned with one another. Now, the ends of the sofa bisected two walls, leaving a triangle of space behind it. The bookcase was freestanding. The coffee table off to the side.

But as she stood there, as the exertion of moving furniture subsided and the blood cooled in her ears, silence descended once again. Suddenly she felt she could hear her own heartbeat.

The Third Wave. Lea imagined what it would be like when Jessie told her. The euphoria of success, being one of the chosen ones. She would go for treatments immediately, at the recommended pace, of course. By the time it got to her turn, she presumed all issues of misalignment and other side effects would have been ironed out. She would emerge from the clinic week after week, each time stronger, glowing, invincible. The blood running through her veins a liquid life force, the stuff of gods. Her skin, dewy and impossibly supple, yet impervious, impenetrable.

She, a goddess. Nothing would ever hurt her again.

Her phone rang. It was her father. For the first time in three weeks, Lea picked up.

"Lea?"

"Hi, Dad."

"Been busy with work? I've been trying to reach you." His voice hadn't changed. There was no accusation in it, no frantic question. It was as if none of it had happened.

Lea nodded, but then realised he couldn't see her. "It's been hectic. New client at work," she lied.

"Oh dear. How's that going?"

"Good," Lea said. "Difficult, but good."

"Well, don't wear yourself out," her father said. For a moment he sounded like Todd and she thought he would say *Healthy mind, healthy body*. But of course, he didn't.

"I won't. Listen, I have to run. Busy day."

"Okay," he said. He paused. "We'll speak again soon, Lea. Whenever you have some time."

They hung up.

Whenever you have some time. Lea looked around at her empty living room. It was silent except for the soft sigh of the ventilation system that pumped fresh air into the apartment. If Lea was very still, if she sat with her arms resting at her sides and her face unmoving, it almost felt as if she did not exist, as if time did not exist. She had never thought that one could have too much time, but suddenly, without the daily activity of work, the years of her life stretched out ahead of her. Was this what her father had felt?

No. She leapt up from the sofa. The Third Wave was coming. She would be part of it, whether Jiang, Todd, the Observers, wanted it or not. She would not languish

251

on the Observation List, her number dwindling as the days went by, until one day it was too late altogether. She would do something they couldn't ignore.

Something her father couldn't ignore, either.

CHAPTER
TWENTY-EIGHT

The meetings were usually held in people's homes, Anja had told her, away from prying eyes. Lea already knew this, of course, but she'd nodded as if she didn't.

This meeting was special, Anja had informed Lea. It was to be in a restaurant.

The place was a nice one, set in the airy archways of an old converted church in Borough Two. It was one of the only low-rise buildings left in the Central Boroughs (even then, ten floors of underground space had been tunnelled out beneath it), undoubtedly protected by a wealthy benefactor with Ministry friends. Surprising that the Club meeting would be here, Lea thought, but then she remembered the party, the comfortable house uptown, the people in their silks and furs. What was it GK had said? *The Jackmans. Let's say they're well connected.*

Lea thought of GK now as she walked into the restaurant. His pale skin, so susceptible to sun damage, his watery blue eyes; recessive genes that would soon disappear from the population altogether. She felt a surge of pity for him, crammed into the tiny office with the huge desk, transcribing mundane details with his advanced degree. Now that they were working together, so to speak, Lea no longer hated him. No, she saw that it was not GK's fault, that he took no pleasure in his work. The thought of AJ though, still brought a flash of anger, the old feeling coursing through her veins. Poor GK, working with someone like that.

Never mind though. Lea brightened and adjusted the mother of pearl button in her chiffon blouse. It was amazing how small cameras could get these days, tiny enough to fit into one of the four eyes in a button. A fisheye lens, guaranteed to capture two hundred and thirty-five degrees in all directions, so she wouldn't have to worry about where she was facing. The microphone was sensitive too, the man on the internet had assured her. It was even smaller than the camera, a wire that ended in a rounded tip no larger than the head of a pin. This was tucked in the cuff of her sleeve.

"Can I help you, ma'am?" The maître d', in an impeccably pressed suit, his hands held clasped in front of his abdomen like an opera singer.

"Reservation under Anja Nilsson, please," Lea said, flashing him a smile. Under the thin chiffon she was sure her heart could be heard pounding in her chest. Antisanct, she heard in her head, antisanct antisanct antisanct.

The maître d' gave a brief, polite nod, indicating she should follow him. No alarm sounded, no glances exchanged, no phone calls made.

The restaurant was a hollow, arched space, all grey stone and warped colourful glass. Since it was just one floor, the ceilings were high, higher in fact than Lea had ever seen. The candlesticked tables and their well-dressed diners appeared tiny in the space, insignificant. Lea noted that it was the usual clientele one found in such restaurants — coiffed, polished lifers, sipping daintily at their flavoured Nutripaks. It was the kind of place her clients would eat at, she thought, glancing around surreptitiously to see if she recognised anyone. She did not.

No one stared as she passed through the restaurant, and why should they? She looked just like them. She *was* just like them, Lea corrected herself, fingering the button in her blouse again.

He led her to a sliding door in the back of the space, knocking gently, two polite raps.

"Come in," a voice called. Lea strained to recognise it, but it wasn't Anja.

The maître d' slid the door open and extended his arm with a slight bow. Lea stepped into the room, and the door shut behind her.

The lights were lower in here than in the main restaurant. When her eyes had adjusted to the dimness of the room, she saw that it was dominated by a long table, with people sitting on either side. The seats were wooden benches that looked as if they had once been church pews.

"Lea. You made it." A hand waved from the far end of the room. It was Anja. "I'd get up, but these benches," she gestured down. "They're such a pain to get out from. Anyway, everyone, this is Lea. Lea, everyone."

A chorus of hellos filled the room. It was a small, echoey space, and the rumble of greetings seemed to come from inside her own head. Lea lifted a hand in greeting. "Hi, everyone," she said. Who was everyone? Did they know her father?

What if her father were here? Suddenly she was struck by panic; she hadn't considered what to do if he was invited tonight. She turned her head quickly, scanning their faces in the dim light. But she saw quickly that he wasn't, for if he was, she would've sensed it right away. Like when she was on that sidewalk, how long ago? Almost two months now. But it was a mere blip relative to the hundred years she had lived, and yet it felt like a lifetime away. How different her life had been then, how certain, with Todd, Jiang, the solidity of her status as a lifer.

Everyone was still looking at her. Lea shook herself and forced a bright smile.

"Where shall I sit?" she said, hoping that Anja would call her over. But she stayed still, made no move to shift and make room for Lea.

"There's a space here," a voice said.

Only after Lea sat down did she realise where she had heard that voice before. The woman who'd spoken had her back facing Lea when she'd come in, so she hadn't seen her face at first. But now that she was seated next to her, the angular cheekbones and dark, liquid eyes were unmistakeable, except she was no longer wearing a red sequinned dress.

"And what is your name?" the woman said.

"Lea," she responded, before wondering if she should give her real name. But it was too late, and Anja knew who she was, in any case. "Lea Kirino."

She thought of the tiny microphone in the cuff of her sleeve, now resting gently on the starched white table-cloth. "And you?" Lea said, boldly. As if she didn't know who she was.

"Cassandra Jackman," she responded. "Mrs Jackman, to most." She smiled. Her teeth were very white but uneven at the edges, as if she ground them in her sleep. Perhaps she did. Perhaps she ground them thinking of all the people she had murdered. Perhaps she ground them thinking of her daughter, Dominique.

"You're new, aren't you?" Mrs Jackman said. "Anja's told me all about you. WeCovery. You poor things, having to go through that tedious 'treatment'. What a farce."

She tapped one long fingernail against the base of her wine glass. The noise was high and sharp. Lea seemed to feel it in her spine. Everything about Mrs Jackman — the smell of stale smoke on her breath, the delicate crepe-like texture of her neck, her strong hands with their white palms that reminded Lea of her own mother's hands — everything about her jarred. Decrepit yet dangerous, carefully preserved yet reckless.

"Oh God, that sideshow. I had to do it too," the man sitting across the table from Lea and Mrs Jackman said. He had the soft, striking features so common among multiethnic lifers, and wore his curly black hair down to the crisp white collar of his shirt. He placed his elbow on the table and his chin in the base of his palm, like a gossipy teenager. "Tell me, does George still perspire as much as he did when I was there?"

"You were at WeCovery?" Lea said. "You were on the Observation List?"

"Aren't we all, darling. How else would the Ministry keep themselves busy?" He laughed, and those around him laughed too.

"I don't understand," Lea said.

But before the man could answer, the waiters arrived, filing in one by one. They stood poised behind their seats, plates balanced on right-angled arms. At some invisible cue they bent down simultaneously, placing the plates in front of them.

"Oh, wonderful," the man across from her said, picking up his knife.

A trad meal, then, Lea thought. Of course. The table had been set with forks and knives of different sizes, rather than the single spoon that would be used for a Nutripak meal. But despite having some interest in cooking trad herself, she couldn't identify the vegetable that was on the plate in front of her. It was a rectangle with neat corners, the colour of a sunset, some way between pink and yellow. A paste, Lea observed, as those around her began cutting into their slabs. Pastes were not uncommon in high-end trad meals, together with foams and gels. Perhaps this was cauliflower or radish, with a hint of tomato, that would explain the colour.

"Bon appétit," Mrs Jackman said, placing her napkin on her lap. She cut a precise square out of her rectangle and forked it into her mouth.

Lea picked up her cutlery and did the same. But as soon as she placed it on her tongue she could tell something was wrong. The paste was heavy, sticky, greasy — it had no discernible smell on the plate, but an overpowering one on her palate. It smelled of sweat and grass. It smelled of an animal.

She wanted to spit it out but it had already dissolved and was everywhere in her mouth, between her teeth, under her tongue, in the corners of her throat. She remembered the smell of steak at the party. This was nothing like it. The taste in her mouth was oily and sweet, almost rotten in its richness. She grabbed her glass, taking a large gulp of water to wash out the taste.

But it wasn't water either. The liquid burned in her throat, and Lea began to cough. Her eyes watered.

"Slow down, darling, we're only on the first course," the man said.

"Are you alright?" Mrs Jackman asked.

The coughing began to subside. "What — what is that?" Lea said, pushing the glass away. "And that?" She pointed down at her plate.

"Only the finest foie gras," the man said, rolling his Rs. "And the drink — that's in honour of our new dear leader. Aquavit, a traditional Swedish drink."

"Manuel." Mrs Jackman shot him a look.

"This is — this is animal meat," Lea said. Now that the burning was gone, the taste of it returned. Disgusting, she thought to herself.

"Not just animal *meat*, darling," Manuel said, offended. "Animal fat. Pure unadulterated fat, from the liver of a free range goose, imported at great expense from one of the last remaining civilised areas in the European territories."

259

"Have you never had meat before, then?" Mrs Jackman asked. Her voice was quiet, the question innocuous. But Lea heard a frisson in her voice, heard the test that was being posed.

"Of course I have." Lea swallowed. "But only chicken and fish. Pork, once. It's so hard to find, as you know. Nothing — nothing like this."

Mrs Jackman weighed Lea's words, her utensils poised in her hands. The dark pools of her eyes, Lea noticed, were flecked with yellow, like a cat's.

"It's an acquired taste," she said slowly. "Try it again. If you want."

Lea thought of the button on her blouse, thought of her father. And she picked up her knife and fork again, cut a larger piece this time, the size of a stamp. Before she could hesitate, she put the whole thing in her mouth and forced herself to chew.

"Mmm," she said, imitating the way Manuel chewed, closing her eyes briefly, sighing loudly. She tried not to think of the triglycerides, the LDLs, the carcinogens and telomere-shortening preservatives. Think long term, she told herself. What's a few years here and there if you can shut down the Club, if you can save your father. Be an Immortal.

"She loves it!" Manuel crowed.

After a long unblinking pause, Mrs Jackman smiled. "Glad you like it," she said, turning back to her own plate.

Lea had passed the test. Still, she forced herself to keep eating, holding her breath as she swallowed each mouthful.

260

"So you know George?" she said, turning back to Manuel.

"Oh, dear old George. I have unfortunately had the pleasure, yes. A couple of years back, when I was first flagged as being . . ." he dropped his voice to a stage whisper, ". . . *Antisanct.*" He gnashed his teeth, then stabbed another piece of foie gras and placed it in his mouth, chewing slowly, deliberately.

Those around him laughed lazily and sipped their drinks. *Oh stop, Manuel, you're terrible. Don't tease the newcomer.*

"What happened?" Lea said, smiling too, like a good sport. "How did you get off the List?"

"Off the List! Off the List!" Manuel howled. "Oh, you're a funny one. You'll be the death of me."

When he finished laughing, he saw that she was still staring at him, waiting for an answer. The smile fell from his face and he furrowed his brow.

"Why are you asking?" he said. "Do you want to get off it?"

"No," she said quickly, shaking her head. "I don't care. I just don't want to have to keep going to WeCovery."

"Think about it," he said, smiling again. "If you stop going, what can they do? Withhold your extension treatments? Cut your number? Let you die?"

Everyone was quiet now. They were watching Manuel, watching Lea.

"Isn't that what we all want, anyway? Isn't that what you want?"

To avoid answering, Lea took another mouthful of foie gras. The taste of it was less unpleasant now. Because she had been expecting it, Lea told herself, because she had braced herself, controlled her gag reflex. But as she cut another square of the processed meat, and another, she felt the saliva in her mouth thicken. She felt the anticipation, the wanting.

Lea attended more meetings. Befriended them, Manuel, especially, for she could see from the way the others listened to him that he was important. Those at the dinner that night were the core members, she learned, the trusted insiders.

Why Anja had invited her to that, she had no idea. Lea still talked to her, both at Club meetings and at WeCovery, but try as she did to continue their friendship in the same vein as before she'd found out about the Club, Lea sensed a chill had fallen between them.

Eventually they started involving Lea more, enlisting her for the logistical tasks that came with any large, sprawling organisation. The things they asked Lea to do were easy, so mundane they made her head hurt. But now that she had been suspended from her job, her days were long and empty, so Lea willingly moved chairs before meetings, printed flyers, arranged for catering. She wore her camera diligently, filming bits of furniture being moved, fragments of conversation, an invoice here and there. But there was nothing that would give her any information that she could bring to GK, nothing like what she had seen at the party. Even as she felt her mind wilting in boredom, she was in some way relieved.

She met other members of the Club, learned their motives through gentle questions. Some wanted to avoid even the possibility of getting trapped into becoming an Immortal, others simply felt they had had enough, and wanted to be in control of their own ends. Others, still, wanted to make a statement. Felt they were fighting for an idea, a fundamental right. Those were the martyrs, the idealists, the principled.

Those were the self-centred, Lea thought. Like her father.

Those days had a strange, dream-like cast to them.

When she went in for her next maintenance appointment, Jessie didn't ask about the Observation or the man who'd come to the clinic looking for Lea, or anything about Lea's personal life at all. She concerned herself only with the practical issues of Lea's body. Lea considered asking her about the Third Wave, but the professional glaze to Jessie's eyes and the quick, matter-of-fact edge to her movements made it clear that there would be no point.

There was a symmetry to her days, buoyed by the steady rhythm of the Club and WeCovery meetings. They were flip sides of the same coin, as Lea saw it. Now that she had decided on her course of action, her mind was focused on execution, on following the path that she'd laid out for herself. It was oddly peaceful. No Jiang, breathing down her neck, no Natalie, trying to steal her clients and take her promotions. No Todd, following her around the apartment with his languid, optimistic eyes, failing to understand. She didn't realise until he left how tired he made her.

So when Lea got the call from Manuel, the call that she had in theory been waiting for this whole time, she felt a surprising twinge. But it wasn't regret, she told herself firmly, it was the pressure of it all, now that the moment was finally here. Now that she would get the material she needed to get her life back on track. She quashed the feeling, ground it out with the heel of her will, and said of course she would be there.

CHAPTER
TWENTY-NINE

The camera the Club gave to Lea was heavy, heavier than she expected. It would require two hands to operate, and she was told to use her shoulder to prop it up. It was intimidatingly built, but they told her it would be easy enough to use. Their regular cameraman, Jonas, had started like that too, standing in at a moment's notice for someone else. And Jonas managed just fine, so fine he went on to become their permanent cameraman when his predecessor's turn finally came. Lea didn't ask what happened to Jonas, only listened to what she had to do, when she had to turn the camera on, where she had to aim it, which buttons to press in order to immediately broadcast the video via the usual channels.

The man who taught her how to use the camera was a nervous, soft-spoken thing, with elegant hands like those of a dentist or a neurosurgeon. He looked like someone who had a good day job, someone who could even be a Tender himself. But what Lea had learned over these past few months was that they all looked like people who could have good day jobs, including her. The man talked slowly, as if she were a child, explaining what the record buttons did, the difference between pause and stop. He didn't know that while he told her all this, her own camera was hidden in the folds of the dark silk shirt she wore, its lens peeking out under the second button from the top, watching and listening to everything he said.

"When it's over," the man said. "Just leave the camera in the room. Lock the door behind you. Clean up will handle the rest."

"Clean up? You mean the people in charge of set up?" Lea asked.

The man frowned, as if she had asked him a personal question he'd rather not answer. Still, he said: "No. Different people."

Lea nodded. She had discovered, from watching and listening over the past few weeks, that that was how it was done. Different people for every step of the process — a loose measure to make sure no one ever had enough evidence to testify against the Club. Though of course, that wasn't what stopped them from doing it. Everyone who was there, as far as Lea could gather, seemed to truly want to be there.

When the day came, Lea arrived at the appointed place an hour early. She'd hoped to catch the people setting up as well, to chat with them and somehow get them on camera, so she'd have the full day documented, the whole process, from beginning to end. But when she got to the building, a nondescript office block on the outskirts of the Central Boroughs, it occurred to her that she hadn't been told what floor or unit they'd be in. Someone was meant to meet her downstairs.

Perhaps, however, they weren't upstairs yet, and if she sat somewhere inconspicuous, she could spot and film them coming in.

The streets were teeming with office workers. She found a bench in a small square across the street, where she had direct line of vision into the lobby. It was abandoned and quiet, with its windows taped over and its glass doors blocked by signs proclaiming its decommissioned status. A single, bored security guard sat at a booth in front of the doors.

Lea sat down on the bench, easing the strap of the camera bag off her shoulder. She rubbed her back, digging her fingers into the hard flesh, enjoying the painful release. She realised it had been weeks since she last attended Swimlates. She would need to go back soon, or it would start showing in her maintenance numbers. Not that Jessie would ask why she hadn't been going, Lea thought.

It was a glorious crisp day, and Lea wasn't the only one who'd stopped to linger in the square. She watched a rounded man dressed in a red shirt and matching red shorts, his stark white socks pulled up high and resolute, stroll by with two large huskies. The huskies had their tongues out despite the autumn chill and they walked reluctantly, pulling at the leash that the man held. Even with their sluggish pace, their bearings were straight and proud, their eyes magnificently dark. Lea wondered what it must be like for them in the summer, and felt a sudden urge to knock their red-faced owner down, undo their collars and set them free.

Lea looked up. There they were, a trim, upright woman in a loose silk shift that billowed in the wind, and a man who was slight and thin, wearing a deep maroon shirt that set off the dark glow of his skin. There was something familiar about the man. It was something about his hands, the way they moved from his hips to his elbows to his face.

After speaking to the security guard briefly, the couple pushed the frosted glass doors open and went into the building. Lea waited a few minutes, then crossed the street.

"Hello," she said to the security guard, surprised at how normal her voice sounded.

He looked up from his tablet, face creased in boredom. "Yes?" he asked.

"I'm with them," she bobbed her head towards the building. "The couple that came in earlier."

"Oh," he furrowed his brow. "Oh, yeah, they said someone would be coming. But later. You're not meant to be here so soon."

"God. They keep doing this! Every single time. I mean, how difficult is it to remember —"

The security guard winced. "Why don't you just go on up? It's no big deal."

"Thank you." Lea flashed him a smile.

"No problem." He turned back to his tablet. "Oh," he said without looking up. "Elevators are off. But three flights isn't too bad a climb."

The lobby was cool, cold even, and the only light filtered in through the grime-covered windows. The way the lobby was laid out was not dissimilar to that of

Lea's own office, with the receptionist's desk in the middle of the large, empty space, and the elevators lining the far wall. It was strange to imagine that perhaps the building of glass and steel where Long Term Capital Partners resided would one day be empty too.

Three flights. The stairs had a musty smell to them. She craned her neck and looked up. They were there, somewhere, maybe already in the room where it was meant to happen. The tessellation of steps blurred before her eyes.

She gripped the cold railing to steady herself. Lea started climbing. When she reached the third floor, her breath came in short, sharp bursts, and her heart pounded in her chest. She stepped out into the hallway. It was obvious where they were, for all the doorways were dark except for one.

She would never forget the look on the man's face when she opened the door. His eyes were dark stars in his face, his full lips curled in a surprised O.

"It's you," he said.

His hands were still now, cupped in his lap as if over a fluttering bird eager to escape. He sat in a chair with a black mesh back and shiny silver legs on wheels, the kind of chair that wouldn't look out of place in her own office. The people who'd worked here must have left it behind when they moved out, Lea found herself thinking. She'd already seen the maroon shirt when he was standing outside the building, but now she also saw that he had on clean, pressed grey pants and a pair of dress shoes, midnight black and so shiny that they almost looked plastic.

"Ambrose," Lea said.

She had seen him just last week, he'd sat across from her at WeCovery, partnered with Susan. She'd thought he'd seemed better, calmer. She'd noticed that his posture had improved. He'd been sitting with his feet flat on the floor, rather than having his knees curled up to his chest or his legs crossed on his chair.

He sat like that now. Again, she noticed that his hands were still.

"Lea," he said. "I didn't know . . ." He stopped. A look of surprise flitted across his face, but just as quickly as it appeared, it was gone. "Well, it doesn't matter, does it. What matters is you're here now. Do you have the camera?" He gestured at the large bag slung from Lea's shoulder.

"I — yes, I do." She fumbled with the strap, lowering the bag to the ground.

Her mind raced. Ambrose. She had steeled herself for this, had watched the previous videos over and over till the sick feeling in her stomach receded, till all that was left was an empty, numb spot. She was ready, she'd assured herself and Manuel, she was ready to watch, to film. More than that, it had turned out that the weeks of footage from other Club events and meetings would be useful after all, for GK had said that they now had inextricable evidence that Mrs Jackman had close personal ties with the lieutenants of the group, those who carried out the dirty work, who made the calls, who arranged for the pills, the cameras, the distribution of videos. Lieutenants like Manuel, whose phone call to Lea stating the place and time of Ambrose's suicide had been diligently recorded, diligently sent along. Now all they needed was the final piece. The proof the act had been carried out.

Her hands were cold as she unzipped the bag and lifted the camera out of it.

"Wow," Ambrose said. "That's a large camera. The tripod's set up right here."

He pointed to the three black legs standing about a metre in front of him. He said it matter-of-factly as if they were setting up for a charity dinner.

She screwed the camera onto the silver base. The screws were stiff, and it took her several tries to get it right. It wasn't because her hands were trembling, she told herself, that was not it at all. Finally she had it in the right place. She tightened the latch slowly, then turned the camera so that it was facing Ambrose, taking great care to make sure that he was squarely framed, that the image was straight. The camera found his face and auto-focused. His sharp features came into view.

Ambrose was photogenic, very photogenic. Lea suddenly saw that he was impossibly handsome. He had cut his hair, no doubt in preparation for his appearance, like the shirt, the pants, the shoes. Now that the black curls no longer obscured his face, she saw that his eyes were bright and intelligent, his soft round cheeks smooth like a baby's. She saw that his dark pink lips were full and plump, his neck solid, his shoulders slim and straight. His hands, now so still in his lap, slender like a pianist's.

She wondered if Ambrose played any instruments. She wondered if Ambrose liked music, what he dreamed of at night, if he had ever been in love.

There was a bottle in his hand. He raised it to his mouth and took a small sip, winced a bit.

"What's that? What are you drinking?" Lea said before she could stop herself. The question sprang from her lips like an accusation.

Ambrose frowned. "Surely you know."

"Of course," she said quickly. "Yes. Of course."

He lowered the bottle to the ground and stood up, walking out of the camera frame and over to Lea.

"Are you sure you want to do this?" he said to her in a quiet voice.

Are you sure *you* want to do this? Lea thought, the panic rising in her chest.

"We can always get someone else," he said. "Postpone it. Another day. Do it — do it another day."

The disappointment in his voice was palpable. She thought of her father and his pain. No, Ambrose was not hers to save.

Lea pressed the record button. "I'm sure," she said. "Shall we get started?"

His gaze flickered over her face for a long moment. Finally, he nodded, and went back to his seat.

He gave a short speech, similar to those she had seen in prior videos. They all said the same things. She wondered how much of it had been scripted, who told them what to say. She wondered if they had been pushed into this final, melodramatic act. Ambrose was impressionable, she knew. He seemed calmer now, happier, but who was to really know? Who was to know what Mrs Jackman or Manuel had said to him? If they had made him feel like he had no choice, like what he was doing was noble in some warped way?

When Ambrose lit the match, Lea wasn't thinking of her father, the reason she was here in the first place. She found herself thinking instead of Uju. She thought of the way her mother had lived her life: life-loving, compliant, never complaining. Strong, striving, always striving. Unlike her father, who had run away once, and wanted to run away again.

She thought of the way her mother had died, at the end of her natural predicted lifespan, in a peaceful end-of-life home. The mechanical parts of her body switched off one at a time, one after another, all within the span of twenty-four hours. Perfectly calibrated. Lea thought of the way her mother had held her hand towards the end. The way she'd stared at Lea without blinking, one long, last stare, drinking in her features, before she'd closed her eyes for the last time. As if she wanted to make sure that Lea was the last thing she saw.

Surely it was an insult, what Ambrose was doing? What the Club, Anja, Mrs Jackman, Manuel, what they were all doing. But as she watched Ambrose lift the match to his glistening tongue, she felt no horror, no revulsion, no fear. The flame was growing now. Ambrose kept his eyes on the camera. He kept his eyes on her.

Lea realised that the window was open. Or rather, it no longer had any glass in it, the building being slated for demolition. Through the window came sounds from the outside world, a world that seemed, suddenly, to be unbearably loud. She felt the violent thrum of every passing car in her bones, the shrill squeal of a baby piercing her nerves. Somewhere outside, a dog began to bark, a low, terrible, hungry sound.

Lea watched as the fire engulfed Ambrose. She watched with a kind of fascination, hands gripping the camera so hard that her knuckles turned white. It was horrifying, yes, watching someone burn to death, but it also raised something primal within her, something she didn't understand, something that kept her eyes open and fixated on the scene before her.

She was reminded of Dwight.

Suddenly the feeling rushed back into her hands. Lea ducked around the camera and threw herself to Ambrose's side. She tried to beat the flames with her bare hands, not feeling the heat, not feeling the pain. The smell hit her all of a sudden. It was a terrible, acrid, bitter smell. She tried not to breathe.

It wasn't working — the fire was still going strong. Ambrose was unconscious now, his eyes rolling up in his head. Lea grabbed the empty bottle he'd drunk from, running out into the hallway, heading for the bathroom. She placed its mouth under the faucet and turned the handle, praying that the water was still running. It was, but only at a trickle. Lea's hands were shaking and the bottle mouth was narrow. It seemed to take forever to fill it just halfway.

When it was full she ran back to the room, spilling water over her legs and feet. But when she got back, the flames had already gone out. DiamondSkin^{TM}, she thought, thank goodness. It wouldn't burn. It didn't work.

Ambrose lay curled on his side, the legs of his pants burnt to ash. She crouched over him and shook his shoulder.

"Ambrose," she said softly. He didn't move. Lea pulled on his shoulder, turning him face up.

When she saw his face, her hands stopped shaking. She placed the bottle of water on the floor carefully, as if all that mattered in the world was that it should not spill.

CHAPTER
THIRTY

Anja was in the kitchen when the officers showed up. The dishwasher had broken down yet again and she had been landed with sink duty. Sweat dripped down her forehead into her eyes as she scrubbed oily plates, her fingers swollen and wrinkled with soapy water. The pile of dirty plates only seemed to get higher, no matter how quickly she scrubbed, so she didn't hear the commotion until Rosalie called her over to the entryway with a low hiss.

She knew immediately that something was wrong. Rosalie never left the fryers during lunchtime, not even to go to the bathroom. Even more ominous was the quiet outside that she only noticed now, several times lower in volume than the usual peak-hour chaos.

Anja turned the tap off and wiped her hands on her jeans. She heard voices coming from outside, but couldn't make out what they were saying. Walking over to where Rosalie was peeking out of the kitchen, she stuck her head into the entryway as well.

There were three of them, two male and one female, all neatly turned out in a mass of shiny buckles and navy blue. Police badges were emblazoned across their hats and sleeves.

276

They stood around Halimah, the daughter of the diner's owner. She twirled a tight curl of black hair around her index finger, nodding as she spoke.

"No, nothing like that at all," she was saying. "He never behaved like anything you're describing."

"How about the people he knew?" one of the male officers asked. He had a mean, squarish face, with the small shallow-set eyes of a hammerhead shark. None of the officers held tablets. They stood with their hands in their pockets or on their hips, as if having a casual chat while picking up some coffee. Still, the diner was quiet, and all eyes were on them.

Halimah tipped her head to the side. "I didn't know who he knew. Do you see the state of this place? We're so overworked, I can hardly keep track of my own acquaintances, let alone all of my staff's."

"Any suspicious characters ever show up to work?" the shark-faced policeman went on.

"Suspicious characters? Depends on what you mean. This is an Outer Boroughs diner, officer, not some fancy Borough Two veggie bar." A note of impatience crept into Halimah's voice. She raised the toes of her left foot, balancing on her heel, a sign that Anja knew all too well meant her temper was flaring.

The policeman blinked. "Do you realise how serious this is? We could have you shut down, just like that . . ." He snapped his fingers. "If you don't feel the need to cooperate. Just the association with someone like him."

Halimah eyed him carefully.

"I am cooperating. Of course I am," she said in a conciliatory tone. "It's just — well, this isn't very good for business, you know." She gestured around at the half-empty diner. The remaining customers barely touched their food, and were all watching wide-eyed.

"I understand," the officer said, not sounding as if he understood at all. He pulled out what appeared to be a postcard. "Have you ever seen this man?"

Halimah studied the photo, her eyebrows and lips pinching together. Finally she shook her head.

"No, never seen him. Who is he?"

The officers looked at each other. They seemed to be able to communicate without speaking. The other male officer, who had an altogether kinder face and voice, said, "Drug dealer. The worst kind."

"Oh?" Halimah was interested now. She peered again at the photo, and seemed disappointed that she'd never seen him before. "And you're saying Branko's mixed up with this guy?"

Anja's heart dropped. *I have a guy*, Branko had said.

Again the officers looked at each other. "Branko was caught buying from him," the one holding the picture said. "We took him into custody. He says the pills were for himself, but, well . . . It doesn't add up. Can you think of anyone he knew who might want something like that? Anyone who showed signs of antisocial behaviour, mental instability, morbidness?"

Halimah shook her head again. "I can't say, sorry. Didn't know him that well. You can talk to the rest of the staff though . . ." She gestured at Raj, who was stacking glasses behind the bar. "They're a tight bunch. Might be able to tell you more."

The officer nodded. "Thanks for your time. We'll hang around for a bit then, if that's okay."

Halimah crossed her arms and nodded. "More of them in the back," she said, jerking a thumb towards the kitchen.

Anja leaned out of the doorway, heart pounding and hands sweaty. She pressed the side of her head against the sticky, oil-splattered wall, and tried to think.

"Cute, isn't he?" Rosalie whispered, still looking out of the kitchen. "I think he's giving me the eye."

When Anja didn't answer, she turned towards her. "Did you see him? The tall one, with the beady eyes? Hey, you okay?"

Anja's head was spinning. The heat of the kitchen seemed to thicken, an animal squeezing her till she couldn't breathe.

Rosalie took a step towards her. "Anja?" she said, reaching out to touch her forearm.

At the touch of Rosalie's cool fingers, Anja snapped back into herself.

"I'm fine," she said. "It's just so hot in here." She made a show of pulling at her shirt collar.

"Now you see what I have to deal with every day. Standing at the hob ten hours at a go, breathing in this rank air, sweating like a pig. And for no thanks at all," Rosalie grumbled. But then her eyes softened. "You're not used to it. Poor thing. Why don't you go out and get some fresh air?"

Anja nodded and pulled off her apron. She shot a quick glance in the direction of the door, her heart still pounding in her chest.

"Don't worry about those guys. They'll probably just ask you the same questions all over again. The whole thing is sad, really, you'd never guess Branko was the sort."

Anja opened her mouth to protest. But then she pressed her lips together and nodded slowly, as if to say yes, you'd never guess. "I'll be back in a bit."

She tore her apron off, dropping it onto the floor. She left through the back door, stepping out into the empty alleyway where they often stood around during breaks, hiding from Halimah.

Branko in custody — what did that mean? Was he locked up? Being interrogated? In prison?

She stood in the alleyway holding her elbows, thinking of Branko alone and locked up. Stupid, stupid, stupid, stupid. Why had he done it? She remembered the look on his face when he had told her about his "guy", the hurt in his eyes when she'd turned him down. Stupid, kind, brave Branko. He hadn't told them about her, she was sure, otherwise they would have already come looking.

He hadn't told them about her. Carrying T-pills was a serious crime, federal, she imagined. Suddenly her bones felt too heavy for her body. She had done nothing to deserve Branko's loyalty. Something swelled in her chest, spilling out of her eyes.

But then she wiped her cheeks. There was no point — she could do nothing for him. Besides, even if Branko didn't give her up, they would figure it out soon. A non-lifer buying T-pills made no sense. They would check the records, find out she was the only lifer he knew, probably find out about her mother, WeCovery, the Club, everything else too. Then she'd be thrown in jail, and her mother sent to a farm to decompose with thousands of other sub-human bodies.

Anja began to walk towards the harbour. As she walked she felt a hot energy humming in her ears, coursing through her veins, and soon, she broke into a run. The tops of buildings were jagged against the spotless blue sky. Nearby, a woman leaned out of a window in a low, skeletal house, holding a bundle of laundry in her arms. A loud cry, the laundry squirmed, and Anja saw that it was a baby. The woman seemed to be watching her run.

When she arrived at the harbour the ferry was poised to leave, the last of the languid crowds slipping off the gangway. Slowing to a walk, Anja boarded the ferry. A lady with raisin skin and a bright fuchsia hat turned to look at her.

"In a hurry, honey?" She smiled, revealing pointed yellow incisors.

Anja smiled back, but didn't answer. Would they question the lady later, when they traced Anja's footsteps, along with everyone else on the two thirty-five ferry? Would they ask if she had said anything, seemed unusual, exhibited signs of dangerous psychosis? She pushed the thoughts out of her mind and headed to the deck outside. It was almost empty, for the day was sharp and cold, and most knew how strong the winds were. The only people outside were tourists, taking videos of themselves with their tablets on sticks, recording their faces against the dull grey steel of the water.

The ferry began moving, and the wind sped up against her cheeks. As the wind gathered strength, it seemed to be flaying off a layer of skin from her face, revealing something soft and new beneath. Anja fixed her eyes on the harbour, watching it get smaller and smaller as they pulled away from the shore. The boat rumbled beneath her feet, sending vibrations through her knees and hips, a comforting engine drone.

She wondered if it would be the last time she saw Staten Island. Her plan seemed more unlikely now, out on the water, as the old ferry groaned and grumbled its way towards the other gleaming shore.

Where would they go, even if she did somehow manage to transport her mother in her current state? Anja felt a sudden chill as she thought of moving her mother.

Anja hadn't touched her in months. The last time she had, it had been shortly after her mother stopped speaking, when she'd realised that she hadn't bathed her for several weeks. So Anja had filled the plastic basin with water from the communal bathroom, waiting five minutes for the hot water to run, and brought it back to their room. She'd placed the basin down onto the bedside table, and lifted the comforter off her mother's chest. This was before her skin had started to turn, back when her cheeks were beginning to hollow out but she still looked like herself.

When Anja had touched her mother's arm, her fingers seemed to come away damp. She'd paused, and touched the bony arm again, this time running her fingers lightly across the crinkled skin. Sure enough, she hadn't imagined it. Her mother's skin was faintly sticky, like old rubber that had started to melt. Anja had pulled her fingers away as if she'd been burnt. She'd examined her fingertips, but they appeared to be clean. She'd examined the place where she had just touched her mother's forearm. There was nothing that distinguished it from the surrounding skin.

Anja had sat motionless for some time, listening to the sounds of the city dimly filtering through the thin walls. Then she'd stood, picked up the basin of water and poured it down the sink. She hadn't touched her mother again.

That had been months ago. Now, she had visions of her fingers sinking into her mother's flesh, of the bones snapping under her weight. She saw her mother's face sliding off when she sat her upright.

"Pretty, isn't it?"

Anja jumped. She seemed to feel her brain bounce against the top of her skull.

"Sorry, honey, didn't mean to frighten you." It was the lady from before, the one with the canine teeth and the crumpled face. She wore a faded blue scarf wrapped around her hair.

"That's okay," Anja said shortly, turning back towards the water.

"Aren't you cold, dressed like that?" The lady unfurled a claw in the direction of Anja's bare arms.

"No, I'm fine," Anja said, adding: "Thank you."

"You foreign? You look foreign," the lady went on, undeterred.

Anja turned towards her. Her eyes, she saw now, were bright and unfocused, darting about even as she spoke, and her hands seemed to have a life of their own. Her fingers shook at her hips, as if playing an invisible piano.

"Not really," Anja said, kindly now. "I've been here a long time."

"Oh. You have family here then?" The lady blinked rapidly. Her eyelashes were long but very pale.

Anja looked down at the grey water again. A plastic bottle bobbed past on the lightly foaming waves.

"I do," she said. "My whole family is here." Her fingers gripped the cold railing, knuckles whitening against her goosebumps.

"How lovely. My family used to be here too, once. Not any more though. Now it's just me." She spat words out in quick succession. "You have a child? Son? Daughter?"

"No," Anja said. "But we're trying, my husband and I. Anyway, we have our parents to keep us busy. They all live in the city too. Sometimes I cook dinner, a nice roast veg pot, and they all come over to visit. My husband, he likes that you know. His brother comes too, with his little niece."

"Lovely, lovely," the lady said, her eyes wide and dreamy. "And what do you drink with these dinners? Do you have a drop then? A nice drop of red? Or white, you look more like a white kind of girl."

284

"Yes," Anja said. Why not go all out, now that she'd started? "We have a bit of red. No more than the recommended monthly intake, of course, but that's the only time we do it, so we can each have a full glass. My husband's father — he has connections in Europe, so he gets bottles sent from Italy."

"Italy," the lady said. "Nice place. Warm. I always thought I'd go, once."

When Anja didn't respond, she turned to look at the water as well. After watching the waves roll past for some time, the lady said: "What's your husband's name?"

"Branko," Anja answered.

The wind whipped her hair about her face, tickling her cheeks. She looked back towards Staten Island, which was only a faint darkness in the fog now.

When the ferry docked in the harbour, Anja bid the lady goodbye. She had been mostly silent for the rest of the trip, leaning her torso over the railings and pushing her face into the wind.

"Goodbye," she said in return, smiling to show those jagged teeth again. "Give my regards to Branko."

Anja nodded and turned away. Soon she was lost in the stream of people coming off the ferry.

The noise of Manhattan hit her like a brick wall, a solid slap in the face. A thick cloud of sound, woven tightly of individual threads — the roar of conversation, the thumping footfall of the walking throngs, the dull gratings and booms of various construction sites, sirens, helicopter wings, music, the great soft whoosh of the Hudson.

285

There was something comforting about being slapped in the face, Anja thought as she plunged into the moving crowd on the sidewalk. Something satisfying about being hit, hard, to emerge ears ringing and nose bleeding, tendons throbbing, alive. How strange it was that it was a city like this that first produced lifers, those smooth-skinned, long-limbed islands, whose entire beings were dedicated towards only ever skimming the surface. How could they do it, she wondered, in a place like this?

She wondered what they would do if they got back to Sweden. Perhaps there, she'd find a doctor who would be willing to put an end to her mother's suffering, have a proper funeral. She'd asked her mother once where she wanted her ashes to be scattered, for Anja had thought it would be nice to have them thrown in the Baltic Sea, next to their home. Her mother had said it didn't matter. She didn't believe in symbolism or rituals or afterlife, and she thought it was a silly, sentimental question. She didn't see how it would affect her, for she would already be gone. She didn't see that it wasn't for her.

Nevertheless, Anja would scatter her mother's ashes in the sea. As she pushed through the afternoon sidewalk traffic, Anja imagined carrying an urn to the beach. She would do it in the morning, just after sunrise. She'd stand on the surf, weak waves caressing her feet, sand shifting under her heels. The water would be so cold it burned, and the jellyfish, harmless and luminescent, would be plentiful. Some would already be stranded and dying on the sand as the tide went out, inert half spheres of solid water, fat droplets of morning dew studding the shoreline.

She'd lift the top off the urn, dig her fingers in, marvel at how light the grains were, more like dust than sand. Then she'd fling one hand out towards the rising sun and the waking sea. Her mother would be taken by the wind.

CHAPTER
THIRTY-ONE

When Anja unlocked the door, the smell of the room rushed out at her, filling her nostrils and head, bringing the usual sense of helpless dread. Her mother lay exactly where she had left her. Everything in the room was exactly as she had left it.

Anja walked over to the corner of the room and knelt down. She prised a floorboard loose and pulled out the stacks of cash within, half-heartedly beginning to count them. She already knew how much was there — she knew that it wasn't enough. She could maybe manage to get hold of a car. But what then? What about the fuel and tolls and food?

She was still there, kneeling on the floorboards, when she heard the footsteps coming up the hallway outside. She could recognise the steps of all their neighbours, and this wasn't any of them. These footsteps were loud and confident, business-like, the gait of someone who felt assured of their place in the world, of their right to walk down hallways.

Anja froze. How could they have found her so quickly? She'd left the diner only a few hours earlier. Surely they hadn't finished interrogating everyone else yet. Or maybe Rosalie had let slip that Anja had left, maybe her disappearance had aroused suspicion.

She listened as the footsteps drew closer, closer still, until they stopped right outside her door. Silence, a pause. Then three sharp raps — *Thock, thock, thock.*

Anja sprang to her feet. Looking down, she realised she was still holding the wads of cash. She stuck them quickly into the waistband of her pants, pulling her loose shirt over the top to hide the bulge. She kicked the floorboard back in place.

They were knocking again. The knocks were more insistent now, in quicker succession, demanding to be heard.

Anja looked over to her mother. At a distance, she could almost imagine she was still herself, taking a nap while Anja tidied the house. From where she stood she couldn't see the translucent skin or the glassy eyelids, though she could still hear her heart, pumping away.

She braced herself — for what exactly? Perhaps they would break down the door, take her away in handcuffs. Perhaps this would be the last time she would ever see her mother. She'd receive an address and a number of months later, in prison, the exact lot in the farm she'd been sent to. She'd never be able to visit, of course, even if she wasn't in prison. People weren't allowed into the farms. It made you wonder what they did there, what was so unsettling that relatives weren't allowed to see.

She would deliver herself into their hands. There would be no more choices to be made, no more responsibility to even try. She'd done her best, surely her mother would understand. So Anja took one last look at her mother's face, then she walked towards the door. They wouldn't have to break it down, there would be no need for noise and violence and struggling.

Anja opened the door, expecting to see the shark-faced officer and his colleagues surrounding the entryway. But they weren't there.

"Anja. Hi."

It took a moment for the slight, dark figure in front of her to resolve into focus.

"Lea?" Anja said. "What — what are you doing here?"

Lea looked down the hallway, as if she expected someone to be there. She tucked a strand of hair behind her ear. Anja observed that it appeared slightly greasy, as if she hadn't showered today.

"Do you mind if I come in?" she said. "If it's not a bad time?"

It was. But something in Lea's voice made Anja forget her own situation for a moment.

"Sure, come in."

Lea stepped through the doorway and closed the door behind her. She didn't go any further, standing as if glued to where she stood, hands frozen to her side. Her eyes darted around the room, from the water-stained walls to the dusty window to the creaking slanted floors. Finally they came to rest on the bed.

"My mother," Anja said. She stopped. How to explain?

Lea nodded slowly, paused, nodded again. Her eyes were still fixed on the bed.

It was odd having Lea there. The soft cream silk of her blouse, the slim tailored drop of her skirt, the tilt of her chin — all of it seemed to call out the meagreness of the room, make the ceiling seem lower and the walls dirtier. Anja shifted from one foot to the other.

"Was there something you wanted to talk about?"

"Is she . . ." Lea stopped. The word seemed stuck in her throat.

"Alive? It's okay, you can say it. She can't hear you, anyway."

"I wasn't worried about her," Lea said. When her eyes met Anja's, they were filled with tears.

Something caught in Anja's chest. She wasn't prepared for this. She was prepared to give her mother up, to turn herself in, to be called a monster and a criminal. To have things taken out of her hands. But not this.

She bit her lip. "How did you find out where I live?"

"George. I called him," Lea said. "He thought I was Susan, at first." A smile tugged at the corners of her lips.

Laughter bubbled up in Anja's chest. It felt good to laugh, felt good to be standing here with Lea, even given the circumstances.

"Of course he did." Anja paused and looked around. "Can I offer you — well, we don't have much, really." She walked over to the sink and pulled out a small tin from the cabinet underneath. Opening it, she saw that there were two tea bags left. "Tea? We'll have to use hot water from the sink though, we don't have a kettle."

"Sure," Lea said, in a low voice.

Anja turned. Lea was no longer looking at her mother. Her eyes were cast to the ground, her arms folded rigidly across her chest. She was kneading the loose skin on opposite elbows with her fingers. A deep frown creased her forehead, something Anja had never seen her do before.

"You alright?" Anja said.

Lea looked up. "Ambrose," she said in a rush. "Did you know?"

Anja looked up from the sink. She thought for a moment and realised what day it was. Ambrose, of course. But how did Lea know?

"Cameraman dropped out. Manuel asked me to fill in," Lea said, as if reading Anja's mind. "So — so I did."

The mug she held under the faucet was now overflowing. She turned the tap off.

Fuck, Manuel. Anja made a mental note to have a word with Mrs Jackman. He'd always been reckless, but this was a different matter altogether.

"I'm sorry, Lea," Anja said. "That never should have happened. Not like that. Not when you're new, not without the training or the preparation. Are you okay?"

The sound of Anja's mother's heart filled the pause that followed. She wondered if Lea could hear it too.

"How can you do this?" Lea said. Her mouth twisted.

"What do you mean?"

"*This*. The Club. Ambrose. Your . . ." The words stuck in her throat. She gestured towards Anja's mother.

292

Anja turned away from Lea's accusing eyes. She submerged the tea bags and watched the rust leak out of them. She brought the mugs over to where Lea was standing and offered her one. Lea stared down at the mug as if she didn't understand what it was. Anja set it down onto the bedside table gently.

"I didn't do this," Anja said, looking at her mother. "My mother did it to herself. Misalignment — that's what happens. You've probably never seen it before."

"So . . . what?" Lea said. "That's why you're running the Club? That's the reason to let vulnerable people like — like Ambrose kill themselves?"

Anja's eyes flashed. "They're not *vulnerable*. They're making a choice. An informed choice."

"Have you seen Ambrose? Have you heard him in WeCovery? You think he's making an 'informed choice'?"

Anja took a sip of the tea. The tepid liquid slipped down her throat, unsatisfying. Her heart pounded in her chest. She didn't need to hear this now, least of all from Lea. What did she know? She was just like the rest of them, all the other self-satisfied, comfortable, unquestioning lifers, pushing their dogma on everyone else. Pushing their dogma on people like her mother.

"Look," Lea said in a low voice. Her eyes flickered towards Anja's mother. "I get it. I think. Where you're coming from. It can't be easy, to have your mother like this. But that doesn't mean the alternative is right."

Anja sighed. It wasn't the first time she was having this conversation, though it was the first time she was having it with someone else. These were the thoughts that raged inside her head every night. As if she hadn't heard it all before.

"You can't possibly understand," Anja said. "I'm sorry you had to witness Ambrose's death, that shouldn't have happened. But you were the one who wanted to get involved, you were the one who asked me to put you in touch with the Club. You came to the meetings, you volunteered. You said yes when Manuel called you."

Lea was silent. When she spoke again, her voice was quiet.

"May I?" she said, taking a step towards Anja's mother's bed.

Anja nodded. Lea walked up to the bed and sat in the chair that Anja normally occupied.

Her gaze took in the stained skin, the hollow chest, the milky eyes, the beating heart. The smell must have been overwhelming for her, Anja thought, for she wasn't used to it. But Lea showed no signs of disgust.

Lea reached a hand towards Anja's mother's face. Anja started to warn her but then stopped. She watched as Lea rested her fingers on her mother's skull, where her hair had once been. Lea didn't pull her fingers away, didn't look at them in horror, didn't scream. She seemed to be listening.

"You're right," Lea said. "I mean, of course you are. She's still alive. You can feel it."

She took her hand away and placed it on her lap.

"I'm sorry," Lea said.

"It's fine," Anja said. She was tired, and wished that Lea would go.

294

"You said I couldn't possibly understand. But I do. I was there, at the party. Where Dominique was — was — well. You know." Lea stopped.

How could she have been there? Anja frowned, running through the sequence of events in her mind. No, she had certainly not invited her. That came only after.

"I followed someone there. You met him, I saw you talking to him," Lea went on. Her voice was calm now, the accusatory note gone. "An older man, monoethnic, Asian. His name is Kaito."

Kaito. Yes, Anja remembered him. The wanderer. The kind, quiet man who you'd have thought would be quite content to be at home. Yet he had gone out into the world, seen all that, decided it was enough. He'd had a lot of pain. Said something about outliving a son, she remembered. A non-lifer.

"Kaito Kirino," Lea said, staring straight at Anja.

"Kirino. You mean . . ."

Lea nodded.

"Oh Lea," Anja said. It all made sense now.

Lea's hands were in her pockets, worrying some fingernail or lint ball, and her teeth ground down on her lips. "Aren't there special dispensations for cases like these?" she said, staring at Anja's mother again. "How many others are there like this?"

She shrugged. "Who knows?"

"And what, you're just expected to wait until she — her body — stops?" Lea narrowed her eyes. "Just like that?"

"No, there are — places. Hospices, they call them, but really they're just warehouses. And they're expensive, non-subsidised, if you have black market replacements. So if you can't pay — and of course most of us can't — you send them to the farms — same thing, but they use the decomposing bodies for nutrients."

It didn't make her wince or cry to talk about it. Strangely, she felt better, stronger, just by Lea being here. She would get a car, she thought, after Lea left. She would go to the Markets.

Lea was shaking her head. "It seems wrong. I wish I could help you."

Anja nodded. There was a lump in her throat.

"Surely in situations like this, the Sanctity of Life directive doesn't hold," Lea went on. "Or the Club could help! Can't they could do something?"

Anja swallowed, still thinking of Lea's father. "That's not the problem."

"You can't bear to," Lea said, the realisation dawning slowly. "You could do it, of course you could. T-pills. But you don't want to."

Anja blinked.

"So then surely you understand?" Lea said, her voice rising. "You know what it must be like, for me? I can't let my father do this. Can't you help? Can't you stop him?"

Anja felt a hot pressure gathering behind her eyes. She didn't know what it was like, no. She'd lost her mother, but it had been a different kind of loss, for her mother was, in theory, still there. It had been a slow, gradual loss. The kind of loss that seeped in from under the door like a poisonous gas, slowly filling the room, killing the plants, making you numb inside before you even realised it was there.

But she didn't know how to tell Lea this. She didn't know how to tell her that helping people like Ambrose was the only thing that, since her mother had taken to bed, had made her feel useful, less powerless. That if she couldn't help her mother die, at least she could help others.

"I can't make him do anything he doesn't want to do," Anja said. "You realise, he doesn't need us to help him die. He could do it himself, easily. He's come to us because he wants his death to be useful, because he believes in something. But even if I say no, even if I didn't allow it to happen, because yes, I could . . . Even then, he would simply find another way."

Anja saw the realisation hit Lea. It seemed strange that she hadn't thought of it before, but Anja understood. She understood the tunnel vision, the sheer force of will that arose in situations like that. She knew what Lea must have been thinking, for she had thought something similar before.

If only I could get hold of T-pills. If only the clinics would help. If only the Club would. If only. If only, if only, if only. It had taken Anja a long time to realise that the problem had never been the rest of the world.

"Right," Lea said. "Right. Another way. I see."

Anja felt sorry for her, but there was nothing she could do. She had her own problems to deal with, for time was running out.

"I'm sorry, Lea," Anja said firmly. "But you'll have to go now."

Lea stared at her, as if not comprehending. But then the air seemed to go out of her. She nodded and turned to leave.

At the door, she stopped, looking at Anja's mother one last time.

"Good luck," Lea said. Her cheeks were flushed and her eyes glittered. What was she thinking? "Good luck to the both of us."

Before Anja could reply, Lea turned and left. The door clicked shut.

And then it was just her again; her and her mother.

CHAPTER
THIRTY-TWO

Back out on the street, Lea shivered in the evening chill that was beginning to descend. Orange rays cut through the slits between buildings, casting long shadows over the streets. The foot traffic was lighter now, it was just after rush hour and people would be at home, downing their daily nutrient rations or working out in their condominium gyms. She imagined her office building emptied out, each floor dimly lit by the soft after-hours light. She imagined Jiang with his wife at home, sitting with his feet up on the coffee table, still reading emails on his tab. She imagined Natalie, probably in a place not dissimilar to her own apartment.

She thought of Ambrose. Of Anja's mother, of Anja. Of Kaito. Lea felt a heaviness in her lower back, as if the weight of all their problems, all their pain, had crept into her body, wrapped itself around the base of her spine, settled there. Calcified, anchored, immovable.

Lea began to walk home. Anja's mother hadn't repulsed her, strangely. She'd been more shocked by the size of the room, the filthy window, the cobwebbed ceiling and dark corners. A contrast with the Club's private dining and lavish parties.

But towards Anja's mother herself, Lea had only felt a pull of curiosity. She wanted to peer into the mechanical workings of that body, to see where the whirrings came from, how tissue welded to silicone, to feel the viscosity of the dark SmartBlood™ that ran through her veins. The same fluid ran through her own, Lea realised with a jolt. She brought a hand to her neck, felt the push of it against the soft hollow under her jaw and imagined the colour, the same thick brown that she'd seen in Anja's mother today.

If it were Kaito lying there, what would she do? Lea pushed the thought out of her head. It was ridiculous, it would never happen. Not with her around. Not with what she was planning to do, now that she had GK on her side. She would make the Third Wave and then she'd ensure that Kaito would make it too.

Lea would fix it.

When she got home, Lea fell into bed, fully clothed. The fatigue weighed on her and she felt heavy, more tired than she had ever been. Sliding her legs under the covers, she closed her eyes with the light still on, falling almost immediately into a deep, dreamless sleep.

Lea awoke slowly the next morning. Despite still being in her clothes from yesterday, and not having brushed her teeth last night, she felt surprisingly fresh, as if a great weight had been lifted. But then she saw Ambrose's eyes, opaque as the night sky, unblinking, unwavering, and it all came back to her.

She sat on the edge of her bed. The weight at the base of her spine had spread to her abdomen, and she could tell it was spreading still.

In the bathroom, she stepped slowly out of her clothes, letting each article drop to the cold marble floor. She would pick it up later, she thought, mentally adding this to the list of things she had to do after breakfast.

As she went to run the bath, something made her turn towards the mirror. She stopped, straightened up and squared her shoulders. Her stomach and her glutes clenched, her hips tilted and her neck lengthened. Still, there was no missing it. Lea saw the way her abdomen and her breasts sagged. She spotted a crease at the base of her neck, and a faint liver spot on her left bicep. A bulging vein crossed the front of one of her shins, a wrinkled worm under the skin.

She drew a finger over the vein, tracing the dark green length of it. When she reached her knee, she started over, harder this time. And then again, with her fingernail. It didn't draw blood, but the smarting felt good.

Lea stepped into the bath. The water was so hot that her limbs felt like they'd been flayed. She pinched her nose between finger and thumb, and slowly dunked her head as well. The heat entered her ears and made her head pound.

She took her time, carefully exfoliating with the loofah that she rarely had the time to use. She scrubbed herself till her skin was red and soft. She imagined scrubbing the vein on her shin away, scrubbing the bulge of her stomach flat. When she was done she unplugged the bath. It made a loud, gasping noise, the sound of a person drowning. Lea rinsed herself off in ice cold water, feeling her pores expand and contract, relishing the numb burn that made it feel like she was wearing armour.

Towelling herself dry, she looked at herself in the mirror again. The vein was still there, as was the liver spot and the soft middle. The image of Anja's mother flashed into her mind suddenly, the raw, translucent length of her.

She would put the furniture back where it belonged, she thought. The sofa legs screeched against the polished floors, and when she looked down she saw a long white scratch across the wooden boards. Lea kicked the sofa leg with the ball of her foot, careful to curl her toes up, but it still hurt.

"Lea?" A muffled voice. Then a knock at the front door.

Lea glared at the door. She hobbled over and looked through the peephole.

A large bouquet of white flowers, peonies or garden roses of some kind, nearly obscured his face. But as he shifted, she saw that it was Todd, dressed in a neat blue shirt and a maroon bow tie, the same bow tie he'd worn at her birthday party not that long ago.

She let the peephole shutter fall.

"What do you want, Todd?" she called back through the door.

"I just want to talk," he said. "Can I come in?"

Lea wondered if it was a trap, if Ministry men in white coats were standing just around the corner waiting to put her into a straitjacket as she came out. She wondered how much Todd had told them about the last time she saw him. Todd was a coward. He wouldn't come back here alone, like this, after what happened.

"I don't think we have anything to talk about," she said, walking back to where the sofa lay askew. She picked up one end of it again. It sagged in her hands. It seemed heavier than before.

"Please, Lea," he said. "I want to apologise."

He wanted to apologise. Lea's lip lifted, baring her upper teeth. She dropped the sofa again. Now this she had to hear.

Lea marched back to the door and opened it with the chain still on.

"Are you alone?" she said through the crack.

Todd lowered the flowers. His face was meek and tanned, as chiselled and square-jawed as she remembered him. Better than she remembered him. Lea felt a tightening in her abdomen.

"Of course I'm alone," he said, frowning. "Who would be with me?"

Lea studied his face for a moment. He was wearing his best child-like expression, eyes unblinking and lips pushed out ever so slightly, glossy with spit.

She shut the door again, unlatched and opened it. Taking half a step out into the hallway, she looked left and right. It was empty. Finally she looked back at Todd.

Annoyingly, he seemed broader than before, more defined in the deltoids and lighter around the hips. He had grown out his facial hair ever so slightly so that his jaw was now covered in even blond fuzz, like neat grass on a rich person's lawn. Lea felt the same tug in the pit of her stomach, and she folded her arms.

Perhaps she would have sex with him, she thought suddenly, in the hallway, there and then. She took a half step towards him, and inhaled the soapy, boyish smell of him. She would push him to the floor and sit on his face. Todd stepped back and thrust the flowers forward. Lea sighed. She took them from him and dropped them on the floor behind her.

"So, tell me," she said. "You're sorry."

Lea placed the tips of her fingers on Todd's hard chest.

"Lea," he said. "It's good to see you. You look . . ." He paused. She saw him take in her tired skin, her limp wet hair. His face softened into something that looked like pity.

Lea let one hand drop to his left nipple, the other to his groin. She felt Todd jump and stiffen, felt a tremble run through him.

"Go on," she said. "Tell me what you're sorry for." Lea felt a predatory urge rise up in her chest. The frustration of the past weeks sharpened to a point. She tightened her grip and smiled as Todd winced. He was hard now, despite the discomfort on his face. She noticed that the maroon bow tie he was wearing was covered in tiny pink dots.

"I'm sorry for reporting on you," he said, his voice uneven, the rhythm of his words unnaturally quick. "I thought — I thought I was helping."

"Really," Lea said, unbuckling his belt now. Todd moved to stop her, but she kept going.

"Lea," he hissed. "What are you doing? I came to talk."

"Then talk." She pulled his cock out. It was in that confused, semi-aroused state, as if held up by an invisible string at its tip.

"Lea," Todd said. His cheeks were red, his eyes blinking rapidly. Such pretty eyelashes, Lea thought. Todd's breath quickened and he flushed even deeper. Was he going to cry?

He didn't try to stop her after that. Lea pulled him into the apartment, closing the door behind him.

They did it on the floor, her on top, him meek and pliable. She almost forgot all of it, Anja and her mother and the Club, as she clasped Todd's rough cheeks between her thighs, bore down on his soft mouth. Sitting on him like that she could break his neck, she thought to herself absently. Lea admired the obedient hard knot of his body bucking beneath her legs. Despite his faults, he was an undeniably beautiful man, she thought.

When they finished she pulled herself onto his stomach and sat straddling him.

"So do you forgive me?" he said, in such a small voice that it almost made her feel guilty. But then she remembered the same look on his face when she found out he'd been reporting on her, and she stayed silent.

"I was saying," he said. "You didn't let me finish. But I thought I was helping. I only realised what I'd done, really, yesterday, when they told me."

Lea stiffened. "Told you what? Who?" she said.

Todd turned his head to the side and spoke quietly, almost under his breath. A lock of curly blond hair fell over his right eye. "I'm not supposed to tell anyone, not until it's all publicly announced. But they've started notifying people already."

Her hands turned cold.

"It's the Third Wave, Lea. Who knew it would be so soon? But they say it's real. And we're to be among the first." There was a quiet wonder in his voice, a seriousness that she hadn't heard before. Suddenly Todd sounded much older, and much more tired.

Lea pressed one hand onto his chest.

"What do you mean?" she said. "What do you mean we're to be the first?"

Todd turned his face back up to look at her.

"I'm sorry, I meant we as in — I'm sorry" he stumbled. "I was notified, you see," he tried again. "And I realised, well, maybe you were too. Were you, Lea?" He searched her face, but the pity in his eyes told her that he already knew. He'd guessed, or he'd asked, or somehow he'd found out.

Lea leant into his face, until her nose was just inches away from his. She placed her hands around his neck and felt how thick and solid it was, but how warm. She imagined the colour of the SmartBlood^{TM} within.

She squeezed his neck a little, felt him start to panic underneath her.

"Lea," he said, eyes widening. She kept squeezing, just gently, just playing.

"Lea!" he shouted, bucking his hips and throwing her off to the side.

Lea tumbled to the cold floor. Her elbow exploded in a burst of pain.

Todd was standing over her now.

"Jesus Christ, Lea. What's wrong with you?" He rubbed the back of his neck and stretched out an arm. "I'm sorry," he repeated, suddenly contrite again. "Did I hurt you? I'm sorry."

Lea grabbed her elbow and tried to straighten her arm. It wouldn't move.

"Come on, Lea," Todd said. "I came to say maybe we can fix it together. Now that I've been notified. Maybe I can put in a good word for you."

Maybe they could fix it together. Maybe they could. She thought of the footage of Ambrose's death, of her conversation with Anja, sitting in the tiny memory card of the buttonhole camera, yet to be sent to GK. What was she waiting for? Why hadn't she sent it yet, exonerated herself, gone back to normal? Todd could move back in. She could go back to work.

But as Lea stared into Todd's perfect, golden eyes, she realised she didn't want to. That was why. Her old life seemed like a distant reality, a hollow one, laughably so. She could not imagine being back in her office, sitting behind her desk, talking to moneyed clients about wealth that was enough to last several lifetimes that they would not have. She could not imagine carrying on with Todd, going to vitamin spritz

— filled parties, gossiping about whose physical trainer had slept with whose client, whispering about each others' numbers in hushed tones behind cupped hands.

What did she want, then?

The answer came in a rush.

"I have to go," she said to Todd.

"Where?" His immediate look of suspicion didn't bother her now. It didn't matter what Todd thought, it didn't matter what any of them thought.

She stood up and began to dress. When she was done, she grabbed her purse and looked around at her apartment. Suddenly she felt an odd sense of loss, as if she would never see it again. But even then she felt the knot in her abdomen lifting, felt a strange, free, reckless tickle in her throat.

"Where are you going, Lea?" Todd said again, still lying on the floor.

"Bye, Todd," Lea said. Not waiting for an answer, she closed the door behind her.

CHAPTER
THIRTY-THREE

The flowers were beginning to wilt. Huge bulbous peonies in violent corals and heavy white roses strained to open, their thick petals peeling backwards obscenely, revealing powdery orange centres. Slumping over in their crystal vases, naked stems starting to give under the weight. The balloons were sinking too, helium leaking into the dense cloud of human breath. While there were so many that the ceiling was still filled, some floated at half mast, their tasselled tails trailing along the floor.

The other children were fidgeting, casting sulky gazes towards the cake. Parents stroked silky heads, cooed into small ears. *Just a little longer*, they whispered. *Be good.* Lea felt they were all looking at her surreptitiously — first at her, then her mother, who fluttered about dispensing vegetable punch and good humour, smoothing tantrums and assuaging concerns.

Her mother was behind her. Lea knew from the smell — a sharp, summery perfume, but also the salty sweet undertone of her body, a smell so indistinguishable from Lea herself that she could not tell if it was pleasant or unpleasant.

"Lea," her mother said, kneeling down next to her.

She looked into her mother's face, tried to find comfort in the golden warmth of it, the dark eyes and full, walnut lips. But it wasn't enough, it was never enough. She couldn't sink into her mother, couldn't bury her face in her shoulder. Her mother was too strong, too solid, too tightly held. There was no opening for Lea, and she dropped her eyes again. She knew what her mother was going to say.

"He's not going to make it, Lea," her mother said. "His flight must have been delayed." She turned to Samuel, who stood at her side. "Tell her, Samuel."

Samuel repeated after his mother. "I don't think he's going to make it, Lea."

He's not going to make it. At those familiar words Lea felt something inside her squeeze, a heat gathering behind her eyes. But she was conscious of the awkwardness hanging in the air, the looks and whispers of the friends and classmates who still sat scattered about their living room, hours after the last games had been played and the vegetable punch was all gone. The sun slanted down in the sky, disappearing into an orange squint between the blinds.

Her legs felt heavy, but she let herself be brought to her feet. A rustle seemed to go through the lethargic room, the guests looking up, alert.

"Time to cut the cake!" her mother said firmly, less to the guests and more to Lea.

A ripple of excitement ran through the crowd. Children got to their feet, abandoning streamers and toys, mothers brushed hair from their eyes and fathers cleared their throats. They all gathered around the pedestal where the cake stood in the middle of the room.

Even as she allowed herself to be steered in front of the cake, as a pink plastic knife was pressed into her small hands, Lea never took her eyes off the front door.

He said he would make it this time. He promised.

But the doorframe, adorned with a rainbow balloon arch, stayed empty. *He's not going to make it.*

"Time to cut the cake!" her mother said again. Under the brightness, Lea could hear the warning, the edge to her mother's voice that always compelled her. Then her mother's hands were under her armpits, lifting her up onto the high chair in front of the cake.

Lea gripped the sticky plastic knife between both hands. She scanned the faces of the crowd in front of her. Maybe he was hiding in the crowd, waiting to surprise her. *As if I would miss my favourite girl's day.* But he wasn't there, she'd waited, she'd made everyone wait and now the balloons were sinking and the ice was melting and they were going to cut the cake without him.

"Happy birthday to you," her mother started singing, still in that loud, bright voice. Samuel joined in, and then the rest of the guests too, an uneven chorus. "Happy birthday to you. Happy birthday to Leee -ee."

Even sitting in the high chair, the table still came up to her chest. The cake loomed over her, tall and white, the red of the flowers as garish as a clown's lipstick.

"Happy birthday to you."

Lea's mother leaned in behind her, wrapping strong arms around her shoulders in a hug. But it wasn't a hug, she was holding Lea's hands too, guiding the knife towards the cake.

Not yet. Lea looked up at the empty doorframe in panic. He wasn't here yet. They couldn't cut it without him.

But the pink plastic blade was already starting to sink into the clean buttercream corner closest to her, her mother's steady hands wrapped around her own small and sweaty ones. Everyone was clapping, the applause like firecrackers going off. It hurt her ears.

Lea tried to pull the knife back, but it was too late. They were through the ivory layer now, and she could see the dark chocolate sponge within. He wasn't here yet. But now it was too late.

Something inside her surged, and she pressed the knife harder, more freely. It went through the thick sponge layer messy and jagged, crumbs spilling out of the cut, until the knife hit the hard surface of the pedestal.

The clapping intensified. Lea's mother took her hands off her, straightening up. "Thank you, everyone," she said, satisfied. The party had been a success after all.

But the guests weren't looking at her. They were looking at Lea, who sat in the high chair, both hands still tightly gripping the handle of the plastic knife. The knife that she hacked into the cake again, making another cut parallel to the first, and again, this time swinging carelessly, going for the second perfect layer of the cake. She sank the plastic knife into the cake's

312

innards, so far in that her fingers were covered in soft buttercream.

The clapping melted away into silence. Lea froze, looking up to meet her mother's eyes.

A flicker went across her mother's face, something she didn't recognise or understand.

"Oh, Lea, look what you've done! Silly girl," her mother said, an easy, wide smile plastered across her face. She prised the knife from Lea's sticky fingers, holding it between her forefinger and thumb, playing to the crowd. "That's the problem with our Lea," she went on. "Always overenthusiastic."

Everyone laughed. It started as a canned, mechanical sound, awkward and forced, but then it eased into something more natural, something more like relief.

Lea sat silently, staring at the dark wounds in the cake's ivory surface. She wanted to plunge her hands into it, grab fistfuls of the creamy, buttery, poisonous sponge and stuff them into her mouth. She wondered what it would taste like, just the smallest crumb.

Lea looked around. No one was staring at her any more, if anything, they were consciously avoiding it. Hats and coats were being handed out, pulled on, kisses being exchanged.

She turned her right hand up. She could feel the oily slick of buttercream in the web of her fingers, could see the crumbs that dotted her palm.

Her mother was taking presents, saying goodbye to the guests. She wasn't looking. Samuel had already started to tidy up, busy picking ribbons and used napkins off the floor. And her father — well, he wasn't even here.

So Lea brought her hand to her mouth, pressing her tongue against her palm. She thought it would be bitter, like all the other things she had been told were poisonous, the acrid burn of her father's black shoe polish, the dull tart of the wetness inside her ears. Bitter was the taste of something going wrong, she understood that even then. And she wanted to taste it now, on the one day that he said he would be home and was not.

But the taste that tingled through her mouth was unlike anything she had ever tasted before. It had the hint of a certain vegetable puree that her mother sometimes fed her, an aspect of it that she hadn't noticed before, blown up and magnified and made wonderful. Lea rubbed her tongue against the roof of her mouth. No, there was no mistaking it. It tasted nothing like poison.

Lea had stuck her tongue out again and was about to bring her other hand to her mouth when she looked up. Her mother was still saying goodbye to guests, who were milling about collecting goody bags and tying shoelaces, but in the midst of the chaos he had managed to come in unnoticed.

Her father stood by the front door. The bulk of his stomach strained against his wet shirt, his coat dangled from one hand. His nose was shiny, shinier than usual, and sweat glinted at his temples.

Part of Lea wanted to run to him, jump into his arms, bury her face in his bulk, but another part wanted to skulk away, crawl under a table and hide.

The look on his face though, kept her rooted in her chair. He was looking at her as if seeing her for the first time. A frown gripped his forehead and his cheek dropped towards his shoulder. He was studying her.

Lea realised her mouth was still open, her tongue still aimed towards her other buttercream-covered hand. She would be in trouble, she realised, now that he had seen her eating the poisonous cake. Strange, though, that he wasn't shouting or running over to stop her. It only confirmed what she already suspected, that it wasn't poisonous after all.

Still, shame of being caught in the act prickled at her neck, and she began to close her mouth, dropping her hand. But then, something about the way her father was looking at her made her stop. She stuck her tongue out and brought her fingers to her mouth again. She did it slowly, so he would have the chance to stop her.

But all he did was stare. He didn't stop her. Something moved inside her belly, a chasm opening up, and she didn't want the icing any more. The sweetness suddenly tasted sickly in her mouth, she wanted to spit it out, to wash it clean with water. She started to cry.

He was beside her in a flash, even before her mother could react.

Why are you crying? There's my birthday girl. There's my little girl. Don't cry now.

His arms were around her, tanned and solid as wood. She eyed the tiny black hairs tufting his forearm, familiar in the way that they stopped far before his wrist. The comforting specks of dark and light, varied in a way that her mother's smooth, poreless veneer was not. The folds of skin inside his elbows.

Shhhhh. That's enough now.

She breathed in the smell of him. He smelled savoury, like a cut onion on the rare occasion that her mother cooked trad. Her head was pressed against his chest, her sticky hands resting around his neck, buttercream mingling with the sweat that seeped through his shirt.

When Lea pulled her face away from the damp fabric of her father's shirt and blinked her eyes open, almost everyone was gone. Quietly ushered out by her mother — *thank you for coming, oh it was just lovely, she's just tired, you know how they get* — who was now picking streamers off the floor with a single-mindedness that Lea recognised as anger. She had done it again, she knew, with a tired sinking feeling in her stomach. What *it* was, she wasn't entirely sure, not yet, but she recognised the stiff angle of her mother's mouth, the tautness of the skin over her collarbones.

"Oh, hello there."

Lea looked up into her father's face, immediately forgetting her mother's anger. There he was, there was the familiar fold of his double chin, the flat, wide nose, the piercing eyes. The indentations on the left cheek that fascinated her so — no one else she knew had holes in their skin. They were caused by pimples, he had said. He'd had bad skin when he was younger, he told her, which mean pores sometimes got infected, turning into red pus-filled bumps that left holes when they popped. Lea had never seen a pimple before.

316

Something rustled in his hand. Lea looked down.

It was crudely wrapped, as if it had been done in a hurry, the gold paper crumpled and folded, the tape ineptly applied. But she grabbed it anyway, a grin spreading across her face.

"You'd think she hadn't got any presents at all," her mother said, an edge to her voice.

But Lea wasn't listening. She was ripping the paper off as quickly as she could, the shiny gold winking as it tore. The tail emerged first, mustard-coloured and plated with fins. Then the legs, the body, the small, pointed head. It was made of a rubbery plastic, as they always were. She saw now that the plates went all the way up its back, from the very tip of the tail to where its head began.

She held the toy dinosaur by the tail, stared into its face. It looked almost human, she thought. She recognised it from the picture books. Lea furrowed her brow in concentration.

"Steglo —"

"Stegosaurus," he said. "That's right."

"Stegosaurus," she said, her grin growing wider. "Look, Mom!" She waved the dinosaur at her mother by the tail. In spite of herself, Lea's mother began to smile.

"Look at that, honey," she said. "How about you take that upstairs and start getting ready for your bath?"

Lea nodded and slipped down from the chair.

She hesitated, turning her face up to her father. "Are you coming?"

It was how they always did it. Most days her mother would bathe her, but whenever she got a new dinosaur, she knew that her father would do it, humming the familiar bathtime song he always did. As he shampooed her hair, he'd tell her funny stories about the plastic dinosaurs lined up against the white bathroom tiles. Stories about the Tyrannosaurus rex who wanted nothing more than to be able to clap his hands, or the pterodactyl who used his wings as sails when he learned to windsurf. Lea wondered what the stegosaurus's story was.

He looked up at Lea's mother, something passing between them that she couldn't read. For a moment Lea felt her mood teetering — if he said no, she knew it would all come crashing down. She knew she would do it again, her mother would be angry again, they would fight. It would be her fault.

But then he gave her a smile that showed his gums and hid his eyes. "Of course," he said. "Why don't you go ahead? I'll be up soon."

A crash of happiness. Lea grinned back and bounded up the stairs, dinosaur in hand.

CHAPTER
THIRTY-FOUR

Anja had never slept well, but that night was worse than usual. That night she dreamt of machines that hankered for her flesh, the coils and scaffolding that lay beneath the floorboards of the apartment building. She dreamed of wires breaking through the ceiling, snaking around her mother. She dreamed of them not crushing her to death; no, that would have been a relief. Instead they plugged into her veins, and in her dream she grasped the terrible truth that this would give her everlasting life. She dreamt of the wires coming down like rain, like a rainforest, knotting and thickening until she could no longer see the door. She dreamed she would be there forever.

When she awoke the next morning, she was covered in a thin film of sweat. She lay still for a moment, staring at the large brown stain on the ceiling, feeling the hard floorboards through the thin mattress. Her spine felt thick and twisted, her neck crunched as she straightened out. The swoosh of her mother's blood and the thump of her heart seemed, for once, reassuring through the silence.

Anja sat up. She couldn't wait any longer. She was lucky that no one had shown up to ask about Branko yet, but she couldn't count on her luck continuing.

She grabbed a towel and the small basket that held her bath things, heading to the communal bathroom. Inside, a cockroach scuttled across a yellow sink. The showers at least were not too bad at this time of the day, far better than in the evenings when the drains were foamy with scum and the tiles strewn with hairs. She stepped in and cranked the hot water up.

The water came out in a slow jet, barely enough to get her hair wet. The only thing that made it bearable was the heat. It was only ever ice cold or scalding, but she liked it scalding, and was thankful it was today. She felt her skin redden in patches, moving her head left and right to let the water dribble down her shoulders and hips.

She was never clean in this place, Anja thought suddenly. How could you be, with this pitiful trickle, where one half of your body was always dry? She remembered the swimming pool at Lea's apartment, all that water in all that space, empty and looking out over the city. She thought of the showers there, the smooth, even jets that pounded your haunches with industrial strength, the multiple nozzles that emerged from the walls, the shower head the size of a dinner plate.

She shampooed vigorously, scraping her scalp with her ragged fingernails to try and get them clean. It occurred to her that there were lakes in Canada. She remembered a documentary she'd seen about grizzly bears, she was sure it had been set in Canada. The image of a grizzly bear flickered, a powerful dark shape crouching against the shining white body of water, sparkling fish trapped between strong jaws. She

320

imagined plunging into a lake like that, glittering and jewel-like, so cold it would take your breath away. She shampooed harder. The foam ran down into her eyes and drew stinging tears.

She was the last person in the carshare when she finally reached the Outer Boroughs. No one who would normally take a carshare would come here, which she was glad for. It meant no judgemental or prying eyes, and solitude for the last half-hour of her journey. It had cost an entire day's wages, but there was no other way to get here. Two days' wages, if you counted the way back.

She smelled the Markets before she saw them. Roasted corn, stagnant water, an elemental, industrial tinge. And as she drew closer, the unmistakeable whiff of human sweat. Here, on the outskirts of the Markets, people sat on the kerb eating charred vegetables on sticks, and children in worn sneakers chased each other. Ahead of Anja, a lone woman in a tight-knit skirt and a ripped leather jacket leaned against a lamppost. She pulled at the ends of her hair in a way that she must have thought was suggestive, but really just looked nervous, as she called out to the men who passed her in the street. On the other side of the road, a man leaning on a stick shook a paper cup at her. The sign at his feet read: "Hungry and alone. Kidney for sale, pls enquire."

Anja hurried on. She was close now. She could hear the shouts and the crashes, smell the smoke and the dust. Finally, rounding the corner, she was there.

The Markets were always a sight to behold. They occupied a broad expanse of low buildings, what must have once been some kind of industrial estate, one of the many abandoned over the years in the Outer Boroughs. The buildings were the size of airplane hangars, their walls rusted corrugated iron or thin, flimsy brick. It was a wonder they were still standing, but standing they were.

Anja didn't even know how large the whole thing was. She'd never walked the entire length of them; she didn't know how far out they went, how many buildings and empty car parks they occupied.

The noise was an assault from all around. Children and hawkers shouted and squealed, wheels crunched through the dusty gravel and machines screamed. There had to be thousands, tens of thousands, millions of people there, more people than Anja had ever seen, even in Boroughs One through Five.

Anja headed east, where the largest and the oldest buildings were, where she knew the warehouses still contained rotting conveyor belts and giant complex machines that an enterprising few put to work for their own purposes. If she was going to find what she needed, this would be her best shot.

Moving through the crowd was slow going. Anja placed one hand on her waistband, where she felt the wad of cash rubbing against her skin. She didn't stand out too much here, not the way someone like Lea would, but her smooth skin and clean clothes were enough to draw stares. Still, she thought, maybe it was a good thing. Even in the Markets, no one would lay a finger on a lifer.

Finally she reached the factories. Here it was mainly men, in dirty singlets and with dark smudges of oil on their cheeks. There were more stares and the occasional whistle. Strangely, though, Anja felt safer here than elsewhere in the Markets, felt that her weakness was so conspicuous that if anyone tried anything, she could rely on mob justice to save her. Besides, it was no worse than being in the diner.

She thought briefly of Branko, and wondered where he was now. Had he come to the Markets too, in search of the pills for her?

"Why the frown, sweetheart?" A man with matted, greasy hair and black fingernails called out to her. He leaned against a stall weighed down with huge nets of nuts and bolts, racks of gears that glinted dully in the sunlight. Despite the autumn chill, his chest was bare and slick with sweat.

"Hello. Where can I find the vehicles?" Anja said, trying to ignore the leer on his face.

"Vehicles! Whoa! What's a girlie like you doing looking for a vehicle?" The man turned to the stall-holders around him, eyebrows raised, conspiratorial. They laughed.

Anja pressed her lips together. "I need a car," she said.

His eyebrows shot up further but he made no comment. "And what would you give me for it?" One of his friends sniggered.

She walked up to the man who had made the comment. At first he held her stare, a smile curling at his lips as his friends whooped and cheered. But as she drew closer, unblinking, her chin held high and her eyes cold, he dropped his gaze and crossed his arms.

"What do you want for it?" Anja said. Her cheeks burned, but for the first time in years, she felt a new strength coursing through her veins.

The other stallholders sensed the change in atmosphere. They saw the embarrassed look that flashed across their friend's face and slunk away, turning to their customers or machines or each other, starting up other, quieter conversations.

"I was just kidding," the man mumbled. "'Course, just joking around." He lifted his eyes, sullen now. "We don't get your kind around here often, is all."

He was not too far off from Branko in age or appearance, Anja realised, this close up. She looked at the rickety stall, at the slings of metal parts and tinny cash box nailed to the countertop. She wondered if the man had a brother too, or even a sister.

"See that pink building over there?" the man said.

Anja squinted. All the buildings looked the same to her, peeling and dirty grey, but then she discerned that the paint on one of them was a faint salmon colour. She nodded.

He wiped his hand on his jeans and stuck it out. It took Anja a moment to realise what he was offering. She reached out and clasped his hand gingerly. It was cold and calloused, like a leather mitt.

"Abel," he said.

"Laurie," she lied.

"Laurie. Pretty name," he said, but then held up his palms to her. "I mean, no disrespect. Hey, you know what, let me take you. You'll get a better deal that way."

Anja protested, but Abel was already asking his neighbour to look after his stall while he was gone.

"Come on," he said.

She followed behind him as he weaved his way between the haphazardly placed stalls. Despite his bulk, his step was nimble, and she almost lost him as he picked his way through the crowd. Still, she stayed close, never straying more than three or four paces away. No one bothered her now that she was with Abel.

It was dark inside the pink building, the only light streaming in through the doorway and the holes in the corrugated-iron roof. The air was hot and stuffy, but at least there were fewer people here, and she could walk unhindered. But coming in from under the shining sun outside, Anja found herself momentarily blinded, the world a flickering, indistinct grey. She blinked, and as her eyes got used to the dark, saw that the room was filled with cars.

They weren't like the cars she saw on the streets of the Central Boroughs though — those were sleek pods of efficiency, yellow and uniform for the most part, stamped with the different logos of companies that owned them.

These cars were bulbous and boxy, in so many different shapes and sizes that it made her dizzy to look at them. She had fleeting memories of individually owned cars in her childhood, but even so, the carshare companies had taken over most of Sweden by the time she had left, rolling out their yellow and grey fleets across the country.

The cars were lined up like slumbering farm animals, some creaking and groaning as dark shapes flitted about them, cranking a wheel here, polishing a mirror there. Anja looked around and realised she had lost Abel. It didn't matter though, looking at the sheer number of cars available. She thought it would be harder than this.

Anja approached a man in overalls leaning against the open hood of a small blue car with round headlights.

"I'm looking for a car," she said.

He eyed her. "Oh?" he said drily.

She bristled. "How much is this one?" she said, pointing to the little blue car he was pressed up against.

The man gave her a long, lazy look.

"Ten thousand."

"Are you kidding?" It was more than twice of what she had to spend.

The man eyed her. "What's a girl like you want a car for anyway? Gift for your boyfriend?"

"That's none of your business," she snapped. "How about four thousand?"

The man's upper lip lifted in a snarl.

"Don't waste my time."

"Maybe not this car," Anja tried again. "But what do you have for four thousand?"

The man let out a sharp laugh. His eyes seemed wary, and they flitted about her, never quite landing on her face. He seemed to be watching something behind her, but when Anja turned around, she only saw the doorway of the building.

"Like I said, I got better things to do." He pulled the front of his cap over his eyes, crossed his arms, and appeared to go to sleep while still standing up.

Anja moved on. Perhaps she would have better luck with someone else. There were so many cars here, so many traders, surely there was something she could buy.

But half an hour later, after talking to countless other men in overalls, Anja was on the verge of giving up. The first trader's price, it seemed, was on the low side. No one else quoted anything below eleven thousand, some asking for as much as twenty. Some didn't seem to even want anything to do with her, moving into the shadows as soon as she drew near.

Anja balled her fists and bit her lip. A wave of frustration rose in her chest. She couldn't leave here without a car — what if the officers came tomorrow? The thought of going back to the apartment and trying to fall asleep that night, waiting with dread, gave Anja renewed resolve.

"Laurie. Laurie!"

It took Anja a few seconds to react. It was Abel, waving at her from across the room. She carefully picked her way over the ground strewn with various car parts and junk to get to where he was standing.

"Laurie, this is my friend, Jerome," Abel said, brandishing an arm proudly.

The man next to him was small and slight, coming up only to his shoulders. He wore a neat blue-checked shirt, buttoned to the collar. His eyes glowed faintly in the dim warehouse, and Anja could just make out a smattering of freckles across the tops of his cheeks.

"Hello." Jerome nodded, but didn't offer his hand. He looked at Abel. "So, anyway," he said gruffly. "What kind of car?"

"I don't care — just something that can get me around. I'm going on a long trip."

"Okay, well, then you'll want something that's not too much of a clunker. How big do you want to go? Any passengers on your long trip?"

Anja paused. She hadn't thought about how she would place her mother in the car. Or how she would get the car back to her apartment, since you could hardly just drive into Manhattan like that.

"Yes," she said quietly. "One passenger. She'll — she'll just need the backseat, though."

"Ah," Jerome said. "Motion sickness?" he asked knowingly. "How much you want to spend?" he said.

Anja's heart sank. Still, she had to try.

"Six thousand," she said.

But Jerome didn't laugh in her face, he didn't do a low whistle to the side or walk away. Instead he nodded.

"Six thousand," he said. "Okay. I think we can find you something."

"Really? No one else would sell me anything back there," she found herself saying before she could stop herself. It occurred to her that this was not the best negotiating tactic.

"Oh girlie," Jerome said. Anja winced, tried to ignore it. "Laurie, is that what you said your name was? Well, you can't just walk into somewhere like this and hope that someone's going to give you a fair price. Especially when you look like you just stepped out of the Ministry."

"So . . ." Anja paused.

Jerome raised an eyebrow. "So why am I helping you?" He looked over at Abel. "Ask my friend over here."

Abel examined a loose bolt on the floor with his toe.

"Anyway," Jerome said. "I assume you're paying cash?"

Anja nodded.

Jerome stuck his hand out. Anja eyed him. "Show me the car first," she said.

He let out a long-suffering sigh and stared at Abel again. "Fine," he said.

Jerome brought them to the very back of the hall. Anja saw that bricks were coming loose in the wall and pinpricks of sunlight shone through. She looked about herself, up at the tin ceiling and at the crumbly pillars with cars and goods stacked about them. It was a wonder it didn't all come crashing down.

"There," Jerome pointed. "Best part . . . it has a skylight."

It was less car and more van. Raised on four large wheels that came up to her waist, the car was boxy and glaring, and to top it off, it was red.

"That's . . ." Anja started. They were both standing with their thumbs hooked into their waistbands as if they didn't care, but their eyes were wide and expectant. "Perfect," she ended.

She pulled the cash out of her front pocket. Their eyes barely widened when they saw the thick wad in her hand, and Anja was reminded of an urban legend that the Market traders were actually the richest men of the whole city. That they secretly visited pay-per-use private clinics and extended their lives past the Ministry-sanctioned numbers, at an exorbitant cost. But when she handed it to Jerome, he snatched it from her in a way that told her he was no secret millionaire. He counted the cash slowly under his breath, tongue sticking out between his teeth.

When he was done, he grinned. It was the first time Anja had seen him smile, and it made him suddenly look twenty years younger. From his back pocket he pulled a ring of keys that was as large as her head. He sifted through them, picking out one identical key after another, finally plucking one out from its loose tag. He handed it to Anja.

"Here you go," he said. As she took it, a thought seemed to strike him. "Can you even drive?" he said.

Anja gave him a withering look.

"Okay, okay," he said.

"Well, thanks," Anja said, truly grateful.

"Hey, no problem, Laurie," Jerome said, elbowing Abel in the ribs.

"Look," Anja said. "My name's not really Laurie. It's Anja. Anja Nilsson."

Abel held out a hand. "Nilsson. Like the opera singer?"

Anja's stomach squeezed. "Yes," she said. "Do you know — have you heard her?"

"Are you kidding? Love that shit," Abel said. Jerome nodded vigorously, pulled out his tablet and tapped its face.

The aria that poured forth was scratchy and jolting. Jerome shook his tab.

"Sorry, not the best signal here," he said.

But even with the jolts and echoes, her mother's voice was unmistakeable. They were silent, all except Jerome, who was humming along. Standing in the crowded Markets, huddled around Jerome's tab, Anja felt with a sudden clarity what she had to do.

Her mother would not have wanted some doctor, up in Canada, to do it.

CHAPTER
THIRTY-FIVE

Lea checked her watch as the floors rushed by. Jiang would have just arrived home, she thought. His wife would be heating the Nutripaks, he would be taking his shoes off, hanging up his jacket, regaling her with the boring events of the day.

Jiang lived in the penthouse, of course he did. Lea noted the dark marble walls, the plush carpet underfoot. The healthy plants in spotless ceramic pots standing outside his front door. She rang the doorbell. It didn't seem to be working, so she rang again, leaving her finger on the button longer this time.

The door clicked open.

"Yes?" Jiang's wife was a large woman, larger than Lea would have expected. She'd never met her before, come to think of it. She had a severe mouth and the hint of a cleft chin. The skin around her eyes dissolved into a fine web when she spoke, but her neck was as smooth as it was long and blemish-free.

"Is Jiang here?" Lea said.

Jiang's wife frowned. "Who are you?"

"I work with him. Is he here?"

She eyed Lea suspiciously, then ducked her head behind the door. "Jiang!" she called. "Someone from — *work*."

Lea heard Jiang's familiar footsteps, heard his tone of annoyance — *what, work, why would they come here, haven't they heard of the phone* — before he appeared at the front door. When he saw her his voice changed.

"Lea," Jiang said. "What are you doing here?" He looked down the hallway, as if checking to see if someone had followed her there.

"I need to borrow your boat," Lea said.

"What? Why? I mean, no," Jiang sputtered. "What boat?"

He shut the door behind him and stepped out into the hallway.

"Just for a day," she said. "I just need it for tomorrow."

Jiang continued to protest that he didn't know what she was talking about, *what boat, why would he have a boat.*

"Jiang," Lea fixed her gaze on him. "If you don't let me use it, I'll walk in there right now and tell your wife about why you have it."

He coughed, and fell silent. His forehead was shiny again. Lea realised Jiang was wearing a large, fluffy bathrobe and bedroom slippers.

"What are you even doing here, Lea? How is this going to help your — your case?"

"Are you going to let me use it or not?"

He glared at her. "Fine," he muttered. "Hold on."

Jiang disappeared into the house. *Who is that, darling? At this time of the evening?* She couldn't hear Jiang's muffled reply, but it was curt. A few moments later, the door opened again.

"Just for tomorrow," he said, handing her a key. "It's down in the old docks. Lot 317. But perhaps you know that already."

She grabbed the key. "Thanks," she said, and turned to go.

"I don't know what you're playing at, Lea," Jiang called after her. "But this isn't the time to do anything stupid. Things are changing. New developments. You'd best keep your head down."

Going from Jiang's home to Kaito's was a shock. The last time she'd been to visit her father it had been a beautiful day out, and the sunshine and pale blue skies had distracted from the dreariness of his apartment block. Lea picked her way over the broken bottles and plastic bags that littered the ground. The elevator was broken. As she made her way up the four flights of stairs, Lea wondered what she would do if her father was no longer there. She hadn't picked up any of his calls in weeks. What if he had moved? What if he had left the city, or worse?

Lea pushed the thought out of her mind, concentrating on the burn in her thighs. Finally she found herself standing in front of Kaito's front door. She knocked.

The door was so thin that she could hear him getting up. She visualised the small room in her mind's eye, the last time she had seen it. She could see it now — the bed, the kitchenette, the oversized dining table. The desk pushed up against the window, with the pile of letters on it. The Club invitation. Her stomach clenched. But it was fine, everything was fine. She could hear her father walking towards the door. He was still here, she had got here in time. She could put her proposal to him, convince him of her plan, change his mind.

The door opened and there he was, standing before her in an old T-shirt and pyjama pants that ended some way above his bony ankles. For some reason the sight of her father's bare feet, spotted and wrinkled and knotted like tree roots, roused a deep sadness in her. She thought of Ambrose's feet, sheathed in shiny leather shoes, laces done with care.

"Lea," her father said. His voice was slow with sleep. "What are you doing here? What time is it?"

She glanced down at her watch. It was past ten — she hadn't realised how long it had taken her to get here.

"I came to see you," she said. "I — I was hoping we could talk."

He rubbed his eyes. "Of course," he said. "I'm so glad you're here."

As she stepped into his apartment, Lea realised that the last time she'd seen her father had been at the party. She remembered the things she'd said to him then, the way they'd separated. Her cheeks flushed in shame.

Never mind. Wasn't she here now? Didn't she have a plan, a suggestion, a solution to both their problems?

"You came. I'm so glad you're here," he said again. He pulled a flannel dressing gown off the hook behind the door and shrugged it on. It was green, with little pink flowers. Lea was reminded of the quilt in Anja's mother's bed.

Kaito perched himself on the edge of his bed, gesturing to the dining table. "You're familiar with the seating options," he said, smiling.

Lea felt her face crumple before she could stop herself. The sobs came in heaving gasps, stilted, awkward, as if she didn't know how to cry.

Her father didn't tell her to stop crying. He didn't say anything. Instead, he came over to where she was standing, and placed one hand on her back. He paused, staring at her face. She wondered what he was thinking; if he thought she was weak, overwrought, an embarrassment. But as the thought entered her mind, he pulled her into a tight embrace, one that crushed the breath out of her lungs and stilled her sobs.

He didn't say anything, but she heard him. Heard his words from a long, long time ago, words that she'd never forgotten.

Why are you crying? There's my little girl. Don't cry now.

His arms were around her, tanned and solid as wood. She eyed the tiny black hairs tufting his forearm, familiar in the way that they stopped far before his wrist. The comforting specks of dark and light, varied in a way that her mother's smooth veneer was not. The folds of skin inside his elbows.

Shhhhh. That's enough now.

She breathed in the smell of him. There it was, that salty, human smell, different now, all these years later, but still some version of what it used to be. She would recognise his smell anywhere.

When her breathing was even again, he let her go. He pulled out a chair from under the dining table and guided her to sit. Then he sat down on the edge of the bed, facing her.

Suddenly Lea was exhausted. The thought of explaining it all was too much, far too much to bear. So instead, she pulled out the key that Jiang had given her.

"My boss lent me his boat for the day. Do you — do you still remember how to sail?" she said shyly.

Her father's face lit up. "Do I!" he said. "I haven't in years; no, the last time must've been when I lived out west. Had a boat of my own then, secondhand and creaky, but a real beauty."

She smiled at his enthusiasm, and for the first time, the mention of his life away from her and her mother didn't cause any spark of anger, any resentment. She would ask him to take her there. To take her to see all the places he had been and lived, to meet all the people he'd known, do all the things he'd done. She'd give him a reason to live.

"Plus," he went on. "You couldn't have picked a better day. Not only is the weather meant to be perfect — seventy degrees and not a cloud in the sky — but, and you probably don't remember this, tomorrow is, well, my birthday."

The thirtieth of October. Of course. She hadn't thought about it in decades, but the date came easily. She knew it as she knew her own name.

"Perfect," Lea said. "A birthday present, then."

She would tell him everything tomorrow, Lea decided. It was too late at night now, they were both too tired. The weather was meant to be perfect, after all, and it was his birthday. There would be no better time.

Lea awoke before sunrise the next morning. She did not jolt awake, did not panic in the dark at the unfamiliar smallness of the bed she found herself in. Although she had slept, it had been a kind of waking sleep, a sleep where she'd never quite lost consciousness of where she was and who she was with.

Her father's breathing was quiet and even, with the faint wheeze of congestion. But even that sounded healthy, innocent, like a child who had forgotten to blow his nose. He had insisted on giving her his bed, and so slept on a thin pull-out mattress on the floor next to her. She'd only accepted on the condition that he take the comforter, which he'd grudgingly said yes to. And so she slept with just a sheet now. It was soft and smooth to touch, the sign of a hundred, a thousand washings. She wondered if her father had carried his bedsheets around with him on his travels, where these flat pillows and threadbare covers had been.

Lea turned and dipped her head over the edge of the bed to look at her father. He slept curled on his side, with his mouth open, his hands close to his face. The picture was off in some way; she realised she'd always imagined her father sleeping on his back, taking up space, arms stretched out.

338

She settled back into bed and shut her eyes. The sound of her father's breathing moved through her body, steady and comforting, lulling her back to sleep. There was a sudden lightness in her soul, the feeling of coming home.

It was, as Kaito had predicted, a beautiful day. Cold, for even as Lea stepped out of the apartment building she felt the chill seeping into the warm spaces between her fingers, in her joints, underneath her clothes. But dazzlingly bright, the sky aglow in a blazing, electric blue. The sea, too, was a shimmering, restless mirror. The glittering dark waves reflected the rays of the sun like the huge scaly back of some ancient, rolling creature.

There was one problem though, Lea thought as they began the walk to the harbour.

"No wind," Kaito said, as if reading her mind. "Guess we'll have to paddle."

She laughed. "Or swim and push."

The boat would have an engine, of course. The sails were just for show. Jiang didn't actually know how to sail, and Lea doubted any of his mistresses did either.

Her father was in high spirits. He'd brought a large, embarrassing ladies' sunhat and insisted on wearing it on the walk there. *The UV rays! The killer UV rays!* He stage-whispered in mock horror, pretending to shield Lea under his hat too. She pushed him away, laughing. Though it was still cold enough that she was wearing her coat, the heat of the sun felt good on her exposed hands and neck.

He pointed at the beach, where a placard was driven into the sand.

"Every winter, a hundred people or so gather here, on this beach. They call themselves the polar bear club," he said, eyes crinkling. "Can you guess why?"

"No," she said. "No way."

"Yup. Water temperature in the high-fifties. Come to think of it, it's probably not far off from that today."

Lea shuddered. "Why would anyone do that to themselves?"

He shrugged.

The walk to the harbour was a straightforward one, straight down the boardwalk for an hour or so. But halfway into the walk, Kaito veered off the boardwalk.

"Where are you going? That's not the right way," Lea called after him.

He smiled and waved her over. "I just want to stop somewhere first," he said. "Come, you'll see."

So she followed him off the path, into the empty streets. The buildings were wooden, squat and white-washed, their windows dirty, gardens crowded with hairy overgrown plants. Where were they going? They walked through the first street, then the next, then turned off into a small side road.

Suddenly they were in a narrow alley lined with shops and crowded with people. It was a makeshift market of some kind. The sellers had their wares laid out on large white sheets — *in case the police come, makes it easier for them to grab and run,* Kaito explained — and they shouted at people going by. They were selling junk, at least it seemed so to Lea. Old household appliances, pieces of cameras, what looked like a canoe paddle. But then her gaze landed on a sheet with stacks of compact discs neatly lined up, their faces dusty but still glinting in the sun, and she understood what kind of market it was. Lea was tempted to stop and rifle through the discs, to see what music they had, if they had anything she could add to her collection, but her father was already way ahead of her. So she hurried along.

"It's very busy," her father said. "Why don't you wait here?" He pointed to an empty spot by the wall. Lea nodded.

Her father continued pushing his way through the browsers, finally stopping at a stall crowded with plastic models — tiny planes, cars, dolls with wide blue eyes and small red lips. He was talking to the seller, a stocky large man who couldn't stop staring at Kaito's floppy sunhat. The seller nodded and squatted down. Lea could no longer see him. Then he stood up again, and handed something to Kaito. Kaito examined whatever the man had given him carefully, turning it over in his hands, and then smiled. He paid the man and began pushing his way through the crowd, back to Lea.

"Okay," he said. "Let's go."

"What did you get?" Lea said, looking down at his hand. It was wrapped in brown paper.

"Not here," he said. "Later, on the boat."

Lea nodded. They made their way out of the crowded street and back to the boardwalk. The empty space was a relief after the scrum of the alleyway.

"Why does no one ever come out here? It's so beautiful, and so quiet."

Her father shrugged. "Had you ever come here before?"

She knew what he meant by *before*; before he brought her here, but also before everything else. Before the Club, before Anja, before Ambrose. Before him.

"No," Lea said. "I hadn't."

She would tell him once they were on the boat, she thought. She would find the right moment, not now, not when they were walking side by side, distracted, with a destination in mind. No, better on the boat, once the engine was running and they were out on the big grey sea, nothing and no one around them.

The boat was smaller than she had imagined. The way Jiang had boasted about it, she'd imagined a luxury yacht, with multiple cabins, decks, coolers. But it was a humble sailboat with an inside space that could only fit one person. Most of the boat was open, and it had low sides. They would truly feel like they were on the water.

"Key," her father said. He was already standing in the boat. She handed it to him mutely, then took his outstretched hand and stepped into its rocking hull.

She perched herself on a small bench at the back of the boat while her father started the engine. It burst into life with a loud roar.

Lea felt strangely unsettled, despite the glorious day and the comfort of being with her father. At first she thought it was nerves, completely understandable,

342

given the magnitude of her decision. But then she realised, as she watched her father guide the boat out of its lot in the harbour, turning the steering wheel with a deft lightness that made her ache for her childhood, that it wasn't even that. What it was, was the feeling of someone else being in charge. Of relinquishing control automatically, of trusting someone else. Lea was not used to that at all.

Once they were out of the harbour, Kaito revved the engine playfully.

"Shall we?" he shouted, twisting his head around to look at her.

He'd taken his coat off and was wearing a flannel shirt and jeans underneath. With the sleeves of his shirt rolled up, his long uncut hair whipping in the wind, he almost looked like a young man again. At the helm of the boat he stood with his back straight, chin up, hands resting comfortably on the steering wheel. From the back, when she couldn't see the folds of skin in his neck and face, Lea could almost imagine she was ten years old. For a moment she believed that Samuel was with them too, sitting at her side, just outside her peripheral vision.

But when she turned, there was nothing but water. Slow, undulating and opaque. They were some distance from the crashing shore now. The waves were smooth and unbroken.

"What are you looking at?" her father said. He turned the engine off and made his way to the back of the boat.

It was quiet now, the space and the silence filling her mind, her heart.

"I've been thinking," she said, before the words left her. "I've been thinking we could — go. Somewhere, away from here. Any of the places you've been, all those years you were away. I want to see it all too."

He stared at her. She saw that he didn't understand.

"Asia, or Europe, even. We could go there. Away."

"You know that's not possible," her father said. "The border sanctions. You'd never be able to come back, at least not to your life as it is now."

She was silent. Was it what she wanted? Around them, the world swayed, back and forth, back and forth, rocked by the invisible pull of the moon.

"Even when I left. When I left here. I never went beyond the borders," he said. "I travelled around the country, but always within it. Never far from a clinic."

"So don't you want to see what's outside of it? Outside of here?"

He shook his head. "I don't think you understand what you're suggesting, Lea. You'd have to give everything up. Live among sub-100s. Sure, other countries have started their own life extension programmes, but you wouldn't be eligible for them. Besides, they're way behind, you wouldn't be able to get the maintenance you need. You'd have ten, maybe twenty years, tops."

"Like you," she said, looking him in the eye. "We could spend those ten, twenty years together."

Her father stared at her for a long while. She held his gaze, feeling the resolve within her solidifying. She

344

wanted to go, yes, but it didn't stop her from tasting the sweet bitterness of self-sacrifice. A small voice inside her crying: *See? See what you made me do?*

Perhaps this was why they did it, the Ambroses of the world. To hold their chins up in defiance. Grand gestures driven by a petty smallness.

No, but that wasn't fair. She remembered Ambrose, remembered the fire burning in his eyes, the conviction in his voice when he no longer stuttered.

"I want to," she said, softening her tone. "Something's changed, ever since — ever since you came back. The Observation List, WeCovery, the Club. Todd. Dwight."

She paused, struggling for the right words. "I guess I just — I just don't believe in it any more. I don't know if I ever did."

Lea saw that he didn't understand. She went on.

"Try as I might, I'll always be that girl who broke Dwight Rose's face, who shattered his kneecaps, who . . ." She stopped, took a deep breath. "Who tried to turn off his life support. I'll always want to break things."

Finally her father dropped his gaze. He laced his fingers together, examined the half moons in his fingernails.

"I don't belong here," she said. "I never have."

When he looked up at her, she thought he would protest, tell her that she didn't know what she was saying, ask her to reconsider carefully. Say that it was absurd and he couldn't possibly condone her plan.

"Oh Lea," he said. "It breaks my heart to hear you say that. If I had known — if I had known, I would have — I don't know, done *something*. I don't know what, maybe taken you away, gone some place else. But your mother was so sure. That this was right. The right thing to do, the right way to live. And perhaps it was. Perhaps it would have been worse if we *had* left, who knows? I couldn't leave either, after all, despite all my talk, all my principles. In spite of myself. Stayed in the country, hiding like a dog, clinging to what little life I had left."

"It's not too late," Lea said. "We could still leave. Start a new life together, away from here."

"No," he said in a strange voice. "It's not . . . We could."

"How many years do you have left?" she asked eagerly.

He paused. "One," he said. "Maybe less."

Her heart squeezed. Suddenly the calm gelatinous beauty of the ocean surrounding them felt unbearably cruel. Seagulls swooped and soared overhead, their shrill cries seeming to mock the tiny sailboat buoyed by the waves, where Lea sat across from the only person left in the world whom she loved. One year, maybe less. She thought of all the decades she would live without him once that precious year was up, the interminable tomorrows stretching forward into the cold, empty future. But then she thought of the eighty-eight years that they had wasted.

"Still," she said as evenly as she could. "One year, that's enough to go to lots of places. Shanghai.

Melbourne. Paris. Maybe Sweden. I've heard a lot about it from Anja, it sounds beautiful."

"Yes," he said thoughtfully. "Sweden. Beautiful countryside, I've heard. We could go hiking. The Road of Kings, that's what it's called. Endless light in the summer, when the sun sets for only an hour a day."

"Right," she said, more hopefully, though the words *One, maybe less* echoed at the back of her mind. "Hiking. I've never been hiking before. Because it's meant to be harsh on the ligaments, or at least that's what the advisories say. I guess it won't matter any more, what the advisories say." She laughed, experimentally.

"Shanghai, too," he said, his face lighting up now. "I've always wanted to see it."

"And on the way there, maybe Tokyo," she said. "That's where your grandparents were from, isn't it? My great-grandparents?"

"It is," he said. "And if you could have heard them, you'd never forget it, too. They were always complaining about New York. The air was too dry, the food portions too large, the people too loud and impolite. Tokyo, now Tokyo was different. City of light. The beacon of civilisation," he said wryly.

"Well then, we'll just have to see it!" Lea smiled, triumphant.

"We will," he said. "We will."

They fell silent. The boat rocked gently and overhead, a seagull crowed.

"I got you something," her father said. He stood up and fetched something from the front of the boat. It was the package she'd seen him holding in the market earlier.

"Oh! Thank you. But it's your birthday, not mine," Lea said, taking the package from him. She felt it. It was small and intricately formed; she thought she felt a tail, legs, a long neck. "Oh no, you didn't!" She ripped the paper open.

"For all the birthdays I missed," he said, smiling at her.

It was a plesiosaur, a sea dinosaur. Had roamed the seas in the Mesozoic Era, before whatever it was, meteor or Ice Age, killed them all. Twenty-five feet long, they said. The size of two full-length cars, they were the giants of the sea, like small whales. Like whales though, they were gentle creatures, speculated to have only eaten sea plants and small fish.

She pressed the dinosaur into her lap. Her eyes felt hot, and she bit her lip to keep the tears away.

"Thank you," she said.

"No, thank you." Her father's voice was tired all of a sudden. *One year, maybe less.*

She thought of Anja's mother, lying in that cold, damp room, her body clicking and whirring long after her soul was gone.

It hit her then that her father was truly dying. That by coming back, by getting involved with the Club, he wasn't trying to die; he was going to anyway. She saw now, finally, what he was really looking for.

They stayed out on the boat for the rest of the afternoon. When the sky began to turn purple, Lea's

348

father asked if they should start heading back. She nodded slowly, reluctantly.

They fell silent as he turned the boat around. Lea realised she was still holding the dinosaur, gripping it so hard that her hands came away embossed with the pattern of its scales. She set it down gently, so that it was standing on the bench next to her. *Give me strength*, she thought to herself.

Strength for what? Lea turned her face into the wind, and thought of the way her father had held Samuel's hands at the very end. Thought of the way her mother had looked at her for the last time, drinking in the image of her face, before closing her eyes forever.

The sun was a low, orange ball on the horizon, colouring the pale pebbles on the shore a blazing red. As they drew closer towards the shore, Lea saw that the city skyline, gleaming in the distance, was aflame too. A city of light.

Kaito docked the boat. He got out first, then helped her over its side. Lea hadn't noticed the rocking of the waves, but now as she stepped onto solid ground, the world began to sway.

He handed her the key.

"Thank you," he said, patting the boat's white hull. He turned to Lea. "And thank you. For a wonderful day. It was perfect."

"We're not going to Tokyo," Lea said in a low voice. "Are we?"

Her father looked at her. She saw him struggling for the words to say.

"It's okay," she said. She gripped the dinosaur in her right hand, by the tail. "I should have known."

"I didn't want to let you down again," he said.

Lea swallowed. She looked at her feet.

"Do you have the pill?" she asked.

She knew he did. Manuel had told her a week ago that their latest shipment had been fully distributed. That everyone who wanted one had one.

Kaito nodded. He reached into the back pocket of his jeans and pulled out his wallet. The leather was worn and soft, so she could see the faint outline of something small making the opposite of a dent in the otherwise flat, black square.

He slid the T-pill out and held it in the palm of his hand. It was oval-shaped and creamy in colour, flecked with tiny brown dots. Nestled in Kaito's calloused hand, it looked like the abandoned egg of a tiny bird.

Her father studied the pill in his hand. "I've had it a long time now. I've been waiting."

"For what?" Lea asked.

But even as the words left her mouth, she knew. Her lower lip began to tremble. To still it, she thought of Anja's mother, and Ambrose, and Samuel. She squeezed the plastic dinosaur toy in her hand.

He didn't answer, but held her gaze. Lea studied the lines of his face. In them she saw again every expression he had ever made — every smile and frown and sigh — saw how they jostled for room on the canvas of his skin, how they'd etched their fleeting existence into his flesh, how they filled it up, made their mark, carved and pulled and twisted until there was no space left. She

350

saw how full he was of the world he had seen, how sated, how tired. Saw, at last, that it wasn't anything to do with her. Had never been anything to do with her. He'd made his choices, and she would make hers.

The steady roar of the waves crashing on the beach filled the pause. "You've been waiting for me," Lea said. Her voice was strong now, and filled with kindness.

They walked back along the boardwalk slowly. They didn't talk about the pill that Kaito had swallowed while standing there on the harbour, as the boats rocked gently around them. Instead her father told her a story. He told her about his childhood, the creaky wooden stairs in his grandparents' narrow house, the balls of rice with flakes of fish in them that only his grandmother knew how to make, the time his father made him kneel on chopsticks outside the front door because he had been caught lying.

He told her about growing up always looking for a way out, finding that way out in her mother, Uju, who was ambitious and loud and strong, and everything he was not. About how it was heaven at first, *before*. He didn't say before what, but she knew it was before Samuel, and before her, before the world forced them to pick sides: trad meals or Nutripaks, jazz or muzak, life-loving or antisanct. He told her about how it fell apart slowly, the pieces of their lives slipping away.

He told her about leaving. About how he'd never admitted, not even to Uju, that it was Lea who had set off the alarms at the hospital. He told her it was the excuse he had been looking for that whole time, that he had been planning an escape for years but could never bear to finally leave. He told her about how it was disappointing, that the life he lived away from them was only filled with more of the same. He told her about realising one day, after seeing a picture of Uju with someone else, that his family had moved on. He told her about the loneliness, the desperation. But also the moments of pure untainted joy, the gratitude for the simple fact of the strength in his limbs as he took a walk outside on a clear blue day. A day not unlike today, he told her.

He told her about coming back. Not knowing, at first, what he was really looking for. Thinking now that it was coming to an end, that he wanted to make a point. To punctuate his brief existence on this earth with *something*. To prove, if only to himself, that it was all for something.

He told her about today. He described the sun and the sea as if she hadn't been there herself. He told her about how the seller at the market said he didn't have any sea dinosaurs, only land ones. About how he made him check again. About the boat they had been on, how easily it steered, how small and light it had felt as it skimmed the waves. How it felt like they had been flying.

He told her about his daughter. About how she was smart and strong and different, how she thought there was something wrong with her because she sought the messy, sprawling innards of life, the flesh beneath the skin, the breakages. That she felt, deep within her, the violence of what it meant to live forever. He told her that she was not wrong, no, she was right. She had been right all along.

When they reached the spot on the beach with the placard driven into the sand, they stopped. Kaito shed his clothes quickly, keeping only his shirt and underwear. He gave Lea the key to his apartment, told her she could do whatever she liked with it. He touched her cheek with his finger.

"Thank you, Lea," he said.

Then he turned away from her and walked into the sea.

CHAPTER
THIRTY-SIX

In the weeks that followed, Lea did her best. She got out of bed each morning and dressed herself as if she was going to work. Some days she even left the apartment, joining the rush-hour pedestrian traffic, sometimes even letting herself be carried all the way to her offices, where she was no longer welcome. Those days she stood outside the glass-encased lobby, watching people arrive with their shiny shoes, snakeskin briefcases and tailored jackets. Other days she stayed at home, sitting on the sofa that she had picked out long before her father had come back into her life. She sat there all day, and then at night she got up, changed into her pyjamas and went back to bed.

Lea stopped going to WeCovery, she ignored the Suicide Club's phone calls. The calls came from Manuel and Mrs Jackman now, never Anja. She wished Anja would call her.

Perhaps she would have gone on like this for longer. But after she'd missed a month of WeCovery, George put in a call to the Observers.

It was GK who showed up at her apartment, and for a strange moment, Lea was almost glad to see him. Then she realised that her father, the problem she associated the Observers with, was no longer a problem. She realised that she no longer had anything to hide. So she told him. Before GK could start speaking, she told him everything. From that first day she saw her father across the road, to finding out what he was planning to do with the Suicide Club, to deciding she wanted to help the Ministry shut them down. But when she reached Ambrose she stopped.

GK was silent. His eyes, Lea observed, were curiously bright, and she realised with a flush of embarrassment that he was close to tears. Suddenly she regretted telling him anything. It had felt good to talk, yes, but she felt the hollowness of the comfort, the distance between her and the stranger sitting next to her. She was very tired now, and wanted to be alone.

So she stood up, went to the bedroom, came back with the memory card that contained the recording of Ambrose's death. The last piece of the puzzle, all the Ministry would need in their case against the Suicide Club.

GK pocketed it eagerly. It would mean rapid promotion for him, no doubt, likely Tier 3 benefits. But when he thanked her, he didn't talk about himself. Instead he said it was time. He would recommend that she be taken off the List, that no further Observation would take place, that she would no longer have to report for WeCovery sessions. Her workplace would be notified, her clinic instructed to lift the hold on new extension treatments.

Given her stats, and her cooperation with the Ministry to shut down the Club, this would mean the

Third Wave, almost undoubtedly, GK said with great excitement.

She would be an Immortal.

He stood up to leave. Wanted to get the process started right away. He would make the recommendation as soon as he got back to the office, she should hear from the Ministry by tomorrow. He grabbed her hand between two of his and shook it vigorously. Thank you, Lea, he said. And congratulations.

It was only when he was halfway out the front door that he realised Lea had never finished her story. Surely, he remarked, she was glad that her father would be saved now. Perhaps, yes, there would be significant prison time for the antisanct act that made him leave in the first place, and for the attempted identity fraud that he'd undertaken to get treatments while he'd been away. Perhaps some extension restrictions. But most importantly, he would be saved. He would not be able to end his life. Surely that was cause for celebration.

At that moment, Lea wanted nothing more than to be alone. So with one hand on the cold edge of the doorframe, she smiled at GK and said yes. It was certainly cause for celebration.

When GK had left, Lea stood frozen with her hand on the doorknob for a long time. The apartment was silent, but her head was filled with the sound of crashing waves, the overhead cry of birds swooping and dipping. Suddenly she felt the wind on her cheeks, smelled the sharp salt, saw the distant, glimmering horizon.

CHAPTER
THIRTY-SEVEN

Anja drew the blade over the base of the mug, again and again. She aimed for the thin circle of rough, unglazed ceramic, knowing she'd aimed right when she heard the drag, when it ended in a point. Funny, how the sound itself was sharp. She imagined the atoms in the knife's blade taking their positions, getting in one straight line.

She'd come close now, several times. But each time she couldn't do it. Either her hands were shaking too much, or she couldn't see through the tears, or she just couldn't. Just found herself taking the step backwards again, going back to the kitchen counter where the ceramic mug lay.

At least if she was sharpening the knife, if the cruel slick of it was echoing through the room filling her ears and her mind, she could pretend she was getting closer.

When the knock came, she thought again that they'd finally come for her. Either the guys from the Markets, or the officers, or George — someone.

A great, lifting relief swept over Anja when she saw Lea standing there, even before she knew what she was going to ask.

"Hi," Lea said, dropping her gaze.

"Lea," Anja said. "Come in."

Lea walked into the room. This time she didn't seem to notice Anja's mother. She went over to the far end of the room and stared out of the dusty window.

"How have you been?" Anja asked.

Lea turned and looked up. There was something different about her. Anja squinted, struggled to put her finger on it. Something about the way she held her neck, the way that focusing her gaze seemed to bring a pained look into her eyes.

"Fine," Lea said. And without looking at her, Anja would have believed her. But her mouth seemed to turn the other way, the skin under her nose wrinkling just a notch. "What are you doing?" Lea asked.

"Oh," Anja held the mug up, flipping it over to show Lea its underside. "See this rough bit of ceramic here? Makes a good sharpener. Works well, since you can't buy them, sharpeners, not without a special permit."

Lea nodded. It seemed to make perfect sense to her. She didn't ask why Anja needed to sharpen a knife.

As Anja gripped the handle of the knife more tightly in her hand, she looked at Lea. Lea would give her courage, she thought, perhaps Lea would watch.

But Lea wasn't looking at her. She had crossed the room and was pushing the window open, sending small showers of dust and wood fragments cascading down its aged sides. The noise and cold of the city streamed into the room, whipping around them and filling their ears with life and sound and thoughts of winter. Lea was still pushing, she pushed the window high up above where Anja had ever managed. She realised Lea had broken the top of the window frame now. It was old wood, but still, Anja stared at Lea's hands, and wondered at their strength.

Lea perched herself onto the window ledge. She didn't seem to be holding on, but it was only when she started to swing one leg out into the cold that Anja realised something was wrong.

"What are you doing?" she said, thoughts racing. Should she rush towards her, grab her arm?

Lea turned towards Anja. Her face was dry, but her eyes crinkled as if crying invisible tears.

"Remember when you came to my apartment? You tried to open the window," she said. "And I told you it wouldn't. Directive 7077A."

Anja nodded.

"What a pity, you said. You'd get such a great breeze up here." Lea turned out to face the city. Across the street was a gleaming office building, people shifting behind the shadowy glass. She closed her eyes, lifted her face to the wind rushing in. "You were right," she said.

Anja took a step towards the window, but she saw Lea stiffen, her knuckles white where she gripped the ledge. She stared at Lea's hands, unusually large for a woman, wired with veins and knobbed with joints. She stared at the lines her tendons made between knuckle and wrist, the solid heft of a thumb hooked around the wooden frame. Anja looked at where Lea had pushed the window up along the crumbling brick and wood.

Anja held up the knife and turned it gently in the light. She saw how clean the blade was, how fine and efficient and perfectly formed it now was for its purpose. She wondered if Lea could see it too, from where she was sitting.

"I realised my mother would want me to do it myself," Anja said. Her hand began to shake. "No Club, no pills, no farms. So I've — I've been trying. More than once. But I just can't do it."

Lea was watching her now. The edge of her skirt flapped in the wind, a tiny parachute, and Anja worried for a second she might be blown off the ledge.

She flipped the knife in her hand so that the handle faced out, and held it out to Lea.

"It's sharp now, as sharp as it can be. But still. With the synthetic skin. I know it will be messy. I know I'll have to use force, to stab and hack and twist. I could have slit her veins, I think that I could have done. But this — I don't have the strength to do this."

Lea stared at her with dark eyes. Anja couldn't tell what she was thinking, if she was thinking of anything at all. When she leaned back, Anja's heart almost stopped, but then she swung one leg over the window ledge back into the room, and stood up again.

It was only when Lea was close enough to grab the knife handle that Anja saw the emotion in her eyes. Lea stared at it for a moment, then touched her index finger to the tip of the blade. When she drew it away, a small pinprick of blood formed.

"It's not about strength," she said. Her voice was suddenly clear and full. "It's easy enough to draw blood. But you have to do it fast enough, rip it fully

360

open, so that the skin can't grow back. You did a good job with the blade."

She took three heavy steps towards where Anja's mother lay. Standing by her side, Lea reached out and touched the base of her neck.

"Here," she said. "But the windpipe is reinforced, so that will need a bit of effort."

Her voice was cold and hot at the same time. She seemed detached, but Anja sensed a simmering fascination under the surface, an old desire.

Suddenly she wanted to wrestle the knife out of Lea's hands. But she was paralysed, her arms heavy, her legs rooted to the ground. She could only watch as Lea examined her mother's neck carefully, the knife that Anja had given her, shiny in her hand.

No, she wanted to shout. No. Not like this. But still she couldn't open her mouth.

Lea turned to Anja. Her eyes were black as coals. Gone was the look of resignation with which she had entered the room. Something seemed to burn within her.

Then, Lea reached out to take Anja's hand. The moment she felt Lea's fingers wrap around hers, a switch seemed to flip. Anja grabbed her hand tightly, and then with both hands, grabbed her arm. She felt the wiry muscles under Lea's skin, a hundred years of good nutrition and maintenance and exercise and technology. She felt how she wouldn't be strong enough to stop her, and the familiar frustration, the helplessness, washed over her.

Lea looked down at her arm where Anja was holding it, then raised her eyes to meet Anja's. Still they burned, cold and hungry, with a violence that Anja couldn't understand. But then, suddenly, they cleared, giving way to a brightness. Perhaps it was the way Anja's fingers trembled as she dug into the flesh of Lea's forearm, or perhaps it was the tears that were beginning to form in her eyes. Either way, Lea seemed to understand.

"Here," she said. Her voice was soft now. Anja could tell she wasn't thinking of her any more, nor her mother. Lea handed the knife back to Anja. Its handle was still warm from the heat of Lea's grip, and as Anja held it now, she felt that something was different.

Anja stepped around Lea and sat down in the chair, the same chair that she had sat in so many times, watching, waiting, helpless. But this time when she brought the blade to her mother's neck, there was no trembling or hesitation. This time, the cold metal touching her sticky skin didn't seem cruel or unnatural. It wasn't even her skin, Anja reminded herself. Her mother wasn't even there. Not any more.

So she ripped into the flesh in the spot that Lea had pointed to, using her other hand to pull the skin apart more quickly. It was slippery and wet, and she seemed to feel it growing back already, back over her hands as they dug in her mother's neck. But then, under the inky thick blood, there it was, the windpipe. She could see it pulsing with her mother's breath, alien and purple and shiny.

You have to do it fast enough, Lea had said. Anja felt her standing behind her, watching and waiting.

The dark blood was trickling down the side of her mother's neck. It moved slowly, like lava out of a crater. When the blood touched the starchy white sheets, it didn't sink in right away, instead sitting for a moment on the surface like thick jelly. But the liquid kept coming and in an instant something gave. The sheets turned deep violet.

Her mother's face was serene and motionless, the same as always. But Anja could still see her windpipe moving under all that wetness, could still hear the thump of her heart.

"What if she's still alive after I do it?" Anja asked in desperation. "What if her heart just keeps going?"

"It won't," Lea said.

She stared at her mother. The windpipe, the heart, the blood. It was never her mother at all. Suddenly she saw them for what they were — alien and cruel. They weren't saving her mother any more than Anja was killing her. Anja dropped the knife.

She went at it with both hands, plunging her fingers into wetness, wrapping them around the warm, rigid, windpipe. The blood seemed stickier now, seemed to already be congealing. It would heal over in minutes if she allowed it to. So she didn't. She felt strength in her fingers, the kind of strength she felt when playing the violin. The windpipe between her hands was like the neck of a violin, the cold metal ridges like strings cutting into her fingers. She squeezed, tighter and tighter, beginning to rotate her hands in opposite directions.

The windpipe was strong, the reinforcing wires rigid, but slowly she began to feel it give under her hands. She thought of the windpipe her mother used to have, a soft, natural thing that would bring such beautiful sound from the depths of her lungs and heart out into the world. This was no such thing. This windpipe only wheezed and crackled, only kept her music trapped inside her.

She twisted harder, feeling her fingers start to lose strength. But then there was a quiet pop and a soft whoosh of air. There was a terrible gurgling noise as the blood seeped into the open channel. Slowly, the wheezing stopped. Her mother was no longer breathing.

Anja dropped her hands to her sides, feeling the sticky blood beginning to harden in the webs of her fingers.

The heart was still beating, its valves whirring and clicking, the liquid spurting out of her mother's throat.

Anja felt a slow dread creep over her. It would never end. She would try and try again, but it would never end, they would never let her mother die.

But then, before she could blink, the floral comforter was being drawn back and the knife was sinking into the flesh of her mother's chest. Lea wielded the knife with a precision and strength that Anja could never imagine. She angled the blade between the ribs, wriggling and manoeuvring until its tip was perfectly positioned at some invisible spot that only she could see.

She turned to Anja. Anja nodded.

Lea gripped the handle of the knife in the heel of her right hand. With one heavy motion, she slammed the heel of her left hand into it, and the knife sank deep and fast.

The heart beat once, twice, then a third time, weakly. Then it stopped, and there was silence.

CHAPTER
THIRTY-EIGHT

The sky in this part of the world was darker and brighter than it ever was in the city. Eddies of colour swirled at night, giving way to a calm, pale blankness when morning fell.

It wasn't just the sky. They caught glimpses of the ocean as they wound up and down between forests and cliffs, and it was large and alive and even more terrifying. Eventually they found themselves on an ocean road that stretched on for hundreds of miles, teetering on the edge of mossy cliffs. They thought the road might lead to where the green disappeared, and ice took over. They thought perhaps they would get there some day.

Sometimes Lea drove, sometimes Anja. The car was a good one, obedient and regular, with a purring engine that sometimes had to be coaxed but for the most part was reliable. It even had a sunroof, a small square of plastic that was permanently open because the cover had broken. The patch of sunlight travelled from the back to the front of the car as the day went by, and as they drove further and further north. The plesiosaur that Kaito had given Lea sat on the dashboard, looking out towards the water.

366

When Anja was driving, Lea liked to push the passenger seat all the way down and back so she could kick her legs out and look up at the sky. There were times when it was dynamic and full of drama, usually the nights and mornings, when the sun did its work of waking the world and putting it back to sleep. But during the day, when they were driving, the opening framed a small patch of blue not unlike the skylight in her old office. Here, like then, she watched as the serene white clouds drifted past.

It came in a rush, suddenly one day, the strange, buoyant feeling. Lea had been lying down, watching the sky speed by. She forgot where she was until she sat up again, and all around them was rolling green and crashing ocean and lighted sky.

Kaito would have loved it, she thought, looking around at the reckless shifting beauty all around them. She looked at the toy dinosaur on the dashboard. Suddenly she felt that he was there with her.

Lea wound down the window, and the wind rushed in, devouring the silence in the car, sending their hair flying across their faces. When Anja started laughing, Lea did too.

Acknowledgements

Thank you to my editors, Melissa Cox at Hodder & Stoughton and Libby Burton at Henry Holt, for bringing *Suicide Club* into the world. Not only did your edits make this the best book it could possibly be, your generosity, enthusiasm and friendship also made the publication process a true pleasure.

To Juliet Mushens — agent extraordinaire, human whirlwind, hard-nosed hustler, insightful editor, unflappable cheerleader, caring friend — thank you for making my dreams come true. You inspire me every single day. To Sasha Raskin, thank you for making US publication possible, as well as for all the great lunches and conversations.

Thank you to everyone at Faber Academy. Special thanks to Joanna Briscoe, for reading the first ten thousand words of what would become this book and telling me not to give up. Thank you as well to Nicci Cloke for encouragement and advice. To my Faber classmates, especially early readers Melanie Garrett and Carol Barnes, thank you for all the feedback and support.

To all my friends, thank you for making me laugh, feeding my brain and keeping me sane through this process. You give me faith that this world is place of adventure and possibility. To Sam and Christine, thank you for fifteen years of communal naps, inside jokes, public screaming and long distance love. To Vadim, thank you for Thanksgivings, Kenya, and all the Things We Did.

To my mother, thank you for raising and loving me. Thank you for reading to me as a child, taking me to the library and letting me use all the library cards. You have given me countless gifts, but the love of reading is one that has shaped my life and made me the person I am today. Thank you to my brother, Kevin, for being my biggest fan since 1993. Thank you for being the smartest, kindest brother I could ever ask for. I love you both.

To Kalle, husband, soul mate and best friend, thank you for telling me on that snowy New York night in 2009 that I should be a writer, five years before I would write my first short story. You understand me in ways that no one does; you read and nurture parts of my soul unknown to even myself. Thank you for being my biggest cheerleader, wisest mentor, harshest critic. I quite literally wouldn't be a writer without you. Thank you for making me laugh helplessly every day, for challenging my mind and my soul, for making me feel a freedom, a lightness I had never felt before meeting you. You are the best thing in my life. I love you.